Listen to the Birds

DEDICATION

This novel is dedicated to my daughter, Virginia, the wind beneath my wings.

PROLOGUE

THE MELT began a century ago. The ice thawed, bit by bit, until a dramatic shift of the ocean's currents moved warm waters to the polar regions. Within a human life-span, the ice caps vanished and the oceans rose, drowning the coastlines of Earth. Sea creatures flourished, whereas the beasts of the land fought for life. And above them all, the moon reigned the seas, commanding the waves along the shore, grinding the new coasts from rock to sand.

In the year 2112, on a rocky beach near Pau, France, two children ran down the shoreline, their laughter muffled under the crash of waves. A reflection in the rocks caught the children's attention. Shrieking gulls circled over their heads as they knelt and dug up a half-buried bronze plaque. Like a pirate's treasure, they took it to the edge of the surf and washed away the crusted mud, revealing etched words.

"C'est de l'anglais."

"Oui!" The boy jerked the sign from her hands. "Il est à moi!"

The girl shouted angrily to her mother, watching from the rocks above them. "Maman!"

Their mother waved. "Venez ici, les enfants."

They raced up the hill to her beckoning hand. The boy gave her the plaque and they sat beside her.

5

"Okay, children, let's practice our English." A smile on her face, she held up the plaque, but her smile faded as she silently read the words.

"Read it out loud, Mommy," the little boy said.

The girl squeezed her mother's arm. "You're crying, Mommy."

The mother blinked back her tears. She touched the name **LONDON** and the date at the bottom of the sign. "Children, this is from the old city of London, England, in the year 2020, before The Melt."

"London is under the ocean now?" The boy asked.

"Yes, Antoine, like so many other cities of the world." She cleared her throat and read the words:

THE AGE OF MODERN MYTHOLOGY IS UPON US.
HUMANS, NOW HALF GOD AND HALF BEAST—WITH
THUNDERBOLTS OF ZEUS AND ARROWS OF ARTEMIS—
HAVE THE POWER TO DESTROY THE WORLD.
THE SIRENS OF EARTH CALL US ONTO
THE ROCKS OF OUR FOLLY.

CHAPTER 1

The solar-powered plane glided silently over a low mountain range and into a valley draped in snow. John gazed out the window. Though it held no warmth, the pale sunlight streamed across the lingering snow, marking the end of the depressing Antarctic winter.

A V-shaped formation of Magellan geese paralleled the plane. John pointed out of the window to his flight companion, Dr. Noelle Clavet. "Check out our escorts."

Like a troupe of dancers, the graceful birds cut through the air, their feathers glistening in the muted light.

"Magnificent!" Dr. Clavet breathed.

"In that species, the males are black-and-white and the females brown. It's a bit early for them, but I suspect they've staked out a home near one of the hot springs."

She cocked her head, listening to the honking geese. "The plane is so quiet, I can hear them."

"Once aloft, the Hawkplane glides silently on the wind."

"If it's solar-powered, how does it fly in the dark times?"

With his thumb, John gestured to the rear of the plane. "We have hydrogen fuel cells as a backup."

The plane drifted above the river and John shielded his eyes from its mirrored surface. A family of otters played on the ice, plunging in and out of a hole near the bank. Just beyond the river, a herd of caribou pawed through the snow, seeking the pale spring grasses underneath.

He turned and studied Dr. Clavet, staring transfixed at the panorama. A professor at Cornell University, she had PhDs in both biology and philosophy. Dr. Clavet was here to lead a group of university students, including his daughter Ginnie, in a study of Antarctica's wildlife refuges. But Ginnie had failed to mention that she was lovely—blue-green eyes set in a sculptured face with curved lips, framed by curly salt and pepper hair.

Dr. Clavet said in a melodious French accent, "So nice of you to arrange this flight over the Concordia refuge—it's simply spectacular." She pointed to wisps of steam drifting across the river. "The geothermal features remind me of Yellowstone Park."

"We have hot springs all through this area. After the Melt, the UN stocked the refuge with cold-climate animals, but the warm currents ensure they have year-round access to water."

The plane banked away from the refuge and started back toward the city of Amundsen.

"Dr. Clavet, I'm curious on the timing of your trek," John said. "It's early spring and there's still a lot of snow on the ground, especially in the backcountry."

"Please call me Noelle," she said. "We have planned a series of these expeditions to track animals and study their habitats through the seasons, though only remotely through the dark time. Less vegetation at this time gives us more opportunities to catch sight of animals. The students will be arriving over the next week or two, and we have orientations and packing to do, so we won't be heading out for a bit." She crossed her fingers. "And I hope for good weather."

With a tilt of her head, Noelle smiled. "I tell you, your work here is incredible, Mr. President. Antarctica is one of the first countries to create a cabinet-level position dedicated to give a voice to the environment and not just shill for big business." She gestured with her hands as if weighing one against the other. "To be able to balance nature and the human population—it's more than any other country has managed in the history of the world."

John arched an eyebrow. "Wrestling match is a more accurate term to describe it."

She chuckled. "I've read about the protests."

"We have a fun-loving group in Antarctica. My vision was to leave the land as untouched as possible. But the real credit goes to our Secretary of the Environment, Elena Brovanec. She was on the original team creating the refuge areas and she agreed to join my cabinet. It's been quite a battle, and we've used tax incentives, land trades, and whatever hammer we could find, to pull off the master plan. But it has to be rational and balanced, or it will fail the test of time."

"Let's hope it becomes a blueprint for other nations."

With crossed fingers, he nodded. "I'm nearing the end of my term, and I hope it will be so ingrained in the political and social fabric that it becomes a permanent legacy."

"A sad day for Antarctica when you leave office. I assume you won't run again?"

"Thank God we have strict one-term limits for political office. I will be delighted to get back to my quiet farm." He grinned. "I won't miss the politicians. Like sharks, they have to keep their mouths moving, or they'll die."

"Sounds like university professors." She looked at him. "The opening of the continent has had its challenges. I read that Antarctica's first president was assassinated?"

"Yeah, Durant was a corrupt S.O.B., so no loss there." He grimaced. "But that's how I got stuck with the job—allowing my name to be placed on the ballot for president of Antarctica."

They soared above the farmlands. John chewed his lip at the sight of the fields now locked under a sheet of snow, veiling the fertile black soil. He missed the smell of the earth as it was laid open by the plow, and the sound of the wind rippling through tall wheat. One year he had been a farmer, the sun on his face, breathing in the clean air. He had flourished as a man.

The farmlands faded from view as the plane lifted over the last ridgeline, and the city of Amundsen came into sight.

John clenched his jaw. While he'd been kickstarting a government, Ginnie had grown up and left for college. After his wife's murder, he and his daughter had escaped the corrupt Old World to start a new life in Antarctica, but now, instead of farming his land, his days were filled with politics. Where had the time gone? He stared out of the window. *All because of one woman—Lowry Walker.*

"Do you know a woman named Lowry Walker?" Noelle asked.

John jerked around to face Noelle. "What are you saying?"

"I said that we've hired a woman named Lowry Walker as our guide for the expedition."

"Oh. I see." Embarrassed, he turned away.

Noelle narrowed her eyes. "Is there something you need to tell me about her?"

He cleared his throat. "No, no, I was just startled to hear her name. Lowry grew up on Antarctica. She'd make a wonderful guide."

"Okay, good." Noelle grinned. "Ginnie was the one who recommended her, but you had me worried for a second."

John turned back to stare out of the window, clasping the arm of his seat.

Noelle coughed. "I hate to be forward, but I seem to have hit a nerve."

It had been ages since he had spoken of his past relationship with Lowry. In Amundsen, by necessity, he had to erect barriers to his feelings and control his reactions. He dug his nails into the armrest. He had loved his wife, but Lowry had been his true love. *Or so I thought.*

He cleared his throat, feeling her eyes study him. Strangely, he found himself trusting Noelle. A fleeting smile grazed his face. "She and I were planning to be married. It didn't work out."

"She fell in love with someone else?"

"Lowry betrayed me." He exhaled, then shook his head. "Not by loving another man, but by betraying the man I had become."

*　　*　　*

The plane landed smoothly. They unbuckled and walked toward the exit. John's security Drots followed him closely.

John waved to the pilot. "Thanks for a great flight, Alex."

She smiled at him. "You're welcome, sir."

When they reached the tarmac, the Drots unfolded from the drone shape into a cascading robot form with mechanical arms and legs.

Noelle's mouth dropped open. "I thought those were simple drones?"

"I'm afraid not." He shook his head. "One of the 'advantages' of the formation of a new country is that everyone wants to give you stuff so they can market their products." John pointed to the Drots as the presidential robocar hovered to a stop beside them. "These are the latest security robots, called Drots: half-drone, half-robot. They're made from lightweight titanium, and in fighting mode, as they are now, they distend into their full form. But as drones, they can travel faster than a hovercar."

Like metallic spider monkeys, they circled the perimeter around him and the robocar faster than any human, their domed oval "heads" spinning as they perused the area.

Noelle looked askance. "They're freaky, but amazingly quiet."

Nodding, John grinned. "Definitely freaky. Part of the stealth aspect is the noise-cancelling design of the hover mechanism."

John gestured to the robocar. "Our chariot awaits."

Noelle grimaced, pointing at the Drots. "Do they ride inside?"

He chuckled. "No, they'll collapse into drone mode and escort us from above."

"Good."

They stepped into the robocar and John gave the order. "Downtown."

Closely followed by his security drones, they hovered from the government hangar toward the road connecting the airport to Amundsen. In the pale sun, they skimmed across a flat barren landscape, dotted with clumps of brush veiled in a glistening layer of ice.

As they passed a dense thicket of Antarctic beech shrubs, a great snowy owl burst from the shadowy branches. The Drots hovered to investigate and the startled bird dodged around them, flying directly toward the robocar. Noelle gasped as the giant owl grazed the window next to her, and poised for a second, wings flapping against the glass, its round eyes staring into hers. With a beat of its wings, the owl soared over the top of the vehicle and disappeared into the distance.

Noelle leaned back in the seat. "Terrifying, but what a beauty!"

John raised his hands with a smile. "Welcome to Antarctica!"

As the robocar hovered onto the main avenue to the city, John said, "This is one of the few roads we have on Antarctica, mainly for heavy trucks transporting materials to and from the airport. Most of the continent is accessed by hovers so we don't have to cut roads across the terrain."

"Excellent."

At the edge of the city, John waved his hand at a large undulating structure of steel and glass rising from the ground. "That will be the new University of Antarctica, hopefully open in a year or so. Maybe you can teach a course or two when it opens."

"Absolutely. We should have our Concordia Refuge study completed by then."

They reached the downtown area, passing modern buildings of glass and stone, connected with arched passageways.

John pointed to the glass channels between the buildings. "Because of the brutal winters, the city has sheltered conduits throughout."

"Makes sense." Noelle nodded. "I love the layout of the city, especially with no wires aboveground."

"Most buildings are designed to be self-contained with renewables and backup systems, but for larger buildings and light industrial manufacturing, we needed a few utility lines, so we used boring robots to drill access under the frost line."

They continued through a roundabout. John gestured to a sculpture rising from a concrete basin in the center of the circle. "All the liquid wastewater is recycled for irrigation and drinking. In the warm times, we have 'recycling' fountains throughout the city." He grinned. "After it's been processed, of course."

"Good. Now I can erase the vision of yellow water shooting into the air."

John laughed. "Yeah, that might not be too esthetic." He tilted his head. "Between the UN and our people here, we wanted to create the first city in the world as self-sufficient as possible. Recycling is mandatory, but we've tried to make it easy to comply, with efficient recovery and utilization, before massive dumps were in place."

"And no unnatural chemicals are allowed on Antarctica?"

"That's correct. Prior to the melting of the ice cap, the UN had a chemical ban which we've inherited and reinforced."

The robocar stopped at Noelle's hotel.

John checked his watch. "I didn't realize it was so close to noon. Would you like some lunch?"

"Thanks so much, but, um, I'm actually meeting Lowry Walker for lunch." Noelle touched his arm. "Perhaps you'd like to join us?"

He coughed. "No, you two will have a lot to discuss."

The door of the robocar opened.

Noelle shifted toward the opening. "Merci for the lovely tour."

"You're welcome, Noelle."

She paused, glancing at him with a kind smile. "John, one thing that I've learned—love is not something which gets damaged. It either exists or doesn't exist. And if it exists, then all else can be fixed."

Frowning, John turned away. "Can it?"

CHAPTER 2

The next morning, John waited in his office for a meeting with Representative Kara Banis. John's Chief of Staff, Kisho Mori, stepped in. "Representative Banis has just arrived and will be here shortly."

"Thank you, Kisho." He nodded as Kisho moved discreetly behind the desk.

Kisho had immigrated from Japan with the first wave of homesteaders and had proven himself to be a diamond in the rough. A nondescript fellow in appearance, but his strength was his intelligence. He had done a superb job of organizing the president's office and he had an inborn political savvy that John needed. He was invaluable.

John rose at the clip-clip of business shoes in the hallway. Head thrown back, Representative Banis strode into the room. She was well known in the assembly as a force of nature.

With a smile on her face and a firm grip, she shook his extended hand. "Good morning, Mr. President."

He gestured to the chair in front of his desk. "Please sit and tell me what you need."

Banis nodded to Kisho, and then sat facing John. She inclined her head. "I'll get straight to the point, Mr. President." Her hand chopped the air like a hatchet. "Our district is expanding, but we can't afford this next set of recycling costs—they're simply too expensive."

John shook his head. "You know as well as I do that if we don't set up recycling as a part of the infrastructure, there's a huge expense of disposal down the road."

He gazed at her. "You're relatively new to our fair nation, but on Antarctica, everything is either recycled or composted—even humans. We mulch the deceased and 'intern' them into our gardens. We won't allow items into the country that don't comply with our recycling systems." He tilted back in his chair. "The UN grants are still available for infrastructure development. Have you applied for one?"

She nodded. "Yes, we have, but that takes time. We want to start right away."

Shrugging, John said, "We can help with a bridge grant if you have all your documents submitted." He studied her closed face. *There's something else she's angling for.*

He coughed. "Let's move onto your next topic."

Banis pursed her lips and leaned forward. "We need power, sir. Mr. President, we want to build an assembly plant for more advanced hovers, both bikes and utility craft. But renewables alone will not completely satisfy our electricity needs. I believe the fusion power plant comes online soon?"

"Yes, within a month."

Her voice rose. "We'd like to be first in line to get a connection to our district."

He twitched a brow. *You and everyone else.*

Behind him, Kisho cleared his throat. "If I could just interject something, Mr. President. The robo-drills are completely booked with current projects."

Banis' lips thinned as she drummed her fingers on the armrest.

John nodded. "I'm afraid you're correct." He tapped his chin. "However, I know the demand will only grow." He turned to Kisho. "We can check with the power consortium in Australia and perhaps get more drills down here."

"Yes, sir."

"Ms. Banis, we'll try our best to fast-track some additional drilling units."

Her face brightened. "Thank you, Mr. President."

He stood and shook her hand. "Team effort, Ms. Banis."

After Representative Banis left, Kisho said softly, "Mr. President, Secretary Lin is returning to the capital and wants to meet with you this afternoon. There's a problem in the Grace Region."

John's brow furrowed. "Did he say what it was about?"

"No, sir, only that it was urgent.

He gritted his teeth. *Fantastic.*

*   *   *

Before lunch, John's virtual assistant, P, alerted him that his daughter Ginnie's plane had arrived at the airport. "Do you want me to arrange a pickup?"

"No thanks, P, I'll pick her up myself." As he walked toward the door, his security Drots floated into a flanking position behind him. He stopped by the apartment, and the door opened. Henry-dog bounded toward him. "I thought you might want to come with me." John smiled at the golden retriever. Henry's eyes brightened.

"Come on, boy."

Wagging his tail, the dog followed him and jumped into the robocar. John said, "Airport," and in few minutes, they parked. John cracked a small air vent for Henry. "I'll be right back, boy, with a surprise."

Flanked by the Drots, now descended into robot mode, he strolled into the airport. Ginnie appeared at the arrival gate, and he waved to her.

She yelled, "Daddy!" and ran toward him, until the Drots stepped forward and she slowed to a walk. She glanced at the Drots. "I'll never get used to those things."

"Me neither." They hugged and he gazed at her. "You cut your hair short."

"I got tired of my hair hanging in my face while dissecting a virtual body."

He grimaced. "What a fun fact to share."

"Yeah, we biology students are just gross, but at least we don't have to cut up a real one."

John said, "Back in the good old days, biology students used to have to dig up cadavers from the cemetery."

She grinned. "Maybe that's next semester."

Her luggage hovered to her and they walked to the robocar.

Ginnie screamed at the sight of Henry jumping up and down inside the vehicle. "You brought Henry!" The door opened and she squeezed into the seat beside him. "Stay in, buddy." The dog licked her face as she stroked him. "I've missed you, buddy."

John got in the other side. "Believe me, he's missed you too." He murmured, "Home."

They left the airport for the city.

The dog leaned against Ginnie, and with a grunt, she gently shoved him away. "Henry, you're suffocating me."

"I know you love her, but don't get carried away, boy." John said with a smile. He turned to Ginnie. "How's school going?"

With a nod, Ginnie said, "Good. I was able to finish my other classes early, so I could take a long winter break for this project."

"Perfect. And I assume not too much partying?"

She glanced at him with a frown. "Dad, I'm not sixteen anymore."

He blinked. *Sixteen.* That was how old she'd been the year they moved into Amundsen from the farm. After the death of her mother, he had tried to be there for his daughter, but in the chaos of jump-starting a fledging nation, he'd spent his days and most nights on the phone or in meetings. Ginnie had been the one to suffer the collateral damage of it all, falling into a group of less-than-desirable friends. John chewed his lip. The guilt of being an absent parent had been a bitter cocktail to swallow.

"Hmm. Sixteen. Do you remember the night I picked you up from that wild party not long after we moved to Amundsen?"

Ginnie laughed. "I remember. It took me weeks to recover from the embarrassment of having to leave because the President of Antarctica was outside waiting for me."

He pursed his lips. "You survived." Smiling he patted her leg. "It's great having you home, Ginnie."

They turned onto the main street of Amundsen and the presidential buildings came into view. She laughed at the cartoonish ice sculptures lining the street, illuminated from within with colorful lights. John gazed at her happy face, like a candle brightening a room—revealing the emptiness of his life.

John turned to Ginnie. "I met Dr. Clavet—she seems to be a woman with a mission." He grinned. "Where is she from? She's drop-dead gorgeous."

Ginnie raised a brow, then chuckled. "She's part Gabonese and French. Her grandfather immigrated to France because of sea-level rise along the coast of Gabon. She met her husband on a tour at the ITER nuclear fusion plant in Provence. He was a nuclear physicist. After the devastation of the Melt, they became involved with a non-profit group called HOME: Humans for Our Mother Earth." She shook her head. "Then her husband died in a tragic plane crash. She's now on the board of HOME and dedicated to population control. They attempt to educate women across the world and give contraceptives, especially in regions where the birth rate is exploding." Ginnie laughed. "During one of her lectures, she brought in a potpourri of birth control, past and present, to show the class."

"Overpopulation was a concern even before the Melt, but now it's catastrophic. Too many people on too little land." He coughed. "Sorry to hear about her husband, but she sounds dedicated to her work."

"Yes, she believes that women can lead the world to a better future—it's her passion in life."

The robocar eased under the porte-cochère of the rear entrance and parked. The doors opened and Henry jumped out.

Ginnie got out and stretched her arms. "It's good to be home."

They strolled to the apartment and sat in the interior garden. John ordered sandwiches and hot tea. The food arrived as a new batch of bird seed dropped into the feeders outside the window.

As they ate, Ginnie pointed to the flock of birds descending to the fresh seed. "They get lunch too."

John lifted the tea pot and gestured to her cup, but she waved it away. He poured himself a cup, then absently stirred in the cream.

Ginnie cleared her throat, then glanced at him. "Dad, do you ever see Lowry? How is she?"

John turned to watch the birds dart around the feeders.

This was the second time someone had mentioned Lowry in the last twenty-four hours. Was his loneliness so obvious? He sipped his tea and then choked as the hot liquid burned his throat. He set down his tea, tapping the side of the cup. A dull ache rose in his chest as he stared at the table. Would he ever heal from that lost love? Odd how your mind thinks like an adult, but your heart stays a teenager forever.

With a grimace, he snapped, "I've heard her name more times in the last two days than I have in years." He raked his hair back, aware of her eyes studying him.

With a tilt of her head, she said, "I know you cared for her, Dad, and I'm gone now. You need to think about your life after the presidency. Haven't you forgiven her yet?"

He met her gaze. "I know you mean well." His lips thinned. "But are you asking me to forget that she fucked up my life?"

CHAPTER 3

Lowry examined her face in the mirror. Crow's feet fringed her eyes. She ran her fingers through her hair and touched the invading silver strands. Not that she minded the gray, but it was a daily reminder of the narrowing window of time for having a child. She'd always been independent and laissez-faire as far as children were concerned, but like waking up with a cold, her biologic clock had begun to tick.

Over the past few years, she'd gone on a few dates: dancing at one of the local fairs, watching movies at the house, but the affairs never lasted beyond a week or two. Lowry had come to realize, almost annoyingly, that she still loved John. With a thick protective shell between them, their relationship had devolved into a neighborly collaboration—and nothing else. She gazed at the sad face in the mirror. *Will he ever forgive me for pushing him into the presidency?*

At her last exam, she confided in her OB/GYN of her wish for children. The doctor had removed her birth-control implant, and then given her a shot of hormones to jump-start her reproductive system. She had raised an eyebrow. "Fair warning, the extra hormones might increase your libido."

Lowry stuck out her tongue at her image. *Great, just what I need, to be hornier than I already am.*

She turned away from the mirror, threw her robe on the bed, and perused her closet to find something decent to wear for her trip to Amundsen to visit her father, Nick. Spring had been erratic to say the least, but the a.m. forecast called for nice weather. With a heavy sigh, she brushed her hair back. *What a beautiful morning to go to a penitentiary.*

The sun was still below the horizon as Lowry left the house. She jumped into the hover and waved to Chuy herding the cows into the paddock for a bit of fresh air. Calves cavorted within the red laser bounds of the fence, happy to escape the confines of the barn.

Lowry swept over snow-covered plains toward Amundsen. In the sky above her, the lattice of sunlight reflectors cast a shimmering pale light across the wind-driven snow ripples, with eerie shadows meandering along the ridges.

With a pinched brow, she thought back to the recent lunch with Dr. Clavet for the upcoming Cornell expedition. The professor had gushed about the flight over the Concordia Refuge with John and then thrown her an odd look. Lowry had finished her lunch wondering if the refuge wasn't the only thing they'd discussed.

Dawn broke as she topped a low ridge near the southern outskirt of the city. The slanted orange rays of sunlight illuminated the razor wire encircling the new penitentiary. The inmate population had exploded after the opening to Antarctica, forcing the government to build this mammoth facility. *How many questionable citizens were dumped on their fair country?*

As the hover reached the front of the prison, Lowry stepped out, said, "Park," and it floated to the parking garage. She walked to the entrance, stared at the heavy doors, and took a deep breath. When the scanner light turned green, she stepped to the second set of doors, opening after another scan completed. At the front desk, the visitation screen flashed a WELCOME sign, and then she sat, waiting with the rest of the families anxious to visit their relatives.

The high windows, covered in heavy mesh, filtered the anemic sunlight into an already dismal room. It was hard to believe that Nick was an inmate; he was such a good man. One of the first inhabitants on the continent, he had been a prominent leader of the miners. But he had killed a man, and had to pay for taking a life, even if it was the crooked politician who had stolen the presidential election. There was no doubt that the "elected" President Durant would have twisted the country of Antarctica like a pretzel if he'd gotten the chance. Nick had sacrificed himself for his nation, at least that was how he felt, and she was convinced he was right in spirit.

The call came for the families to proceed into the visitation area. Lowry stood and shuffled through the interior security doors and into the large room with the rest of the crowd. Nick waved to her from one of the booths. With a big smile, she sat across from him. Her smile faded at the sight of bruises and cuts on his face.

In a worried voice she asked, "What the hell happened, Nick?"

He shrugged. "Boys will be boys. A couple of Durant's former henchmen were caught embezzling funds from the hospital, and arrived a few weeks ago. Once they figured out who I was, they gave me a 'lesson,' as they termed it."

Lowry's mouth twisted in anger. "Do the guards know about this?"

He laughed. "Those two regularly 'donate' to the staff. The guards won't say anything."

"I'm going to the warden to see if we can get you moved away from them."

Nick looked at her intently. "Lowry, I know you want to help, but if they catch wind of it, my ass is dead."

Lowry's lips quivered. "We've got to get you out of here. Maybe I can speak with John…"

"NO!" He leaned forward and repeated, "No, Lowry. If John pardons me, his political sway will go right down the toilet. You can't destroy him by trying to save me, or all of my sacrifices will be thrown away." He stared at her. "Do you understand me?"

Her shoulders sagged. "Yes, Nicky. It makes me sick you being in prison, and now getting beat up by thugs."

"A small price to pay for Antarctica and for you to live in a country not corrupted by Durant."

"I'll try to get you moved if it can be done under wraps. Nicky, please let me know what's going on, if you can." Lowry shook her head. "I thought most of Durant's entourage had left or been kicked out of the country?"

Nick shrugged. "Most did when the gravy train stopped, but a few started their own little underground mafia for drug trafficking and god knows what else."

A bell rang, signaling the end of visitation. Lowry placed her hand on the thick glass between them and he put his hand over hers from the other side. His hand caressed the window and her fingers replied as if the unyielding pane was absent.

She bit the inside of her lip. "Bye, Dad."

Nick blinked, his eyes reddening as he whispered, "Goodbye, my beautiful daughter."

Her legs shook as she left the penitentiary, steeling herself from cracking until she reached the hovercar. She stumbled inside and broke into tears. Nick, the man she had thought was her uncle and a stalwart surrogate father for years, had an affair with her mother, who was married to her "father," who was really her uncle. *Jesus, it sounded like a crazy soap opera.* Her mind numb from emotion, Lowry dried her face, then murmured to the hovercar, "Home."

If only she could find a way to have him moved out of the reach of Durant's men. But Nick was right—John was limited in what he could do for him. It would be political suicide for him to pardon the assassin of the President-elect, and by killing him, conveniently leaving a spot vacant for John to fill. John's task was difficult enough without throwing the government into more chaos.

Lowry breathed easier as she reached the open plains outside the city but felt guilty going home to the farm while her father sat in a prison cell. She blinked back tears at the memory of the times she had been overwhelmed with work, forgetting about him for days while he withered away. And a nice twist of fate for her as well—she was made fatherless twice: the now real one in jail, the now-uncle, dead of suicide. Just makes life worth living, doesn't it? At least she was free, not like poor Nick.

*   *   *

When she returned to the farm, Lowry parked the hover beside the house. She stepped out and breathed in the fresh air. *Don't dwell on the past.* She walked to the house, changed into her work clothes, then went to the kitchen for a quick lunch. Her eyebrows furrowed at the sight of a gray cloud bank edging over the western horizon. *Damn.* She called out to the house. "Weather report, please."

A forecast popped onto the monitor. Spring had teased them with a brief warm-up that morning, but now another winter blast was sweeping across the homesteads. And she still had to check John's orchards while the sun was above the horizon.

She threw on a jacket and jogged to the hover. Leo trotted after her and cocked his head as she got in the hover. "Come on, boy," Lowry said. He jumped into the seat next to her and they hovered past the laser paddock, now empty of lowing cows. Anticipating the storm, Chuy had snuggled the cattle back into the barn.

They floated across her empty pastures, her grass waiting patiently under in a crust of hard-packed snow, but now, the only living things in sight were knots of ice-covered tussock grass shivering in the frigid winds.

At the boundary of her property, she slowed the hover and turned to follow the fence line. A short melt earlier that month had thinned the snow, revealing the damage that winter had caused to the laser fencing and irrigation systems. With her watch, she noted the coordinates of areas needing repair after the spring thaw and sent them to the farm cloud account. Only a few more weeks and the final melt would begin at last.

Lowry reached the gap leading to John's homestead. She stopped the hover and gazed vacantly at the river that connected their tracts. Thick ice still lined the banks, but water bubbled in the center where the veil of ice had broken. Weighted down with snow, branches of scrubby evergreens bowed over the water's edge. With a sigh, she grabbed the thermos and drank some coffee, remembering the day John left his farm to become the reluctant leader of Antarctica. After his accidental win during the special election for president, Lowry had agreed to care for his orchards while his other neighbor, Bill Taylor, opted to lease his wheat fields. Lowry closed her eyes, recalling the pain on his face the day the leases were signed. He had shaken Bill's hand, but he'd refused to look at her. They had barely spoken since—the wounds between them had crusted over, but never healed.

Lowry put the thermos into the cup holder and patted the dog. "Leo, are you ready to check John's orchards?"

Leo's eyes brightened.

"Okay, let's go."

They hovered along the riverbank to John's land. At the edge of the orchard, the bare branches of the apple trees shook in the brisk wind. She stopped the hover beside the first row of trees, zipped up her coat, and she and Leo stepped into the cold. She inhaled the crisp air as Leo bolted after a flock of crows picking at the ground.

"Don't go too far, Leo."

The dog halted and stared at the crows flying into the distance, cawing their annoyance. Then he circled and sniffed his way back toward her until another scent lured him to a scraggly patch of frozen brush at the edge of the orchard.

The icy crust crunched under her boots as she walked along the apple trees. The sun peeked through the clouds and lit up the elegant limbs reaching toward the sky, waiting for the warmth of the sun to spring into action.

A wind rose in the distance, the sound building at its approach until it whipped through the orchard, branches flailing as it passed. Like ballet dancers, the trees bent to the will of the wind, but with a crack, a large branch snapped off a nearby tree. Its outstretched limbs dry and brittle, the tree had surrendered to the harshness of Antarctica. She moved to the tree, reached out a gloved hand and tested another branch. A cold wind rose again and charged across the orchard, snapping the limb off the dead tree and into her hand.

Like a gust of wind, a wave of sadness hit her. Tears sprang to her eyes, and angrily, Lowry threw the dead branch onto the ground. Exhaling, she wiped them away before they froze to her face. She caressed her stomach. The time had come for her to decide whether she would be a mother or face a future as barren as this tree.

CHAPTER 4

John settled Ginnie into her room in the presidential quarters, then returned to his office to meet with Lin. He had grown used to the harness of work, putting his shoulder to the yoke twenty-four-seven. Or had he merely become addicted to it, covering the emptiness of his life with exhaustion?

Bent forward, he strolled along the hallway with his hands clasped behind his back, his face pensive as thoughts of Lowry Walker resurfaced. The vision of her naked body flashed into his mind. The sex had been torrid, to say the least. He shook his head, trying to clear away the cobwebs of the past, and bumped into his Secretary of State, Rua Patel.

He coughed in embarrassment. "Excuse me, Rua."

Patel beamed. "No worries." He glanced at John. "Sounds like Lin has a report for us?"

John blinked. For some reason, Lin must have felt Patel should be involved as well. "Do you know about this?"

He shrugged. "I heard a few tidbits." Patel matched his pace.

Ignoring him, John gritted his teeth. *Great. Let's add Patel into the mix today.*

Patel had immigrated from New Zealand, but he'd lost his homestead by reneging on his contract and then drifted into politics. When John was assembling his cabinet, Patel had been the only candidate with diplomatic experience as New

Zealand's ambassador to Chile. But to John's annoyance, instead of developing trade with other nations, he had spent most of his term perfecting his virtual golf score.

As he passed the reception area, John nodded to his com-secretary, Julia.

"Good morning, sir. Secretary Lin will be here shortly," she said smoothly.

"Thanks, Julia."

John walked into his office, sat at his desk, and silently perused his messages. Patel plopped into a chair facing him. Out of the corner of his eye, he noticed Patel touch his eyebrow, and then his eyes shifted back and forth as if he was reading something on a screen.

Wrinkling his brow, John turned to him. "What are you *doing*, Rua?"

In an excited voice, Patel said, "I just got the iBrow implants."

He squinted at him. "iBrow?"

"They're the newest tech thing out there." He rolled the chair toward John and leaned into him, pointing to the two tiny beads embedded neatly into his eyebrows. "They correct vision, of course, but they are my phone as well. All my messages, voice, videos, games projected in front of my face. I can even video without anyone knowing it!"

With a frown, John leaned back in his chair. "That sounds scary. Don't video anything sensitive—including me," he said, pointing to his chest with his thumb. "I can be pretty damn sensitive."

Patel chuckled, then abruptly stood as Peter Lin entered the office.

John tilted his head. "What's going on, Peter?" He crossed his arms, studying Lin's stoic expression. Lin had become a shining star when he joined John's administration as the Secretary of Defense, and someone he could always count on for advice. Of Chinese descent, he had grown up in the States and enlisted in the American army before the merge of America and Canada. After the creation of Amerada, and like many fleeing the corrupt new country, he left the U.S. for China, and renounced his U.S. citizenship.

With his military training, he had taken a security job in the capital of China: Chongqing. During the Land Rush, he came to Antarctica as the head of the UN security forces. Afterward, he stayed on, setting up the fledging police force in Amundsen. In the chaos of forming a cabinet, Lin had been introduced to John as a possible defense minister.

Lin swept his finger across the virtual tablet in front of him. "A man named Ivan Zoric has come to our attention. He's the new leader of the breakaway Christian religious sect from Eastern Europe that settled next to the Concordia Refuge."

"I remember earlier this year that fur traps were discovered in the streams along their border with the refuge. Zoric's gang was implicated in smuggling furs to outsiders, but no proof has ever been established." John tapped the top of the desk. "Zoric's group is starting to sound like a cult, and one that doesn't bother with legalities."

Lin glanced at Patel. "Sir, I hope you don't mind if I invited Secretary Patel, but we believe the furs are being sold to foreign actors, and we may need help in stopping the trade from outside our borders."

Patel jabbed his thumb toward Lin. "The UN stocks the refuge and Zoric's men steal the animals, selling them on the world market."

With studied dismissiveness, Lin ignored Patel.

John bit his lip to keep from grinning. He was well aware that Lin despised Patel.

Lin continued. "We're still trying to get proof for the trapping, but now a new problem has arisen."

John clenched his jaw. *I don't want to hear this second shoe drop.*

"For several weeks, the neighboring regions have complained of strange activities in the Zoric camp, reporting sounds of gunfire and bizarre internet outages over the Grace Region. We've received news from the district bordering Zoric's." Lin grimaced. "Yesterday, an industrious Labrador

Retriever dug up part of a human skeleton. Someone may have been murdered."

*   *   *

Two days later, John stood under the flap of a crude tent, staring toward the border of Grace Region. The sky was steel gray, spitting cold rain. Grimacing, he shoved his hands back into the warm pockets of his coat. A gust of wind buffeted the tent, and he flinched as the awning snapped.

Where was Ivan Zoric?

For years, Grace Region had been benign, peaceably living with their neighbors. With the recent takeover of the group by the evangelical leader Ivan Zoric, all bets were off. Had there been a confrontation with the former leader of the group, his brother, Anton Zoric? The authorities ran the DNA of the bone marrow in the forearm and found a match to Anton, but the rest of his body had not been discovered. Without evidence, they couldn't get a warrant, and without a warrant, Ivan couldn't be brought in for interrogation, nor could the authorities search private property within his district.

Kisho stepped beside him and handed him a cup of hot tea. He said under his breath, "Mr. President, do you think this jerk is going to show?"

"He'll show." John laced his freezing fingers around the cup and sipped the hot liquid.

The rain changed to sleet, bullets of ice striking the covering of the tent.

Kisho shook his head. "We've been here over an hour—we can't wait forever."

John grunted. "We'll give him ten more minutes, and that's it."

The police had investigated a call from a terrified family after their black lab had proudly deposited a dirt-encrusted human forearm onto their kitchen floor, hand and bony fingers tenuously attached. They had tracked the dog back to the border of Grace Region, but when the two regional deputies had attempted to access their domain, a group of armed men had blocked them from entering, saying the deputies were trespassing.

When Ivan had been contacted, he had refused to come to Amundsen, so Lin had arranged a meeting with him to discuss a growing laundry list of weird events in and around their region. Zoric had sent a message that he would be willing to meet on the border of their lands. Now he was late.

A poke in the eye to begin the games?

The sparse information on Zoric portrayed a man of humble beginnings morphing into an intelligent, charismatic fanatic. An exquisite manipulator to be sure, but was he the madman others rumored him to be? Though Lin had warned against coddling Zoric, John hoped that rationality would win the day. Now he wondered if Lin was right.

John strained to see through the veil of sleet. His heart beat swifter as hovers appeared over the ridge. The hovers stopped and the doors opened. Even with the poor visibility, he recognized Ivan Zoric standing in the driving sleet. Zoric paused, scrutinizing his adversaries, then his men gathered into a loose formation of "captains" and "lieutenants" and they walked toward the tent.

The Drots hovered quietly in "Diplomatic" mode. John didn't want them to challenge Zoric and his men at this critical meeting.

Lin slid over to him and in a low voice, said, "We have enough firepower to take him out here and now, sir."

"As yet, we have no evidence against the man," John replied. "If we drag him into custody, the judge will have him released before morning."

Zoric approached the tent with a sneer on his grizzled face. Under his fur cap, beads of water from the mist clung to his long brown hair. Tall and lean, Zoric bent his head as he ducked under the awning. His piercing eyes locked on John.

John steeled himself—whether madman or not, he knew he had a formidable adversary on his hands.

Zoric swept off the fur cap and knocked the sleet off the beautiful pelt. John's lips thinned. *Ermine fur.* It looked like the rumors of illegal trapping of animals were true, at a time when stabilizing the animal population was paramount. Leave it to this asshole to flaunt it.

One of the local magistrates introduced them. "Ivan Zoric, this is John Barrous, the President of Antarctica."

He turned to John. "Mr. President, may I present Ivan Zoric."

He reached out to shake hands. Zoric removed his glove and shook his hand with a purposeful grip. The rest of Zoric's group remained huddled behind their leader.

John waved toward the table. "May I offer you, and your men, some hot tea?"

"Yes, thank you."

Warm cups of tea were passed around, then John gestured to a seat on the opposing side of the table.

He sat facing Zoric. "Illegal trapping of animals is forbidden inside of the refuge, and even beyond the refuge boundary until the animals are established enough for a reasonable harvest policy." He waved to the ermine cap on the table. "That cap of yours cost the people of Antarctica tax money to replace the animal hide warming your head."

Zoric's eyes glittered, his head tilted back with a sneer. "'And God granted man dominion over the beasts and birds.'"

John clenched his jaw. *I hate people who pretzel religion for their own selfish interests.* He leaned forward. "Mr. Zoric, a black Lab dug up the skeletal parts of a human arm. This dog was seen crossing the border from the Grace Region. Can you explain this?"

With a shrug, he replied, "How do I know where the bone came from? And why was the dog wandering on our land? Maybe you should interrogate the dog."

John observed his impenetrable face. "To catalog the population, every homesteader had to give samples of their DNA. We ran DNA on the bone marrow. The arm belonged to your brother." He pursed his lips. "Did you happen to notice if he was missing his left forearm?"

"Ah, my brother. Now the mystery is solved." Zoric sighed. "The day of that unfortunate accident is burned into my memory." He wagged his finger. "He was a sinner who drank too much. Last fall, he went to cut brush, and in his drunkenness, sliced off his own arm. We were able to stem the bleeding, and of course, buried it." He waved his hand. "Then, he returned to Serbia, a depressed and broken man." His mouth twitched into a gruesome smile. "After all, it was his favorite arm."

John balled his fist. This son of bitch was a pathological liar. "The medical examiner didn't mention that the limb had been cut in any way. And we have no record of him leaving Antarctica. He would need documents in order to return to his home country." He tilted his head. "If he has died, you cannot deny us access to your region to search for his body."

"Just because we don't know where he is doesn't mean he's dead. He was a funny guy. He had mentioned wanting to travel a bit, perhaps he flagged down a fisherman and caught a ride to South America on his journey to the home country."

"Or perhaps he swam there with one arm missing?" John tapped the table with his finger. "We're only asking that a group be allowed to inspect certain areas within your region. You can accompany us at all times, but we need to have full access to any area we deem necessary for this investigation."

A hush fell over the meeting as Zoric glared at John. He folded his arms across his chest. "You have no evidence that anyone has even died, therefore, we see no reason to allow intruders into our domain."

Lin walked up to the end of the table. "We'll find the evidence that your brother is dead." He jabbed his finger at Zoric. "And that he was murdered."

Zoric met Lin's look with a snarl. "Good luck, my friend."

With a frown, John shot a look at him. Lin narrowed his eyes but remained quiet.

Abruptly Zoric stood, his lips tight with anger. He cocked his head, signaling his group to leave.

John called to him, "We haven't finished our discussions of the fur trapping issue."

Zoric didn't turn but snapped his fingers to one of his followers. A twisted smile on his face, the man approached John and laid a small wooden box on the table in front of him.

As they walked away, John opened the box. He swallowed hard at the dried carcass of a skinned ermine. His hands shook with anger as he slammed the lid of the box shut. *These people are truly sick.*

Zoric's troupe reached their hovers. Zoric turned, glancing at the group under the tent. He threw his head back in laughter, and when the wind shifted, John heard his roar.

CHAPTER 5

Kisho walked into his office. "Good morning, John. I thought I'd run through the agenda for today."

John grinned. "Sure, let me have it—as long as no dismembered body parts are involved."

"Not this morning." Kisho tapped his watch and a virtual screen solidified in front of him. He swept his finger across the screen, and the agenda appeared on John's wall monitor. "At ten a.m. is the ribbon-cutting for the new fusion power plant, followed by a news conference."

"I assume that Dr. Becker is going to be there to handle any technical questions?"

He nodded. "Yes, she'll be there. And the press releases went out last week with an overview of nuclear fusion energy." Kisho smiled. "It's fantastic that we've been able to get one of the new fusion power plants."

John leaned back, cradling his head in his hand. "Yes, it will check a rather large box off the to-do list for my presidency." He mused. "It took over a century to develop a working fusion reactor. It makes you wonder if the Melt would have occurred if we had figured it out in the 1960s."

"And the decades of wars in the Middle East over oil."

"Exactly." He looked at Kisho. "Any update on Zoric?"

Kisho shook his head. "Not yet, sir. We're tracking down information on whether Ivan's brother left Antarctica or not.

I'm betting on the 'not' answer, but we can't get a warrant until the authorities finish their investigation."

Leaning forward, John tapped the desk with his knuckle. "Yeah, I doubt his poor brother is still with us, and what's left of him now moved to a different location or thrown into the ocean. It's a wonder that God doesn't send a comet this way and get rid of us for good." He cleared his throat. "On that cheery note; anything else for today?"

Kisho glanced at the virtual tablet. "Nothing scheduled after the news conference."

"Excellent, Kisho. I don't know what I'd do without you."

"Thank you, sir." He swiped the tablet image and it dissolved back into his watch. Kisho glanced at John. "Would you mind if I take off a bit early today? I'm taking Douglas to the doctor."

John nodded. "Of course; taking care of your spouse comes before work. I hope he's better?"

"He's recovering, partially in self-defense, I think. Sick of me fussing over him."

"Good. That was a nasty flu bug going around." John chewed his lip. "I forgot to mention that I have an appointment at the farm. I'm bolting out of Amundsen at noon."

"The weather should clear after the news conference; just in time for your escape from the city." Kisho turned to leave, then pivoted back. "I forgot, there is one other item—the Secretary General of the UN called. She wants you to give a speech at the 'State of the Earth Conference.' This year it's being held in Summit, New Jersey. It would be a great opportunity."

"Yeah, I could give a thrilling oratory on recycling manure." He grinned.

"That and all of your other accomplishments, sir."

"*Our* accomplishments, Kisho." He swept his arm wide. "Everything we've done took a team dedicated to balancing the needs of the people with our responsibilities to the Earth."

Kisho smiled. "Well said, Mr. President." He tilted his head. "I'll have them bring the robocar around to the door."

Flanked by the security Drots, John and Kisho hovered to the power plant. At ten o'clock, John and Dr. Becker stood facing a group of reporters and spectators in the entryway of the nuclear fusion plant.

John raised his hand to the group. "Thank you all for coming out on this dreary morning." With a smile, he waved at the donut-shaped 3-D hologram image of the fusion reactor. "Welcome to the future!" He gestured to Dr. Becker. "I'd like to introduce Dr. Becker, who's the nuclear physicist leading the power plant. She will give you an overview of nuclear fusion as an energy source." John pointed to Kisho, standing to the side. "And we have a press release on the power plant and nuclear fusion energy, if you didn't receive one."

Dr. Becker stepped forward with a broad smile. "Nuclear fusion is how our sun works, and is simple and elegant. When enough heat and pressure are applied, two hydrogen atoms are fused together and form helium, and in this way, energy is released in the form of heat. This heat turns water into steam, which spins turbines and produces electricity."

She pointed to the image behind her, now a diagram of a simple fusion reaction. "In nuclear fusion, there are no emissions and no radioactive waste produced. One of the reasons it took us so long to develop nuclear fusion energy, is that the fusion reaction itself is difficult to keep going, so the reactor doesn't go out of control like the old nuclear fission plants." With her thumb, she pointed to the coast behind them. "We use sea water as a source for the heavy hydrogen molecules, which is the particular type of hydrogen that is used in the process."

A reporter held up his hand. "What's the downside?"

"The only downside is minor radioactivity buildup of the container around the fusion reaction, but the timeframe for a return to background levels is approximately fifty years. Nuclear fission waste takes thousands of years to become safe." Dr. Becker smiled. "Fusion is the holy grail of energy and a long time coming for mankind. It's as much of a game-changer as the discovery of fire."

A young reporter shook her head. "It sounds almost too good to be true. What about continuing with the sustainable sources we currently have—solar, wind, and geothermal?"

Dr. Becker gestured to John. He stepped forward and replied, "Those energy sources are tiny in scale compared to fusion. As we know, solar is not available for months at a time on Antarctica, though the wind is fairly continuous. But both are dependent on the weather, time of year, and on the capacity of batteries to store the energy when the source isn't available. We'll still need renewables, but we've already had issues with heating homes over the winter." With a smile, John gestured to the hologram behind him. "Fusion is the ultimate solar power."

Another reporter raised his hand, and John pointed to him. "Mr. President, what's happening in the Grace district? We've heard rumors that Ivan Zoric has established a cult?"

With a nod, John said. "We recently met with Mr. Zoric and an investigation is underway."

On the edge of the press pool, a woman stepped forward and asked, "Mr. President, can you give us confirmation of a report involving strange ships, lights, and possible off-loading of items on the western islands of Antarctica?"

John swallowed hard. *What the hell?* He kept his face impassive and replied with a confident smile, "No update as yet. I'm waiting for a report from our Secretary of Defense, Peter Lin."

Kisho walked to the front of the press. "Thank you for coming."

The news conference ended. Kisho and John stepped into the robocar and started back to the presidential offices.

He leaned toward John, and whispered, "What's this about the western islands?"

John shrugged. "I have no idea, it's the first I've heard of it. Lin better have an answer." He tapped his leg. "Contact Lin and have him meet me in my office this afternoon."

"Lin won't be back until the morning. He's inspecting the port today."

He grimaced. "Let's see if we can get up to speed with whatever information the reporter has found. I've depended on Lin keeping me in the know."

CHAPTER 6

Every spring Lowry and John's neighbor, Bill Taylor, met with John to review plans for the upcoming season. Bill had just messaged that he'd twisted his ankle and couldn't make it, and Lowry and John should meet without him. She and John would be alone. Fate had signaled that today was the day to discuss their future—if they had one.

Biting her lip, Lowry stared into the mirror, brushing her hair with quick strokes. Her heart beat wildly as she set the brush on the vanity. She closed her eyes, breathing in and out to calm herself. She glanced back at her image, touching her cheek with trembling fingers. *Would John notice the tension in her face?*

Her desire for a child had clarified her mind—John was the man she wanted, both as a husband and a father, and she had to deal with it before her window of fertility closed. Artificial insemination was one route, even if John was willing to donate sperm, but she wanted the natural way or no way. She wished to raise a child with him, not just have his DNA. Despite his hatred, she'd never stopped loving him.

Lowry tucked her blouse into her slacks, grumbling to herself, "I hate being in a position of weakness." A line from a poem popped into her mind: *Like a tide, love raises you in frenzied waves, then recedes, leaving you abandoned on a solitary shore.* Was it possible that John felt the same way?

She pulled on her boots and grabbed her coat, zipping it up as she walked to the stables. The sky began to lighten behind a screen of low clouds. Lowry slipped on her gloves. With the sun's reappearance, the snow had begun to thin, but the cold wind reminded her that winter had not conceded to spring's debut.

She led the new Belgian horses she had purchased into the grooming stalls. She grabbed the shedding blade and began to pull it across the long rough coat of the first horse. With short, quick strokes she drew out the long winter hairs. *What if he never forgave her?* She moved along the barrel of the horse. He turned his head, giving Lowry a baleful stare as she hit a ticklish spot. *Even if we restarted our relationship, would John want to remarry at this stage of his life—and have another child?* The horse shook his head as Lowry worked the blade back and forth near his flank. "Sorry, buddy." Lowry said softly, stroking him as she gazed at the large pile of hair on the ground.

After she hitched the pair to the new sleigh, Lowry jumped in and clucked her tongue, signaling them to move out. With tinkling bells, they swept toward John's farm. The sun burst through the cloud bank, the slanting rays turning the snow from silver to gold, like crystallized honey. Lowry smiled. The overhead grid of artificial lights could never equal the breathtaking sight of the sun.

The team slowed as they moved into the pass and followed the river. As they reached John's land, she clucked them into a steady trot. She scanned the barren fields, ready to be awakened by spring. Like a day-old beard, the stipple of last year's crop stuck above the frozen earth.

Lowry chewed the inside of her cheek. The violent death of John's wife, though years ago, had scarred him. To risk love and marriage again must be frightening. Perhaps that was the real reason their relationship never coalesced?

She hummed, realizing the team had passed John's house. "Whoa, boys," she called out, pulling back on the reins. She turned them in a wide circle and halted them near the front porch. "Love makes you do stupid things," she muttered, stepping from the sleigh.

John appeared at the doorway. "Um, I just got the message from Bill. I guess he's not coming."

"Yeah, a twisted ankle."

He coughed, then gestured to the team, staring at him with ears pricked. "What a beautiful pair of horses—gold like Palominos."

"Yes, they're a matched pair of Belgian draft horses. I bought them and the sleigh from a farmer going back to the States." She hobbled them and put feedbags over their heads. "They'll be happy enough while we discuss the orchard."

"Since Bill is not here, we can meet in the house instead of the barn. It's a little warmer."

They walked into the house. Lowry glanced around—it looked abandoned. Dust covered everything, a reminder of the time that had passed.

John glanced at her with a shrug. "Sorry it's a mess. The housebots went out during an electric storm and I haven't had a chance to get them repaired."

With a smile, Lowry said, "It's close to noon. Why don't you come over to my place and we'll have lunch? We can stop by the orchards on our way."

"Okay," he mumbled and grabbed his coat. He opened the door, and the security Drots zoomed behind him.

The Belgians shied as the Drots circled them. They shook their flaxen manes as their hoary breath wreathed around their heads. John walked to the huge beasts and rubbed their foreheads. "I'm sorry. You're okay."

"If you want to ride with me in the sleigh, you can hitch your hover to the back and we'll tow it to my house."

John brought his hover to the back of the sleigh and attached it, then climbed in beside Lowry.

She poured warm brandy from a thermos into a travel cup and handed it to him, then wrapped a blanket around his legs.

He raised his eyebrows. "Even has room service."

The snow sparkled in the sunlight. She picked up the reins and settled herself on the seat of the sleigh, tucking a blanket around her body. With a cluck, the horses moved off to the jingle of bells. The Drots followed closely behind the sleigh.

The horses pricked their ears at a humming sound. Lowry pointed to the flock of drones slowly moving across the snow-covered fields. "Bill's 'swarms' will melt the remaining snow before planting."

His face turned pensive. "At least the farm isn't falling apart while I'm gone."

They halted at the orchard. John stepped from the sleigh and scanned the lines of dormant fruit trees. Lowry followed as he walked toward the row of apple trees, their umber branches lifted in pray toward the sky.

"The orchard looks great." He gazed at them with a smile. "They've doubled in size since I left the farm."

"Yes, I fertilize them and check the irrigation system on a regular basis. They produced a bumper crop last year."

"I appreciate the baskets you send to the office." He shrugged. "Of course, the check for my half of the proceeds goes directly to Ginnie's tuition."

"I'm glad I could help." Lowry stared at the lifeless tree she had seen on her previous visit, its broken limbs hanging to the ground. She chewed her lip and pointed to the dead tree. "We'll cut that one down and plant another sapling to replace it."

John walked to the tree and caressed the limbs like a doctor examining a patient. "The bark is peeling away." He shook the trunk and broke off several more branches. "Yep, it's dead all right."

Lowry swallowed. "We'd better keep moving."

They returned to the sleigh and started across the snow. The jingling sleigh bells wore on her nerves and she started at John's voice.

"How's Nick?" he asked, glancing at her.

With a frown, Lowry replied, "Not so good. Two inmates from the old Durant gang found out who he was and jumped him." She looked at John. "They beat him up pretty badly."

He shook his head. "I'm sorry to hear that. Maybe I can pull a few strings and move him into a safer situation."

"That would be wonderful, but please be discreet, whatever you do. He's worried that someone will rat and the next time might be worse than just a beating." She raised an eyebrow. "Any chance that Nick could be pardoned?"

"I'll try, Lowry, but it will have to wait until the end of my term. Less than a year to go and I'll be free, and hopefully, so will Nick."

With a smile, she touched his arm. "Thank you, John."

They moved into the valley between the farms. The ice over the stream had collapsed during the last warm spell, and the brook gurgled pleasantly as they passed. They reached the wide pastures of Lowry's farm and curved toward her house.

"Dr. Clavet mentioned that you'll be guiding the Cornell expedition." With pinched brows, John looked at her. "I want to tell you about a problem with the Grace Region."

She glanced at him. "The cult?"

"You've heard?"

"A little. Ivan Zoric sounds crazy. And a lovely rumor that a Lab dug up part of a human arm?"

"Good news travels fast." He shrugged. "The police force is gathering evidence to bring charges. Lin is chomping at the bit for a full-scale invasion, but beside a little item called a warrant, I'm worried about collateral deaths of innocents. We're trying to decide the best path forward."

John glanced at his watch. "P, can we get a photo of Zoric?"

A photo of Ivan Zoric projected in front of them.

"Thanks, P."

Lowry studied the image. "He looks like a dick."

He chuckled. "That says it in a word. We also have stories of illegal fur trapping near the Concordia Refuge. Until we can resolve the situation, I want the expedition to stay far from their boundary."

She nodded. "Aye, aye, Captain. I'm packing a gun regardless—wolves might be an issue."

"Absolutely. I'm going to ask Hank if he can join the group. Just as a precaution."

"Hank would love an excuse to get out of Amundsen."

The Belgians trotted across an open snowfield and past one of the laser corrals. The brown, long-haired cows relaxed in the sunlight, happily eating from the giant hay rolls scattered around the pen.

"Your Highland cattle look good," John said.

"With the harsh winter, we almost ran out of feed, so we had to send half of the herd to market. We kept the best momma cows and one bull, and they wintered well." She pointed to a couple of baby calves stretched out on a scattering of loose hay, asleep in the sun. "We already have a few calves."

The Belgians trotted up the hill to the horse stables. The horses lounging in the paddock whinnied as the team slowed to a walk.

They passed Lowry's house, encircled with orchards and a myriad of fallow gardens, with bare trellises waiting patiently for rising tendrils.

"Lowry, the place looks great."

"Thank you. It's been a lot of work, but we finished putting in the gardens." She smiled. "Now we just need spring to wake them up!"

She stopped the sleigh and they got out. The Drots descended into their fighting form and surveyed the perimeter of the barn. The horses ran to the other side of the paddock.

"Those things are creepy." Lowry said, jabbing her thumb at them.

"I'm afraid so. I won't miss them once I'm out of office."

Lowry unhitched the horses and released them into the corral, while John draped the cover over the sleigh.

He glanced at the clouds now advancing across the sky and grumbled, "Stay with us, sunshine." He pulled his coat together against the wind. The Drots returned and followed them to the house.

At the front door, John turned to them. "Exterior drone patrol only."

They collapsed into drone mode and buzzed around the house. After they hung their coats near the door, John followed Lowry into the kitchen. She waved to a chair at the table. "Sit, and I can make coffee?"

"I'd love a cup. Especially after that brandy you slipped me."

Lowry called out to the house, "Start coffee, please."

"Certainly, Lowry." Her virtual assistant's voice floated in the air.

John raised an eyebrow. "I thought you'd refused to have a virtual assistant?"

"Yeah, I did. Then I was forced into it by an upgrade to the house computers."

She walked to the refrigerator. "How about a roast-beef sandwich?"

"Perfect."

He sat at the table as Lowry sliced the roast beef and bread. She glanced at him. "Tell me how you've been, John."

"Surviving day to day in a glass cage. Most of the time, I feel like I'm driving a bus at the edge of a cliff and can't get back on the road." John turned over his hands. "See my hands? They're soft and white, no longer the hands of a farmer."

As she assembled the sandwiches, her breath caught in her throat at the bitterness of his voice. *Lowry, would you like a side of guilt with your sandwich?* With a grimace, she sliced the sandwiches in two and plated them. Her hands trembled as she brought the tray to the table. Lowry passed John his coffee and sandwich, pulled out a chair and sat, scooting up to the table with a screech. She lifted her cup with shaking fingers, took a sip of coffee—and choked.

"That hard stuff gets to me too." John studied her. "What's eating you, Lowry?"

With a shrug, Lowry set her coffee cup on the table. She tapped the side of the cup, then blurted out, "John, we had left things at loose ends, but I want to know . . . have you forgiven me?"

John put down his half-eaten sandwich. Lowry chewed her lip waiting for him to speak.

With a pinched mouth, he faced her. "You are such a fine woman, and I wish all the baggage between us was in the past, but I can't honestly say that." He gazed at her. "From my point of view, you sacrificed me, and our relationship, and Ginnie as well, for an abstract idea called Antarctica. It's very hard for me to forgive you."

He turned away from her and stared out of the window. "I had dreamed of a simple life. A safe country school for Ginnie, with me teaching her about the world—not being raised by a housekeeper who ferried her to school events and social outings while her old man traveled or worked ten- or twelve-hour days. There are so many moments we cannot get back. Time flows one way."

"You accomplished a great deal for Antarctica."

John shot her a look. "I've tried my best to do what's right for the big picture, but I've made personal sacrifices on the way. Ginnie's starting her own life—we'll never be a family again."

Lowry dropped her eyes, staring at her plate. She had played god with his life, shoving John onto a path that he didn't want because she felt the ends justified the means. Who was *she* to decide someone else's fate?

She dug her nails into the palms of her hands. "You're right, and frankly, I don't deserve your forgiveness." She sighed. "I've anguished over this ever since the election, though I felt there was no one else."

He cleared his throat. "I'm not sure I agree on that last item."

Lowry gazed vacantly out of the window. "This may not make any difference, but I need to tell you something that impacted me as a young woman." She clenched her jaw, forcing herself to relive a past that she'd spent a decade forgetting. Tears welled in her eyes, but she blinked them back.

She drew in a deep breath and exhaled, glancing at John, now staring intently at her. She whispered, "The fear of that time changed me as a person." Her voice broke and she stared at the table. "It was long ago, but do you remember when the ISS crashed into the Atlantic Ocean?"

He furrowed his brows in confusion. "Of course."

Her lips taut against her emotion, Lowry met John's eyes. "I was the only survivor."

CHAPTER 7

John's mouth sagged. "*You* were the survivor of the ISS crash?" He stared into her anguished face, revealing both the pain and the truth of Lowry's story.

He remembered the ISS disaster, but at the time, the lone survivor had not been identified. In a world of constant social media, it was odd, but the survivor's name had virtually been erased, or so it had seemed, as the manhunt for the culprits ensued. Regardless, he and Helen had been raising Ginnie. Kindergarten, lacrosse games, school events, all the usual family stuff, with no time for an exciting detective story.

Lowry shrugged. "In the weeks before the ISS was thrown into the sea, I became a pawn in a political-corruption web. Halder, the attorney general of Amerada at the time, was a manipulative bastard—a Machiavellian to a T." With a slow shake of her head, she whispered, "I am still haunted by my inadvertent role in the charade."

John opened his mouth and closed it. *Wow.* Blinking, he studied her tense face. "You must have been young?"

"Yes, I was a grad student—and very naïve."

"What was the final outcome?"

Lowry raked back her hair. "Oh, the usual: those in power squashed those unable to defend themselves. Greed overcame justice." She leaned forward and covered his hand with hers. "Within a corrupt political system, human vices run amok, and in my mind, Durant and his crowd were the same as Halder. I just could not allow my homeland to be raped by the Russian mafia."

John stared into his cup of coffee. "I wish you had told me this earlier." *It must have been traumatic for her. How would Ginnie have reacted?* He blinked in confusion, then shifted his gaze to the rolling fields and scattered puddles where the snow had melted. In the silence between them, the cattle lowed and water gurgled from the ice melting off the roof, flowing to the cistern of the house.

He clenched his fist. *What happened in the past still didn't excuse her throwing him under the bus even if he had been stupid enough to allow it to happen.* For years, he had bottled up his anger and resentment toward Lowry. With a set jaw, he faced her. "No matter what, damage was done to our relationship." Frowning, he snapped his fingers. "You can't simply say 'poof' and all the pain disappears."

A twinge crossed her face, and she drew her hand from his.

He shoved the cup aside. "I had broken free from a warped society that I hated, and started my life over in the wilderness of Antarctica. I became the man I wanted to be." He met her eyes. In a voice hard and flat, he said, "You betrayed that man."

Lowry dropped her gaze to the table. "I know. I'm trying to explain why." Her fingers trembled as she clutched the mug. "I was shell-shocked. Everything in my life flipped upside down and I panicked." She sighed. "After Durant stole the election and then was assassinated—"

John cocked his head. "—by Nick."

"—by Nick," Lowry replied. She shot him a glance under furrowed brows.

He shrugged and gestured for her to continue.

"—and the man who I knew as my father commits suicide."

John mused, "Ironically, Duff was the only one who got what he wanted."

"You asshole."

"If I wasn't a gentleman, I'd say, 'back 'atcha.'"

Lowry stared out of the window, then turned to him, her eyes fixed on his. "John, you're the only man I've ever truly loved. I know that external circumstances got in the way of our personal lives, but I must make a decision soon. I want to have a child . . . and I want that child to be yours."

Jesus Christ. He dropped his gaze to his half-eaten lunch. *So that's it. I should have known there was something else, besides my magnificence, creating this sudden wish for love.* He shifted in his chair and exhaled, drumming his fingers on the table. God knows once Lowry decided on her path, there was no stopping her. He glanced at her, and pushed his cup toward her. "How about a warm-up on that great coffee—and a double shot of whiskey?"

"Shut up and answer me, John."

His mouth twisted in anger. "Are you asking me, in a 'subtle' way to marry you? The last time I asked you, the answer was no."

"I never said no. I said the time wasn't right. I was wrong. Does that make you happy?"

"Yes."

"John, I love you. I want us to marry and have a child."

He cleared his throat. "I'm getting a bit old to think about that."

She snorted. "You're only forty-nine."

"Only forty-nine, looking down the barrel at the big five-o."

"I'm looking at the big four-o, myself," Lowry said softly, intently stirring her coffee.

John narrowed his eyes as he gazed at her. "I do see some gray, Madame."

"Fuck you."

A lopsided grin sprang to his face. "If I'm reading you right, that's what you have in mind."

"Ha, ha." She leaned forward. "John, half of your life is ahead of you. I'm in the same boat. Whether I like it or not, my biological clock is ticking. I need to get on the stick—literally."

"You're so romantic, dear." John drained the rest of the tepid coffee and put the mug down with a clunk. "Honestly, this has hit me like a train." He lurched up, shoving the chair back with a squeak. With outstretched arms, he stared at her. "You can't throw this on me and expect an answer. I need time to unravel the anger over what happened." With a puckered brow, he said, "If I say no, who's next? For that matter, I'm not sure if I'm number one."

Lowry's eyes grew wide. "Don't be a jerk." With a scowl, she turned away, her hands balled into fists.

John moved to her side of the table. "You're right, I *am* being a jerk." He placed his hand on her shoulder. "I'm sorry. You didn't deserve that."

She snapped, "Thank you," but refused to meet his gaze.

He chewed his lip. "Lowry, even if we could resolve our issues and restart our relationship, I'm in office until next year. What about your farm? What about the expectations for a president's spouse? And facing the people who remember the events of four years ago?"

She glanced at him and he saw a glimmer of hope in her face. "I realize that I changed your life by pushing you onto the ballot." She rose, lifted his hand and squeezed it. "I am asking for your forgiveness." She touched his cheek. "If you can forgive me, and we can love each other again, then we'll overcome any obstacles."

John looked into her eyes and felt himself falling into them. With a cough, he turned away, clenching his fist. "It's not a done deal. I need to digest all of this."

She tilted her head toward his half-eaten sandwich. "The roast beef wasn't that tough."

"Ah, but the conversation was."

CHAPTER 8

John returned to the presidential offices, sorting through his intense lunchtime conversation with Lowry. He walked along the hall absentmindedly, nearly running into a robo-cleaner that promptly flashed a red light at him. "Sorry," he muttered as he scooted around the robot vacuuming the floor with precise determination.

John walked into his office and plopped into his seat. With a heavy sigh, he drummed his fingers on the desktop, shoving his disparate thoughts into cubbies in his mind for later scrutiny. He shook his head and said softly to Julia, "Sort messages in priority, please."

Holograms of messages with red banners across them popped up in front of him. He leaned back in his chair and swept through them, answering a few, throwing some to Kisho, and the rest to a back-burner folder. He quickly progressed through the less-important yellow messages, sending most to Kisho to handle.

Lin walked into his office. "You wanted to see me, sir?"

John glanced up at Lin and, with a sigh, whisked away the green messages for a later date. He tilted back in the chair and studied his Secretary of Defense. No expression on Lin's face. It was odd that he hadn't reported the ship incident on the western islands. Like a dog roving a perimeter, Lin was a territorial beast, barking and running the fence line—it was strange that he might miss a possible intrusion. His eyebrow twitched. *I may need to keep an eye on Mr. Lin.*

John took a deep breath. "I was blindsided by a reporter during yesterday's press conference at the fusion plant. She asked a question on suspicious activities on the western islands of Antarctica." He furrowed his brow. "Do you know about this?"

A thin smile flashed onto Lin's face, then dissipated. With a wave, an image of a document appeared in his hand. "Yes, sir, I have the report with me. I just found out yesterday that a Chinese cargo ship went aground near Graham Island." He chuckled nervously. "A fishing boat saw her and mistakenly radioed in that it was a large ship offloading onto smaller boats."

"Do we have any imagery?"

Lin shook his head. "Not much. It was foggy." He swiped his finger across the document, flipping vague images of a cargo ship onto the wall monitor. "These photos were taken by a drone, after they set sail. I assume that when the high tide came in, the ship was able to dislodge and continue on without incident."

"Did the captain of the ship contact the Antarctic authorities?"

"No, it doesn't appear that they did. Maybe they were embarrassed or didn't want to get in trouble with their bosses."

"We need to get all the facts on this." He glared at Lin. "I don't like hearing a ship ran aground or anything like that from a reporter before I hear it from you."

Contritely, Lin tilted his head. "Yes, sir, I apologize. I had just received an initial report while I was heading to the port for the inspection. I didn't think it was serious."

John snapped, "It's serious. What if the ship had capsized and sank? Lives could have been lost. Can we find out whose ship it was?"

"I magnified the images, but I can't read the ship's identification numbers."

John pursed his lips. "Let's start patrolling more often and keep better track of shipping in our waters."

With a sigh, Lin dropped his gaze. "Yes, sir. Again, I'm really sorry."

"Okay, let's get a report together for the press, but run it by me and Kisho first. Then we can release it to the public."

Lin's mouth twitched as he stared at the ground.

John narrowed his eyes at Lin. For years he'd been his most trusted cabinet member and was the one always warning John of trespasses into their domain. With a sigh, John folded his hands. *At least the thumping was over.* "What's the latest on Zoric?" There was an almost audible sigh of relief from Lin at the change of subject. John bit his lip to keep from smiling.

"Not much. I sent drones to reconnoiter within the Grace Region, but once they reached the border, they stopped transmitting. When the operators found them, they were dead on the ground, but there's no explanation as to why the drones' power died. We tried pinging the internet transmitters for that area, but apparently the internet web is completely out." With a slight shake of his head, Lin said, "I recommend we put a force on the ground and find out what's happening in there."

"Do we have any more information on the cult and Zoric?"

"Only that his family had established a religious group in Serbia, then were kicked out for stockpiling arms and fomenting ethnic violence. But besides that, nothing more than our original report." Lin shrugged. "You would think that with the internet nothing could be hidden, but if you know what you're doing, you can erase anything."

"How did a cult like that get a foothold in Antarctica?"

"Governments love to scrub the background of questionable characters and dump them onto unsuspecting countries."

Grimacing, John said, "Yeah, now they're our problem. Let's keep digging on Zoric's past and get a few extra eyes patrolling the Grace border with the Concordia Refuge."

"Yes, sir." Lin gestured with his hand. "Also, the report came back from the Amundsen city veterinary who did the autopsy on the ermine body in the box that Zoric's man dropped onto the table." He raised a brow. "It died from old age, not from trapping."

John grunted. "He's a wily son of a bitch—loves to keep us off balance." He shook his head. "Regardless, the expedition is heading out in the morning, and I don't want any issues popping up—I want them safe." With a sigh, he stared at his desk. *I'm going to be a basket case until they return.*

With a concerned look, Lin nodded. "Yes, sir, we'll step up patrolling in the area." He turned to leave.

John held up a finger. "Oh, Lin, before you go, I forgot to mention that the police chief of Amundsen caught someone you may know in a drug sting. A guy named Zhang Tao?"

Lin's back straightened abruptly, then he pivoted back and stared at John. He blinked in shock and then nodded. "Zhang is a distant cousin of mine. When I returned to China, he found a security job for me in the capital, Chongqing. Unfortunately, he has had an off-and-on addiction to opioids, but I was under the impression that he had cleaned up his habit. As a return favor, I hired him to help with the Land Rush security."

John coughed. "I'm afraid he's in jail at the moment."

For a moment, Lin stared vacantly ahead, his fists clenched. With pinched lips, he met John's eyes. "Most disappointing."

CHAPTER 9

John knocked on the doorframe of Ginnie's room. "All packed?" With a twinkle in his eye, he perused the bed covered in clothes, surrounding an empty duffel bag.

Ginnie stuck her tongue out at him. "You're too funny, Dad."

"You give me so much good material." He leaned on the jamb. "Don't forget the foot and hand warmers I gave you."

She held up the socks and glove liners. "Those will definitely get packed." She shrugged. "It looks worse than it is. I just have to throw everything into the bag and hope I can zip it."

"It's the zipping event that has me curious." A cup of coffee floated in on a tray, stopping in front of John.

Ginnie gasped at the burnished metal tray hovering in mid-air. "What the hell is *that?*"

He lifted the cup from the tray, murmuring, "Thanks." He sipped the steaming liquid as the tray floated into the hall on its way to the kitchen. "The Japanese ambassador gifted us one of their new inventions. It's called a Hovler—a hover butler."

With a grin, she gave him a thumbs-up. "I love it!"

"I'll admit it's handy. I ask P for something and it magically appears wherever I am in the apartment." John sat in the dressing chair facing the bed. "Back on the subject of the trek." He leaned forward. "Even though Dr. Clavet is the leader of the expedition, she's not familiar with the trials and tribulations of Antarctica. You and Lowry are experienced trekkers, and I've asked Hank to join you."

"He would be great to have on the trip." Ginnie folded her clothes into piles.

He tapped the edge of the cup. "Honey, I want to discuss a problem that has arisen. A religious cult has set up in the Grace Region, led by a nut, Ivan Zoric. The expedition route takes you near the Grace border, but you must not cross into their territory."

Nodding distractedly, she began stuffing the bag.

John's voice rose. "I'm not kidding—I want you to stay away from that boundary. They are under investigation for possible crimes—including murder."

She stopped packing and looked at him. "You're serious?"

"Yes, I am."

"Does Dr. Clavet know?"

"I briefed her on it, but I'm not sure it penetrated."

"Yeah, she can be rather 'focused' on her work."

Chuckling, he said, "'Focused' is a good way to phrase it. That's the other reason I've asked Hank to join the group. He'll be armed against wolves, both the four- and two-legged ones. As will Lowry."

"Wow. So much for a fun college outing."

"Welcome back to wilds of Antarctica." With a shrug, he lifted his hand. "If the expedition doesn't cross him, I don't think Zoric will be any threat."

He set his coffee onto the nearby desk, stood and watched her sort, fold, and pack the bag. With a little cough, he shifted on his feet. Then he blurted out, "There's something else I want to discuss with you."

Ginnie glanced at him, narrowing her eyes at his pensive face. She sat on the side of the bed with a tilt of her head. "True confessions?"

"Not quite." He cleared his throat. "Um, Lowry wants to get married."

Guffawing, she jabbed her finger at him. "I *knew* you still had feelings for her."

John scowled. "She filled me in on some background as to why she nominated me. I understand her point of view better." He gazed at her. "She asked me to forgive her."

With a grin, Ginnie said, "Lowry would be good for you, Dad."

"It's a tiny bit more complicated." He rubbed his forehead. "She wants a child."

Her brow twitched, and she looked away, blinking slowly as she digested the news. After a moment, she turned to him. "A baby is a big decision. And you both have to agree, of course."

He sighed. "Yes, I'm still sorting the child issue out in my mind."

She picked at the fabric of the comforter. "You were a great father to me. Whatever you choose, Mom would want you to be happy." Ginnie looked at him. "She loved you very much. I know you tried to hide it from me, but she told me how you hated corporate life. Mom said that one day we'd be able to get out of Pittsburgh and move somewhere safe and quiet."

He gazed into her eyes, swallowing hard. She reminded him of Helen when she was Ginnie's age, almost thirty years ago.

Fresh out of college with an environmental engineering degree, John had been hired by an environmental firm in Pittsburgh. As a part of his training, he had been brought onto a case in which one of the principals was an expert witness. Helen was a young attorney with the law firm that had engaged John's company. Their eyes had met across the conference table and he asked her out in the break room that afternoon. They had married a year later.

Ginnie rose and wrapped her arms around him. "I think Mom would approve of Lowry and whatever decision you both make as to having a baby." She laid her head on his shoulder. "And so do I."

He blinked back tears as he hugged her. Until he had become a father, he hadn't realized what being a parent truly meant. A child was the greatest joy and the most devastating heartache wrapped into one little human. When Helen had lost her first pregnancy with the twin boys, the searing grief had nearly ripped apart their marriage. Somehow the strands of love had lasted long enough for Ginnie to be conceived, and their relationship had survived. He closed his eyes. *Until death do us part.*

John caressed Ginnie's hair. "Thanks, I'm glad you approve—it means a lot to me. Your mother was an amazing woman, a wonderful wife, and a great mom." He sighed. "Though I'll never forget her, as a human being I need companionship and love."

With a slight shake of his head, he said, "And despite all that has occurred and how frayed the bonds between us have gotten, I still have feelings for Lowry."

CHAPTER 10

John gazed at the Presidential dining room, decorated with elegant table settings and exquisite flower bouquets. On the eve of their journey into the wilderness, his staff had done an extraordinary job on the dinner party for the university research group. He stared at the flickering candles, trying to shake his disquiet. *They're leaving tomorrow morning for the refuge.* Like fussing at a painful hangnail, his mind kept returning to worry about the impending trek.

He gripped the back of a chair. A nightmare had woken him at three that morning—his heart pounding as he dreamed of the night, years ago, when the police called, informing him of his wife's murder. He had stared at the ceiling, slammed with the memories of shock and grief, and the terrible emptiness that had followed.

Leaning over the chair, he inhaled and exhaled until his anxiety faded. To truly live, one had to take risks. He could not keep his daughter in a cage, nor would he want to try. He had to admit that he was concerned for Lowry as well, though she was a grown woman capable of handling herself. There would always be a connection with her no matter how their relationship progressed. He shook his head. *I'm being ridiculous to be this nervous.*

Lowry arrived, and like the sun breaking through the clouds, John's mood lightened at her smiling face. She glided toward him in an elegant black dress. It had been ages since he'd seen her in anything other than rough farm clothes. He could not keep his eyes off of her, and by the twinkle in her eye, she knew it.

John cleared his throat. "You're simply stunning, Lowry."

Her smile broadened. "Thank you, kind sir."

After their meeting at her farm, his mind and his heart had been in turmoil. In his loneliness, it was easy to pull the rock of anger out from time to time, gazing at the pain it had caused, but quite another to face a lover who fully acknowledges the damage done and asks for forgiveness. Especially with the way she looked tonight.

"Will Hank be able to join us?" He gestured with his thumb at a small bar set with various whiskeys. "I made sure we had his favorite adult beverage."

Lowry smiled. "He's loading the last items onto the hover carrier, and then he'll be here."

"I'm glad Hank was able to come on this trip." John grimaced. "I may be able to sleep slightly better knowing he's with you—and armed."

Her brow twitched. "I'm glad he's coming as well." She squeezed his arm. "We'll keep in touch. I know how worried you are about Ginnie."

A quick smile flashed on his face. "It's not only Ginnie." He shrugged. "If we didn't have a planned cruise to 'show the flag' as it were, I'd go along."

"Show the flag?"

"Yes, there was a recent report of a foreign ship around our western islands, so Lin felt that we should cruise a few islands on one of the Coast Guard ships to assure folks that we were on guard. We head out tomorrow afternoon for a couple of days, then I'll fly back."

Lowry nodded. "I think we'll be okay. Surely Zoric isn't so stupid as to bother with us if we stay away from the Grace Region."

He crossed his fingers. "Let's hope."

She brushed back her hair and turned to muffled voices in the foyer. Her scent drifted to him and he closed his eyes. Could he forgive her? Or perhaps a better question—was he willing to risk love again?

The university group meandered into the room and John touched Lowry's arm. "I need to get into host gear." He met them near the door with a smile. "Welcome to the President's Stateroom."

Ginnie beamed. "Dad, the place looks beautiful!"

Noelle stepped to him and shook his hand. "Yes, quite lovely. It's very nice of you to throw a party for us."

"It's the least we can do for our honored guests."

Lowry joined them. Noelle turned to her, a smile on her face. "You look gorgeous tonight."

"So do you, Dr. Clavet."

"Thank you, but I'm afraid this is the last dressing-up for a while."

The room buzzed with laughter and excitement. John waved to the refreshments table. "Please, feel free to have something to drink before dinner."

Dr. Elena Brovanec walked through the doorway.

"Elena!" John called to her. He turned back to Noelle. "I want you to meet Dr. Brovanec, the Secretary of the Environment I mentioned."

Noelle's eyes brightened. "Bon! I can't wait to meet her."

Elena joined them and John did the introductions.

"Dr. Clavet, I'm so thrilled to meet you," Elena said. "I've read your articles—John and I used several of your ideas in our plans."

Noelle bowed her head. "I'm honored. And please call me Noelle."

A snapping sound came from the entryway and they turned to see Hank shaking sleet from his coat. He hung the coat on one of the hooks in the hallway, and with ruffled hair, strode into the room.

John grinned. *Ever the rough old miner.* "Hank, so glad you could make it. I made sure that your favorite whiskey was here to warm your bones." He poured a tumbler and handed the glass to Hank.

"Thanks, John." Hank tilted his head toward the door. "Starting to sleet a bit, but the weather is supposed to clear by morning."

The maître d' signaled to John that dinner was ready. With a smile, John motioned to the gathering. "Please make your way to your seats, ladies and gentlemen."

The group ambled toward the large dining table, seating themselves amidst the sound of scraping chairs and animated conversation.

John took his seat last. The adults had congregated on one end of the table and the students on the other. Noelle sat to his left, Elena to his right, with Lowry next to Elena. Ginnie sat beside Noelle, the link between the adults and students, but chuckled with her fellow classmates. He gazed at his daughter's profile as she smiled at a fellow student's antics. She was an intelligent twenty-year-old beauty, full of vitality—and the spitting image of her mother.

John nodded to the maître-d' to begin serving. Salads were brought out, and the room was filled with tinkling sounds of utensils.

Lowry glanced at Noelle. "How did you become a naturalist?"

Noelle inclined her head. "A winding road to be sure. I was majoring in biology, which I adored, but it was sparse on mental stimulation. I took a philosophy class my sophomore year. My professor blew away any rigid thoughts I may have harbored up to that point. I've never forgotten his favorite saying: 'Generalities are the refuge of a weak mind.' I decided to pursue a dual major in both subjects. I think naturalist was the only 'job' available to me when I graduated."

After the salads were taken away, the head waiter set an exquisite rack of lamb on the table. He sliced a chop, set it on a plate and offered it to Noelle. She grimaced and waved the plate away.

John asked, "Is something wrong?"

"Um, I guess no one told you I'm a vegetarian."

He glanced at Ginnie. "No, no one told me that."

"Sorry, Dad, I forgot to mention it," she said meekly.

"It's not a problem," Noelle said, picking up a bowl of wild rice and scooping up a large serving.

After the guests were served, the waiter bowed, saying, "Bon appétit," and withdrew.

John sliced into the chop. "I feel that livestock is like a cultivated crop. They're grown for a purpose—for humans to consume. On Antarctica, once the imported wild animals have been firmly established, in order to manage the numbers, wild-game hunting permits might be considered, outside of the refuge areas, of course."

Noelle pursed her lips. "Hunting wouldn't be my first choice as a tool to manage herd sizes. There are other management techniques, such as a proper balance of predators to prey, that can stymie overpopulations of any one group of animals." She sighed. "If only proper management could be applied to one beast that is proliferating beyond all others . . ."

Lowry looked at Noelle and asked, "What animal is that, Dr. Clavet?"

She turned to Lowry with a grin. "Humans."

John chuckled, then shrugged as Lowry narrowed her eyes at him.

Noelle smiled at Lowry. "And we're going to spend several weeks together, so everyone please call me Noelle." She served herself a fork-full of green beans. She glanced at Lowry. "Ginnie tells me that you've had an extraordinary life on Antarctica?"

Lowry wiped her mouth on her napkin and draped it across her lap. "An ordinary story in an extraordinary place. My mother had passed away a few months before I came to Antarctica, so the transition wasn't easy. The emptiness of the land matched the hole in my heart, but in time, it healed me." She shrugged. "But at home, my life was complicated—I don't know if any of you were aware that my uncle Duff was the provisional governor of Antarctica, before the initial Land

Rush occurred?" She lifted an eyebrow. "Let's just leave it that his skill set was limited as both a governor and a pseudo-father."

Hank snorted. "I'll drink to that," he muttered, and drained his whiskey.

Lowry glanced at him, then continued. "When it came time for my college, I chose to return to the States and attend my mother's alma mater. I majored in geophysics, and after graduate school, I worked on mapping the surface geology and waterways of Antarctica. When the news came that they would open Antarctica to homesteaders, I decided to return and stake a claim."

John smiled. "Ginnie and I met Lowry on the ship bringing the first homesteaders to Antarctica."

Lowry squeezed Hank's arm. "Hank was here at the opening of the continent, and one of my father's closest friends."

Nodding, Hank said, "Yep, I was part of the original Antarctic expedition. Lowry's uncle, Nick—I mean, father—and I were on the same ship." He grinned. "I still remember that day. Cold, windy and miserable—and the start of an amazing adventure. Those first months, we lived in insulated tents, slowly building the mining town from scratch. Nick was a young geologist, but he became much more than that." He looked down and shook his head. "Until fate handed him a dreadful duty." He tilted his head toward Lowry. "It was tough on little Lowry when she arrived to a rough mining town and no momma."

The waiter refilled their wine glasses and Hank's whiskey. The staff cleared the table, followed by a dessert cart and coffee.

Noelle sipped her coffee, then turned to Elena. "I'd love to hear about Antarctica's environmental policy."

"It was a challenge, but our goal was to balance the human development with the environment. In drafting the Constitution, we modified an existing UN doctrine, adding it as a clause into the Antarctic Bill of Rights: *All citizens shall have the right to a healthy environment."*

John counted down with his fingers. "Safe water, no toxic dumping, and no warfare that causes damage to the environment." He grimaced. "Which means *all* warfare."

Elena nodded. "Our goal was to ensure the right not only to life, but to a healthy one, internally and externally."

John tapped the table. "And permanently written into the constitution, so the next president can't overturn it."

With a smile, Noelle said, "That's why your work here is so important."

"We didn't do this to save the world. We just tried to develop a rational plan," John said.

"One person's rationality is another's insanity. It's the small pushes of good that might one day create an avalanche in the right direction. Most people just see the ground in front of them. You have shown people what could be."

Hank stared at her with a grimace. "What about the mining operations?"

Noelle raised a brow and shook her head. "Mining is very polluting."

Sliding his glass back and forth on the table, Hank leaned forward. "We have to have minerals."

She turned to Hank and they locked eyes, neither one retreating. Then with a faint huff, she shrugged. "I remember a saying from my studies of the American Indians: 'We dig small holes and you [the whites] dig big holes.'"

"Farming is worse for the environment than mining," he muttered, crossing his arms with a frown.

To keep the fight from escalating, John held up his hand. "It's a double-edged sword. Fossil fuels brought us into the modern age, but when the population exploded, we didn't move to a green power source quickly enough." He rotated his hand. "What we must find is balance; we need to farm to feed ourselves and dig in the earth for the resources to run our world." With his other hand, he pantomimed an old balance scale. "But you have to require environmental measures for everything that humans touch over its entire life-cycle." John glanced at Hank. "The UN has had inspectors for the Antarctic mines from the beginning. I've personally toured the mining operations and they're run properly."

Noelle folded her napkin and placed it on the table. She ignored Hank's scowling face and smiled. "In just living, humans overuse precious resources and create pollution. That's why I'm working on population control."

Elena raised her finger. "Your ideas on the necessity of limiting human population are part of how we developed our tax code. Over two children in a single family, and the family has to pay additional taxes. We try to discourage large families. Especially on Antarctica where the climate is harsh and so the land needed to support an individual is greater."

Hank lifted his glass in a mock toast. "I guess you were delighted that the Melt drowned the millions of folks that it did." With a grotesque smile, he shrugged. "Got rid of some humans, though I guess the shark population rose."

In the stunned silence, Lowry glanced at Hank, and then cleared her throat. "I wonder if the battle of humans against nature stems from our need to dominate?" With a pensive look, she shook her head. "Perhaps it's fear that makes people want to control their surroundings. No bugs, no large animals, and controlled landscaping. A deep instinctual fear of being out of control."

John scanned the faces around the table. Hank stared at the empty tumbler in his fist and Elena nodded solemnly. But it was the pain on Noelle's face that reflected the searing veracity in Lowry's statement.

"On that cheery note." John raised his glass. "To a successful and safe trek into the, as yet, uncontrolled wilderness of Antarctica."

The others around the table raised their glasses, with a few muted "Cheers."

Solemnly, Noelle lifted her glass. "Here's to the evolution of the human, from instinctual beast to a thoughtful being— before we destroy the Earth—and ourselves."

Hank shot her a look, then dropped his empty glass onto the table with a clunk.

The staff began to remove the dishes. As the students rose from the table, their effervescence revived and they talked excitedly of the next day's start.

John's unease returned as the students chattered nearby. He turned to Noelle, voice low, "As I mentioned earlier, whatever you do, stay away from the Grace territory. With this unresolved situation with the leader of that region, Ivan Zoric, it would be imprudent to cross into his district. The refuge is large enough to stay away from the boundary."

"I have no interest in political situations, just the wildlife."

John glanced at Lowry with a raised eyebrow. She gave an imperceptible nod of her head.

After the table was cleared, Noelle stood and said to John, "The students and I thank you for your lovely hospitality, but we must take our leave and get some rest. We have an early call in the morning."

The students groaned.

"I want to thank you for coming this evening," John said. "I wish you all the best and please, *please* be careful."

The students thanked him for the dinner, then headed toward the door.

John wrapped his arm around Ginnie. "Young lady, you take care of yourself." He bent down and whispered, "And I want you to listen to Lowry and Hank."

She smiled up at him. "I will, Dad." Slipping her arms around him, she said, "I love you very much."

He lifted her into a bear hug. "I love you, too, sweetie."

Laughing, she said, "Dad, I can't breathe!"

He released her and tugged a lock of her hair. *Be safe, my beautiful daughter.*

Ginnie waved at Lowry. "See you in the morning," she said, then joined the students as they left the dining room.

Hank ambled over and glanced at John. "I hope I didn't mess up your party." He darted a look at Noelle. "She's one of those environmental human-haters."

Chuckling, John squeezed his shoulder. "I don't think she's actually *hates* people." He shook his hand. "Take care, Hank, but try to chill it on the trek—promise me?"

"I'll try." He frowned. "But it won't be easy." Hank headed to the door and waved to Lowry. "Lowry, I'll see you bright and early."

"I'll meet you at the hovers."

Lowry walked up to John. "Nothing like a good discussion to stir the blood." She sighed. "Unlike me, who inadvertently shut down the party, I'm afraid."

He tilted his head. "Truth cuts deep. Human nature is the real reason we can't seem to stop 'engineering' the world into oblivion."

"Perhaps one day humans will stop being stupid."

She turned to go, but John whispered, "Wait, Lowry, I want to talk to you."

The robo-crew finished clearing the table, and the room quieted.

He touched her shoulder. "I want you to watch over Ginnie, Lowry, as well as yourself."

"I have a pistol."

"Good, and Hank is also armed, though I hope it's not Noelle he shoots before the end of the trek."

Lowry furrowed her brow. "Yeah, I hope that relationship smooths out, or it's going to be a long trip."

"Like oil and water, I'm afraid." John reached into his pocket and pulled out a small globe. He handed it to her. "Hopefully, you won't need it, but I want you to take this combird in case you have to send an emergency call. There have been internet outages in the Grace Region, stretching into the western part of Concordia, though I hope the expedition will stay away from the border."

Lowry looked at the globe with a frown, then studied his face. "You're really worried."

"You and Ginnie are abandoning me to have a lark in the forest, and you wonder why I'm a little anxious?" He sighed.

"It's this Zoric situation. There's something weird going on in the Grace Region that I'm afraid isn't going to end well."

She slipped the combird into her bag. "This trip is getting more exciting by the hour."

John cleared his throat. "Lowry, be careful, please?" He tilted her chin up and she met his eyes. "When you return, we'll discuss everything else."

Lowry's jaw muscles tensed as her gaze shifted to the exit. "Until then."

CHAPTER 11

Lowry inhaled the crisp air of the wilderness in early spring. A late winter storm had dropped a blanket of fresh snow overnight. After lunch, the clouds broke, and the sunlight sparkled on the snow as she glided across an open snowfield on her hovershoes. They had been in the backcountry for a week; she'd forgotten how much she loved the dappled light in the forest and the sound of birds calling to one another. The tranquility was lovely—unlike the brewing tensions within the Concordia expedition.

Lowry shook her head as her thoughts returned to the traps they had discovered earlier in the day. The second trap they'd come upon contained an arctic fox leg. She'd heard tales of the gnawing off of a limb by a trapped animal, but this was the first, and with any luck, the last time she would ever see it.

Another held a beaver, drowned as the ensnared animal had been swept under the ice by the current. They had pulled the beaver out and buried it as best they could in the frozen ground, so at least it wouldn't benefit the trappers. They documented and destroyed every trap they found. *Quite a report for John.*

As she moved toward a grove of spruce trees, Lowry pondered her relationship with Ginnie. She hadn't spent time with her since their first year on Antarctica and before John's election. She'd been a teenager, grieving her mother's death, and after Lowry's break with John, any developing friendship had been nipped in the bud. On this expedition into the hinterland, Lowry was delighted to reconnect with her. An intelligent young woman armed with a charming sense of humor.

Her hovershoes sank in the snowdrifts between the trees. The sun warmed her shoulders as she knelt and adjusted them for the depth of the soft powder.

A silence fell in the forest and she raised her head. In the shadows, a pair of gold eyes stared at her—an enormous wolf sizing her up for a potential meal. Lowry held her breath. He studied her as she rose. She reached for her bear banger, but hesitated to use it, since the wolf stood quietly and didn't approach her. He was a beauty, silvery gray with black guard hairs, his wispy breath furling around his muzzle. She puffed herself up, stretching her arms out slightly, making herself more imposing. The wolf blinked and cocked his head as he scrutinized her. Then he turned and trotted away into the underbrush.

With a sigh of relief, Lowry glided toward the camp. The wind whisked the snow from the spruce trees, the flakes glittering as they drifted to the ground. She came around a bend and stopped to watch a Rough-legged hawk glide through the trees. The raptor swooped down as a vole scrambled across the powdery snow. The vole screamed as the hawk's talons bit into its fur. It struggled briefly and then ceased to move. The hawk lifted the rodent and disappeared over the hill.

Lowry approached the scene. The tracks of the vole ended at the zone of impact and drops of blood froze onto the icy crust. She shivered and looked back to where she had seen the wolf.

The forest was balanced. Life and death, celebrated and accepted. This was life, simple, as it should be. Survival of the fittest. Better to be eaten by wolves than die in a hospital bed, and be buried in a hole, providing no sustenance to the creatures of the earth.

She approached the campsite and slowed her pace, listening to the raised voices in the camp.

"Wanton killing of animals for fur! It's an outrage!"

Lowry recognized Noelle's voice. She paused at the edge of the clearing to hear the gist of the argument.

Hank's voice rang out. "We know it's against the law. I'm sure John is trying to stop it."

"This is beyond law enforcement. This is an offense against nature!"

Lowry proceeded into the camp. Noelle and Hank faced each other, the tension between them palpable. Hank shot an exasperated look to Lowry, then threw up his hands and stalked away.

Noelle strode to her. "Were you aware of the illegal trapping of animals by this fellow, Ivan Zoric? This area is not even in his region. He is not only trespassing, he's killing the wildlife breeding stock. For God's sake, this is supposed to be a refuge!"

With a slight shake of her head, Lowry replied, "I'm as shocked as you are. Zoric is the leader of a crazy religious cult and, I'll tell you straight, this guy might be insane. John is trying to control the situation, but he doesn't know the extent of the fur trapping."

Noelle fumed. "Insane is right!"

Lowry glanced over her shoulder. "We must be careful. I think we need to move away from here. Let's hike northeasterly and we can complete the survey as we return to Amundsen. I doubt he would trespass too many miles out of his territory."

"He's the criminal. Why should *we* run?" Noelle turned and stormed to her tent.

Frowning, Lowry grabbed a cup of coffee and sat next to Ginnie.

Before she could speak, Ginnie gestured with her hand. "I know, Professor Clavet is very opinionated."

Lowry said under her breath, "If she's more worried about the animals than the humans—that's her prerogative. But my first duty is to you. Your father asked me to watch out for you. I'll try my best to persuade the others but, if not, you have to come with me. Frankly, I'm as upset as Noelle is. I need to get this information back to John."

Ginnie looked at her. "You think if it's Zoric's group who's illegally trapping, that it might be dangerous for us?"

She shrugged. "Once they find out that we spent the day destroying their traps, they won't be happy." Lowry touched her arm. "Don't worry, but I'm going to discuss our options with Hank."

Lowry found Hank behind the camp collecting elk dung for the fire.

He shook a large piece of dung and spit on it. He snapped, "That lady has shit for brains," and jammed the dung into the sack.

"Hank, she's passionate but not stupid."

"Sometimes passion *makes* you stupid."

Lowry blinked. *Ain't that the truth.* She picked up a few pieces of frozen dung and stuffed them into the bag. "Burying those poor animals reminded me of the day Annie passed away and you helped bury her while Nick was gone."

He glanced at her. "She was a good dog."

"The ground was almost as hard as it was today. I'm sure it was a chore to dig a hole large enough for her."

"Yep, she was a big-un." Hank nodded. "Took more than an hour with a pick and shovel. By then, she was froze solid. I had to break her tail and fold it over her."

She grimaced. "I guess I wasn't aware of that part of the story."

"Oh, sorry."

A smile on her face, she squeezed his shoulder. "Regardless, you were a good friend to do it."

After they filled the bag, they started back to the camp.

Lowry whispered, "Hank, the hair on my neck is standing up and it's not because of the cold. I think we need to move out of here first thing tomorrow morning."

He nodded. "I agree. Especially since the internet signal is down again in this whole area and we can't get a message out." He gazed around the camp. "We're pretty vulnerable in this meadow. You have a pistol?"

"I'll be sleeping with it tonight." Lowry inclined her head toward Noelle. "Do you want me to discuss our plans with her or do you want that honor?"

Hank snorted.

Lowry chuckled. "That's what I thought. I'll go smooth her feathers down and tell her that we're moving out in the morning."

*   *   *

At dusk, the group sat quietly around the campfire. Noelle had retired early after supper to pack specimens and organize her files. With a crunch, the fire fell into a heap, and the flame died. The cold eased into the meadow, and with contagious yawns, the students wandered to their tents.

Lowry squatted next to Ginnie. "You need to sleep, too. Don't worry, we're leaving in the morning."

She glanced at Lowry with a crooked smile on her face. "It's been an adventure, but I'll feel better when we see the homesteads." She rose and ambled to her tent, crawled in, and after a wave to Lowry, zipped the flap.

Lowry stared into glowing embers as everyone settled down to sleep. When the students had quieted, she scooped up a handful of snow and dumped it on top of the hot coals, which hissed in protest. She rose and Hank waved his flashlight at her from the front of his tent. He lifted a large automatic pistol.

With a nod, she gave him a thumbs-up sign, then turned and crawled into her tent. Her stomach buzzed with apprehension as she dug into the bottom of her pack for the hard-plastic gun case. She drew it out and clicked it opened. She swallowed hard, staring at the pistol glinting in the light of the dim camp lantern. She bit the inside of her cheek, pulled out the cartridge and popped it into the handle. After a vicious attack from intruders years ago, she regularly practiced shooting. Any attacker would pay dearly for an attempt on her life.

Exhaling, Lowry slipped the gun under her pillow. With trembling fingers, she swept back her hair and then shoved her pack toward the edge of the tent. The bag fell to the side and the combird John had given her rolled onto the ground. Blinking, Lowry gazed at it—was this a sign to use it? They weren't in an emergency situation, but she couldn't shake her unease. At last, she picked up the little bird and examined it. It was a marvelous invention; it flew at the speed of light but unlike a light beam, it auto-corrected for the arc of the Earth. No detection system was set up to intercept it. Once it had been released to deliver its message, it was invisible to all, except to the person receiving it.

Lowry pivoted the bird's static face toward her and spoke quietly. "Record."

A light flashed three times and the bird replied, "Ready for your message."

She cleared her throat. "Ready."

The light flashed twice and she began her message. "John, this is Lowry. We're located at the southwest border of the refuge, near Zoric's territory. The combird will give you the exact lat/longs. We're fine but have discovered many fur traps in the refuge waterways near the edge of Zoric's region. We assume they were set by his group. We've been documenting and destroying them as we go. Hank and I are worried by the incursions of Zoric into the refuge—and for our safety. I've spoken with Noelle about moving away from the area. She wasn't happy, but willing to hike northeasterly from our current location near the Grace Region, then return to the homesteads. Ginnie is fine and surprisingly, Hank hasn't killed Noelle as yet, though a few times it's been touch and go." She whispered, "I love you."

She said to the bird, "Finished." The light blinked one more time. "Go to John Barrous in Amundsen."

The bird twirled and zoomed through the flap of the tent.

Lowry rubbed her forehead, then gazed at her trembling fingers. With her outer clothes still on, she scooted into the sleeping bag and zipped it. Lowry stared at the ceiling of her tent, listening to Hank's muffled coughs in the tent across from hers. The camp quieted, and she slipped into a fitful sleep.

Lowry bolted up at a loud snapping sound. A branch breaking in the trees? Her heart beat a staccato rhythm and she held her breath in the darkness. *Perhaps it was just a dream.* She reached under the pillow and touched the cold metal barrel of the pistol. She stiffened as Hank called out to her. "Lowry!" Lowry grasped the gun and wriggled out of the sleeping bag. With pistol in hand, she scrambled to the entrance of the tent. She eased open the flap and peered toward Hank. She could see nothing in pitch-black of the night.

Hank's disembodied whisper drifted to her. "Someone's in those trees at the back of the camp."

An intense light stabbed across the center of the camp and spastic shadows darted among the tents. Lowry gasped as flashes of gunfire blasted from Hank's tent. She flattened herself on the ground as beams of light swirled to find him. Furiously, he shot another round into the lights. Lowry clenched her teeth at the sound of shattering glass. One of the lights died, followed by groans of the wounded.

But the beams coalesced to expose Hank kneeling at the flap, gun in hand. He ducked back into the tent. A deafening rat-tat-tat of automatic fire swept across him. He cried out as the bullets struck him, his body pulsing against the sides of the tent. As Hank fell forward, the nylon tent collapsed around him, and he lay supine and bleeding in the snow.

Lowry leapt from her tent and shrieked, "Hank, No!"

The beams of light pivoted, illuminating her as their next victim. Figures ran toward her. Blinded, she fired her pistol at the motion. A groan and a thud as a man fell. The yelling figures raced closer, and she shot again. With a scream, another dropped to the ground. Then they were on her. She yelped as a sudden chop knocked the gun from her grip. A gloved hand snatched her arm. She kicked hard, and a grunt answered her blow.

"Bitch!" a deep male voice bellowed.

He knocked her in the side of her head with the barrel of his gun. Stunned, she collapsed to her knees in the frigid snow. She blinked to clear her vision, rubbing where the barrel had struck her. A man wearing a ski mask held a pistol to her temple.

"Get on your coat and shoes," he hissed.

She stood, swaying on her feet.

"Hurry up!" He shoved her toward her tent.

Lowry crawled inside, while the man knelt at the entrance with his flashlight shining on her. Squinting against the light, she pulled on her coat and boots. He dragged her out by her arm.

"Get up and walk." He kicked her.

"Kick me again, mister, and you'll be sorry."

He grunted. "You killed one of my friends and badly wounded another."

"You murdered my friend Hank, so we're even."

She stood, and zipped her coat with shaking fingers, not sure if it was from the cold or from shock. She'd killed a man.

Lowry moved to the huddled students. In the darkness she could hear frightened whispers and muffled sobbing. Then a beam of light illuminated the group, revealing the terrified faces of the students and Noelle. Lowry shook her head. Everyone in the expedition had coats and boots. Their entire party was being kidnapped.

She nodded at Ginnie, sidling closer to tell her about the message she'd sent to her father.

One of the men jabbed her arm with a stick. "No moving around."

From the shadows, a gruff voice barked, "Let's go."

On the horizon, a strip of gray signaled the dawn and the kidnappers hurried them to the edge of the camp. The students cried out, covering their eyes as they passed Hank's corpse, lying in a pool of frozen blood.

Choking, Lowry stopped beside him, swallowing back the bile in her throat. His contorted face had frozen into a last cry of rage and pain. Bullet wounds freckled his clothing, and his legs were tangled in the tent fabric like a ripped shroud. Lowry groaned as the butt of a rifle struck her between her shoulder blades, shoving her forward. Her guard knelt and jerked the pistol out of Hank's half-frozen hand. With a grunt, her captor pushed her again, and she stumbled past his body. Hank had died a true hero—a better death than most.

The kidnappers extinguished the search lights and herded the group into the forest. The prisoners stumbled over snow-covered rocks as they made their way in the dim light.

"Stop here." One of the men called to someone. "Turn on the lights."

Small lights floated above a set of hoverbikes, parked under the branches of the spruce grove.

"Stay put," her captor said gruffly, then wagged his pistol at her. "I'm a very good shot, lady." Lowry stood still as he walked to his bike. She thought of bolting, but she couldn't leave Ginnie. Even in the faint light, Lowry could see Ginnie's guard gesture to her. Ginnie climbed onto the back of the bike and he strapped her wrists. He mounted in front of her and started the motor.

Lowry's captor returned with a hoverbike and growled, "Get on," waving to the rear seat. There was no way out. She exhaled and straddled the bike. He jerked her hands behind her back and zip-tied them together.

The leader shouted, "Let's go!"

The headlights shuddered as they sped away. Lowry struggled to stay on board. The chill wind bit into her face as they headed into the abyss.

CHAPTER 12

In a rough-hewn stone cabin, Lowry and the group huddled in the darkness around a small heater. The guards had thrown them worn blankets, too thin to fend off the penetrating cold. Noelle had urged the others to rest and, one by one, they'd fallen asleep on the hard floor, bathed in the eerie light of the woodstove. With a blanket across their shoulders, Lowry held Ginnie as she dozed.

Exhausted, Lowry stared blankly at the cement floor. Over and over, Hank's death replayed itself in her mind. Perhaps if they had surrendered at once, he'd still be alive. But Hank had done his duty in attempting to protect them. And so had she, though the idea of killing another human was abhorrent to her.

Lowry chewed her lip. She wasn't looking forward to telling Nick that Hank had died. A constant friend for most of Nick's life, Hank had been one of his last remaining colleagues from the mining camp on Antarctica.

She eased Ginnie down onto the blanket covering the concrete floor. She stirred, then fell back to sleep.

Lowry lay next to her, shivering as she pulled the tattered blanket over her shoulders. It would do no good to fret about things she couldn't change. She had to focus on their present predicament. The others weren't fully aware of the danger. She stared at the rock wall and tried to think of an escape. Without weapons or provisions for a trek across Zoric's territory, there was little chance of success.

Soft snoring sounds from the others lulled her to sleep as fatigue won over anxiety.

At dawn, Lowry opened her eyes to pale sunlight filtering through the windowpane at the rear of the cabin. Without moving, she examined the window and saw metal bars welded across the frame. She swallowed hard. This cabin had been built as a jail.

Ginnie lay next to her, still asleep. Overnight, the small room had finally warmed between the feeble stove and body heat. She yawned and inhaled, then sputtered against the odor of unwashed bodies, tinged with sour notes of a dead rodent wafting from god knows where.

The sound of muffled voices drifted into the cabin. Lowry lurched upright, listening as the voices approached the massive front door.

She shook Ginnie, whimpering in her sleep. "Wake up, Ginnie, but be quiet."

Ginnie's eyes opened sleepily at first, and then wider as she realized where they were. "I guess it wasn't just a bad dream?"

Lowry squeezed her arm. "I'm afraid not." She leaned over and whispered into her ear, "They're coming. I want you to be very careful and follow my lead. Do nothing to bring harm to yourself. And don't tell them who you are."

With a nod, Ginnie sat up, her face pale as she clutched the blanket.

The bolt in the doorjamb snapped and the heavy door creaked open.

A guard, dressed in a heavy coat and scruffy fatigues, strolled in with a frown plastered on his face. His eyebrow twitched as he kicked one of the sleeping boys sprawled on the floor.

The boy grunted. "What's going on?" He looked at the guard's threatening mien and scrambled away.

The guard examined the room and nodded to someone outside of the cabin that all was secure. A tall man appeared in the doorway, his dark eyes scanning the despondent captives, the hood of his coat lined in doubtless Concordian Refuge ermine.

Lowry's heart thumped loudly. She knew that face from the photo John had showed her—Ivan Zoric in the flesh. A smirk on his face, he sauntered into the room, pivoted toward them and his smirk faded into a scowl. "Who is the leader of this *illustrious* group?"

In the hushed room, Noelle stared at Zoric, her face still and calm. She dropped the torn blanket from around her shoulders, and unhurriedly, rose and faced him. With disheveled hair, Noelle glared at him. Lowry held her breath at the elegant defiance she projected. Gaia, the goddess of the Earth, facing Hades of the underworld.

Her head erect, she replied, "I am."

Zoric inspected her like a bug. He snapped, "My men have reported that you've wantonly smashed our fur traps. Why were you trespassing into our region and destroying our property?"

With a slow blink, Noelle inclined her head. "We are on a research field trip, sponsored by Cornell University, studying the animals and plants in Antarctica's Concordia Refuge *adjacent* to your territory." Her lips thinned as she leaned slightly toward him. "The area we were in was *not* within your region, sir, and the destruction of illegal traps in a designated wildlife sanctuary should be applauded by any legitimate authority."

Zoric narrowed his eyes at her audacity.

Lowry's brow twitched. Here was a man unused to being challenged.

In a flash, he strode toward the professor. Lowry clutched Ginnie's hand. *You bastard, don't hurt her.*

He halted in front of Noelle, staring into her face. "Legitimate authority?" He pointed up to the sky. "The only legitimate authority is God. And God gave us the animals of the earth to harvest."

Noelle fluffed Zoric's ermine-lined hood. "There won't be any animals left to 'harvest,' if you keep killing them."

Zoric's mouth curled into a snarl. His chest expanded as he stared at the diminutive Noelle before him. He clenched and unclenched his fists, his face turning scarlet with rage. Then, with gasps from the students, he lifted his arm and backhanded Noelle across the face. The crack of the blow echoed in the room. Noelle grunted and hit the floor with a thud. Lowry held Ginnie back as she reached her arm toward Noelle with a shriek.

The students scuttled back in fear. Noelle glared defiantly up at Zoric, blood flowing from her mouth. One of the girls edged closer, wiping the blood from Noelle's lips with a corner of the tattered blanket. The girl's hands trembled in shock.

Zoric's lip twitched, his eyes roving over the terrified students. He grabbed the boy next to him, shaking him back and forth. "Why did you trespass on our land? Did you destroy our property?" The boy's face was ashen with fear. "Why are you here and who sent you? Tell me!"

Lowry shivered at the savagery of Zoric. Something had to be done. She pushed Ginnie away from her and rose. In a clear voice, she said, "Do unto others . . ."

Zoric stopped as her words penetrated his madness.

She faced Zoric. Taking a deep breath to calm her heart, she gazed at him and repeated, "Do unto others . . . as you would have others do unto you."

He pivoted to Lowry, his mouth wrenched in fury. He dropped the boy onto the ground. Noelle pulled the young man away from Zoric's reach.

Inwardly trembling, Lowry grit her teeth as Zoric came toward her.

He stepped in front of her, staring at her with eyes bulging with anger.

She dug her nails into her palms, gazing back at him. Her heart raced, but she couldn't afford to show fear—not now.

Zoric's hands shook at his sides, aching to strike her. His long brown hair fell across his brow as he leaned into her. He panted like an agitated animal; she tasted his breath. His eyes bored into hers, flicking back and forth, studying her. "You were the one who murdered one of my men and wounded another."

"*Your men* invaded our camp, firing automatic weapons at us. *Your men* killed a dear friend of mine, who died protecting us."

With his hands balled into fists, he said, "That sounds more like 'An eye for an eye' rather than 'Do unto others.'" He tilted his head. "According to our laws, you, my little friend, are a murderer." He crossed his arms, staring at her with a menacing smile.

Her eyes narrowed. In her past, she had faced men like him. Puppet masters, such as the corrupt attorney general of Amerada, Elliot Halder, and even the man she thought was her father, Duff Walker. Duff, in his playbook of deceitful machinations, had inadvertently taught her the wiles of countering his despotic behavior, stemming from an abusive childhood and alcohol.

But was Zoric a cunning bully or truly insane? In this charged atmosphere, angering him would not be helpful. The best course in their vulnerable position was to lessen the tension in the room.

Lowry extended her hand toward him. In a calm voice, she said, "Ivan, let us go. Take us back to our camp or the edge of Grace and we'll return to Amundsen. After all, you didn't personally pull the trigger that killed my friend." She shrugged. "Who knows, these things might yet be worked out."

She could see the wheels of his mind turning. Fur trapping in the refuge and a question of human remains was a magnitude different than gunning down a man and kidnapping an entire expedition from Cornell University.

Zoric squinted at her. A smile flashed on his face and then faded. Perhaps he had come to a decision, but was not revealing it. Would they be pawns in some negotiation?

He rotated on his heel and stomped through the open door. The guard threw them a threatening glance, followed him out and slammed it shut. After the echo of their footsteps died away, Lowry swayed, breathing in and out, then sank to the floor.

Ginnie crawled to her. "That was terrifying, but you were amazing." She touched her arm and then joined the students crouched around Noelle.

Noelle smiled wanly. "It's okay, we'll be okay."

With Noelle at the center, the students held each other, sobbing in fear. After a few minutes, the group quieted. Noelle pointed to a bottle in the corner. "Bill, can you grab the water, please?" He brought the bottle and they passed it around the group.

After the students calmed, Noelle came over and took Lowry's hand. "Are you all right?"

Lowry nodded, grimacing at the sight of Noelle's injured face. "I should be asking you that question."

She smiled, touching her cheek. "I'll live."

"Noelle, you were magnificent the way you stood up to that bully."

"I was pissed." Noelle shrugged. "But I'm afraid my anger juiced him up." She shot a glance at the students in a circle. "He could have hurt these kids." With a smile, she said, "You saved us by confronting his religious authority."

"That may only last a moment."

"A moment might be enough."

Lowry glanced at the door. *Yeah, enough time to charge, convict, and execute me for murder.*

Noelle squeezed Lowry's hand. "I'm sure that John has the police looking for us." She returned to the huddled students.

Ginnie came back to Lowry and wrapped her arms around her. They sat motionless, like frightened animals in a trap.

Lowry's mind flashed back to the wolf she had faced in the wilderness. The insanity she had just witnessed wouldn't be tolerated in the brutal, but rational, world of nature. In nature, it was eat or be eaten, but no animal had the energy to waste in madness. A deranged animal would be expunged, one way or another.

She focused her mind on taking out Mr. Ivan Zoric.

CHAPTER 13

John stared at the bedroom ceiling, rubbing his knuckles against his forehead, unable to erase the uncertainty from his mind. With a sigh, his thoughts returned to last night's message from Lowry.

The little combird had appeared before him like a moth hovering near a light. When it opened its mouth, Lowry's voice spoke through its tiny beak. She had calmly detailed Zoric's intrusion into the refuge and the illegal trapping they had discovered, but an undertone of fear came through loud and clear at the end as she whispered thinly, "I love you." Then the combird had shattered into a thousand virtual pieces and faded away.

After Lowry's message, he'd tried to call her cell, but no answer. John had messaged Hank on his emergency beeper, but there was no response. He'd contacted Lin to get in touch with the police nearest the refuge, but as yet, they hadn't been able to contact the expedition. Lin told him he'd handle it and for John to try to sleep.

But sleep had evaded him. He felt certain there was more that Lowry hadn't said. The fact that she used the combird made him doubly afraid. His throat constricted as if someone was throttling him. Gasping, he sat up in bed. *What if they've been killed?* He moaned. *Surely even Zoric wouldn't just kill them.* But perhaps an avalanche or a pack of wolves? He shook his head.

Hank and Lowry had brought guns and could handle any animals, but an avalanche might bury the entire expedition in seconds.

He tossed back the covers and sat on the side of the bed, his stomach twisting like a pretzel. Exhaling, he rose, went into the bathroom and gazed in the mirror. If his daughter and Lowry were dead—what would he do? How could he live without them?

John stripped and got into the shower. Under the steaming water, his legs trembled, and he knelt, nauseous with worry. The hot water flowed over him as he stared at the shower floor. He shook the water from his hair, breathing in and out to steady himself, then stood and finished bathing. He turned off the water, stepped out and dried off briskly with the towel.

P called out, "Your coffee is ready, John." A mug of coffee floated to him.

"Okay, thanks." With shaking hands, he sipped the hot liquid, then dressed quickly.

"Would you like some breakfast, John?" P said, breaking into his misery.

"Later. But another cup of Joe, please."

He walked to the door and nodded thanks to P for the to-go cup waiting for him. "Send breakfast to my office. Just a banana and a brownie."

"I'll make that an energy brownie with a banana."

John walked to his office through empty hallways, gripping the coffee mug. *God, when are we going to hear something?*

The party's disappearance had struck him to the core. But in the midst of fear for his daughter, an epiphany had hit him. He loved Lowry—with all his heart, he loved Lowry. No doubt the pain of his perceived betrayal had put a schism in their relationship, followed by the overwhelming effort of jump-starting a nation. But once the crises were over, he had gathered his hurt and resentment, like bits of old lint and broken string, weaving them into a hair-shirt for his monkish lifestyle. And now she might be dead.

He shook his head. All his stupid, childish whining about her pushing him into the presidency. In reality, she had believed in him to be the right person to guide a nation into the future, and wasn't that in and of itself a sign of her faith in him? And Lowry had gained nothing from it. He kneaded his forehead with his hand. *You're really pathetic.*

A few dim lights lit the presidential offices. No one here at this early hour. The door to his office opened, and he put the mug on his desk. He messaged his pilot Alex. *The Cornell expedition has gone missing—get the Hawkplane ready for a search mission.*

He paced back and forth behind his desk, calling the district representatives near Concordia to organize full-scale searches for the expedition. His breakfast floated in and he shoved the brownie in his mouth, chasing it with a shot of coffee.

Lin arrived and stood at the door of his office. John's stomach knotted at his pinched look.

John swallowed hard and asked, "What is it?"

"Um, Mr. President . . . I'm afraid I have some bad news."

He searched Lin's eyes. No hint on that deadpan face. His heart raced as he licked his dry lips. "Let me have it."

"As you know, I tried to reach the expedition last night, but there was no response. This morning, we sent drones to investigate their last known location. Once they were close, the drones tried to contact Hank on his emergency radio beeper, but nothing." Lin inclined his head. "With searchlights, the drones sent back videos of a campsite with tents in disarray, but until daylight it'll be hard to tell what happened." He cleared his throat. "But there was no sign of the university research party."

John's face paled as he gripped the arms of his chair. "My God! It has to be Zoric. Lowry said they had destroyed traps near the Grace border."

Lin stared at him. "It's possible, but why would he kidnap an entire research group? The drones are still searching in the proximity of the camp, so perhaps they're on an early-morning trek."

"Pray that you are right, Lin." John's face was taut. "But if he has kidnapped them and harms a hair on their heads, I will personally—" He pressed his fist to his forehead. If that was the case, they must find them and quickly before Zoric hid them away, and especially before he realized the prize that had fallen into his hands: the president's daughter. John touched his pilot's number on the phone. "Alex, I'm heading your way."

John stood and hit the desk with his fist. "Time is of the essence. I've called the authorities near Concordia to start a full-scale search." He grabbed his coat. "Alex and I will scan the area with the Hawkplane." He raised his hand against Lin's protest. "All of them, including my daughter, could be in the hands of a madman. I'll be in touch as much as I can, but I'm leaving Patel in charge, in case I can't be reached."

"Mr. President, I cannot let you go. It's too dangerous."

John pushed past him. "Try and stop me."

The Drots trailed him as he bolted down the hall. He jumped into the presidential robocar outside the building and zipped to the government hangar. He waved at Alex, moving the Hawkplane onto the tarmac. He crawled in, nodding to her as the Drots hovered behind his seat. She throttled forward, and they took off as the Antarctic dawn broke over the horizon.

CHAPTER 14

The plane swept over the bleak landscape as John stared from the window of the cockpit. Spring had arrived on the calendar, but the land was still frozen. They crossed the Adélie River, covered in ice, except for pockets where steam rose from subterranean geothermal plumes.

He swallowed hard, thinking of the terror the group might be experiencing. No telling what would happen if they'd been ferreted away into Zoric's domain.

Alex broke into his reverie, saying quietly, "Mr. President, we're receiving a message from the person who found their last camp. I'll turn it on speaker."

John leaned forward as a crackly voice came into the cockpit. "I'm walking into the campsite. There are five tents, some collapsed. Provisions scattered around. Maybe a bear rampaged through here? But odd there would be no effort to clean up."

There was silence, and then a gasp.

Alex shouted, "Go on!"

The voice came back, thin with shock. "Sorry. I see two bodies—my God, they're dead—frozen into their own blood. Looks like multiple bullet wounds—" The sound of retching echoed in the cockpit. "I'm going to be sick."

John turned to Alex. "Jesus, Zoric's men must have attacked the camp." He gripped the arm of the seat, shouting, "The dead—male, female?" pressing his hand onto his head.

The sound of coughing. Then his voice croaked out, "Two men."

John closed his eyes. *Ginnie and Lowry were alive.*

The voice came over the intercom. "I'll try to take photos." The crunch of his boots, then silence. The sound of his boots on the snow. "Okay, got both bodies documented. I'll upload them and the GPS locations." They heard his labored breathing. "I'm now circling the camp. Hey, I just found a whole set of tracks leading south. More people than in the research group. I'm following them now. Still going south."

John murmured, "Zoric's territory is south."

Alex glanced at him with a nod.

The crack of an explosion burst through the speaker. At the blast, John and Alex jolted upright, and stared at each other in alarm.

Alex shouted into the mic, "Are you still there?"

They heard groaning, then silence.

He shook his head. "Those sons of bitches must have booby-trapped their trail," he said, slamming his fist into the dash. "See if there's anyone near that location who can help him."

"Yes, Mr. President." Alex radioed back to the capital.

As they approached the campsite, Alex said, "I'll drop altitude."

John put on his binoc-glasses. He sucked in his breath, staring at randomly collapsed tents and abandoned clothing blowing in the wind. Red stains caught his eye. He shuddered at the sight of two bodies crumpled on the frozen ground.

Past the campsite, Alex banked the plane. John pointed to the trampled snow leading away from the camp, and they turned southward to follow the trail.

John leaned forward. "Shit. I see another man lying on the ground, but I can't tell whether he's dead or alive. I would guess the one who took the photos."

Alex furrowed her brow. "As a battle tactic, the main reason to booby-trap a trail would be to slow a rescue team."

She glanced at him. "It *does* look like the expedition's been kidnapped."

He raked his hair back. Lin had urged him to take Zoric out while they had a chance. Had lives been lost because of his hesitation? And even if his daughter and Lowry were alive for the moment, it was becoming increasingly apparent that Zoric's group was capable of much more than illegal trapping. Perhaps the mysterious body part had been a harbinger of doom.

A message from a search party came back. "We have been patched through to you, Mr. President. We're near his location and will assist. We have the internet functioning again over Concordia and we'll contact you as soon as we know something."

"Thank you and be careful."

He sat silently, then turned to Alex. "Let's follow their trail."

Alex shot a glance at him. "Yes, sir." She turned the plane toward Grace Region.

P said, "John, the photos have uploaded."

"Thanks, P." A file marked Cornell Expedition Attack appeared on his watch screen. He took a deep breath and said, "Play."

The first photo opened. A man lay with his head sideways on the snow, a ski mask askew on his head exposing his face. John didn't recognize him.

"Be glad you don't have to see these," he said to Alex.

"Yeah, I saw enough carnage in the war to last me, so you can keep all that to yourself."

He flipped through the poses until he reached the photos of the other man who'd been killed in the attack. The first image assembled in front of him. John felt a deep pain in his gut, like a fist had slammed into his solar plexus. "Jesus, it's Hank."

Poor Hank lay in a pool of crystalized blood, one hand stretched out grasping the snow. His contorted face, veiled in ice crystals from his dying gasps, revealed his final agony. John gritted his teeth, scrolling through the carousel of images. After the last photo, he tapped the screen of his watch and, with a whoosh, the photos returned to the virtual folder.

He gazed out of the window. *I'm so sorry, my friend.* John had personally asked Hank to join the expedition. *If I hadn't, he would still be alive.*

"Sir, Hank may have saved lives out there. He's a hero." Alex glanced at him. "It's hard to send someone out, but as a commander, it's a part of the duty."

"He didn't need to die by the hands of a crazy cult to be a hero." With pinched lips, he snapped, "If I had fully recognized the danger of Zoric's group, he might still be alive, and the expedition blithely studying the wildlife." John cleared his throat. "Now we've got to find the rest of them. I hope to God they're safe."

John rubbed his chin. "They had to return to Zoric's stronghold." With a grimace, he looked at her. "Alex, I want to fly to his compound, approaching it from the rear."

She blinked. "But sir, Zoric has disabled the internet in Grace. No one will know where we are, and we don't have any backup. This type of operation would take special ops to carry out."

He gestured with his thumb to the Drots. "We have two security robots that can each outfight three soldiers. Time is of the essence and to put together a team of special ops might take, at a minimum, hours and possibly days. We've got to find and rescue them before more people are killed. This is an order, soldier, from your Commander-in-Chief."

They approached the border to Grace Region. John searched the ground for any sign of the group. Sporadic marks from hover airflow, but no clear trail.

"The Hawkplane runs completely silent and can fly under any sensing equipment they may have," Alex said, tilting her head toward the Drots. "But you may want to put the Drots in a silent mode, so they don't inadvertently give us away."

"Good idea." He turned to the Drots. "Drots, go into Hibernation."

Blinking lights ran across their control panels, and then went dark.

He looked at Alex. "My proposal is this. You land the plane and I walk to the compound. Alone, I might be able to find them without detection."

"Or they might be able to capture the president of Antarctica and have a real prize."

John gestured with his hand. "I don't want to risk more lives, including those in the expedition group, if we tried to mount a large force against them. One person could pull it off. And does it matter if they caught me as well?"

Alex pondered for a second. "There are four students, Dr. Clavet and Lowry, is that correct?"

"Yes."

She shook her head. "The Hawkplane is only rated to take six passengers, Mr. President."

"I know."

After a moment, she continued, "Sir, in the States, I was a captain in the Air Force for six years. Three of those years were in Special Forces training. I want to come with you on the rescue."

John smiled. "Sounds like you outrank me, Captain."

She grinned back. "I need a course, navigator."

He glanced at his GPS. "Turn south, fifteen degrees."

She dropped altitude as they entered a narrow glacial valley.

John bit his lip at the closeness of the valley walls. "Kind of like a toboggan ride, isn't it?"

She chuckled. "As long as we don't have any downdrafts, we're okay."

He took another reading. "Turn two degrees west. We have maybe thirty minutes at this speed."

"From this point on, whisper and only when necessary."

"Aye, Aye, Captain."

The wind swept them close to the steep walls. Alex veered away while John gripped the seat. They moved into a rough ridge and valley system and she kept the plane low, leaping from valley to valley, until they came to the rugged stretch behind Zoric's compound. John surveyed the jagged rocks surrounding them. It was an area where no one in their right mind would try to land.

Alex lifted the plane over a grove of small trees, then pointed to a tiny flat spot. "We'll land there."

John swallowed. "There?"

"Only level place, I'm afraid. It looks like a frozen lake."

With a grimace, John muttered, "I'd call that a pond."

She slowed the plane and glided onto the frozen surface. John held his breath as the plane skidded to a stop. They scrambled out and listened for any commotion from the camp over the ridge. The only sound was the wind.

Alex whispered, "Help me push the plane around. I want to get it set for takeoff. When we return, we may be in a hurry."

With his thumb, he gestured to the hibernating Drots. "What about the Drots?"

"I think they'd only attract attention if they tag along."

They unloaded the backpacks of emergency supplies from the hold and shouldered them. A gust of wind slammed the door of the plane shut. Alex and John froze as the noise cracked through the air. They listened but heard no outcry from the camp.

He checked the GPS screen on his wrist. "This way."

They moved out. John grimaced as his hovershoes brushed against a frozen bank of snow. The wind, at least, was on their side, coming from the direction of the compound and whisking away any sound.

They slowed as they neared the camp.

His heart raced. *What if they weren't here—or worse?* He breathed deep, clenching the ski pole. *Please be okay.*

He whispered, "Alex, remember the pickup point if we get separated."

"I have it."

They made their way to the ridge overlooking the camp. As yet, they had seen no guards patrolling. Perhaps they assumed a rescue would take time to launch. The wind swirled the snow kicked up by their hovershoes. Alex signaled with her hand to drop to the ground. They crawled up the ridge and eased over the top to get their first look at the compound.

They pulled out their binoc-glasses. Lines of primitive rock cabins faced the center of the village, dominated by an austere stone church, topped with a half-domed cupola and wrought-iron filigree cross.

She wriggled toward John and whispered, "Sir, check out the third cabin from the tree line. See the guard out front? That may be where they're keeping them. We need to observe who goes in and out of that cabin. If it appears that's where they are, we'll move behind it tonight."

John nodded. He searched the dirt streets and empty yards. It struck him as odd that there was no music, only an eerie silence, punctuated by muffled voices. Furtive shapes scurried from one destination to another. No chatting among friends, no children playing in the snow. He chewed the inside of his lip. A village of despair. Zoric knew how to control his people—with fear.

A woman brought a container to the cabin. The guard lifted the top and searched the contents.

John dialed up the magnification on his glasses. *Food.*

The guard gestured and the woman entered. After she left, he walked the periphery of the cabin, then returned to his position at the front.

Alex nodded to John. *Tonight.*

In the short days of spring, dusk fell early. Hiding behind the ridgeline, they crawled across the snow, toward the back of the cabin. Alex signaled to halt with her hand. They froze. On the edge of the camp, a guard without hovershoes struggled through the deep snow. John held his breath as he passed close to them. When the guard disappeared, they inched to the slope behind the cabin and waited for darkness.

The sun fell behind the ridge. They tobogganed down the icy hill and crawled through the ice-covered underbrush to the rear of the cabin.

A small light was visible in the back window. At the sound of Ginnie's voice, John grabbed Alex's arm. She nodded. The light went out. A door shut and footsteps crunched in the snow. The guard circled the cabin, then disappeared to the front.

John felt Alex's hand on his shoulder and he leaned toward her. She whispered in his ear, "We'll check his nighttime cycle before we move."

The cold seeped into his body as they waited in the snow, but at least Ginnie was alive. He strained to hear Lowry's voice, but only heard muffled sounds with the deepening night.

An hour later, the guard circled the cabin.

Alex whispered, "On the hour, like clockwork. We'll take him on the next circle. Let's go."

She motioned John into position in the shadows. She gave him her pistol. "Whatever you do, don't shoot it, just knock him out. But you'll have *one* chance at it."

John nodded, steeling himself to the task. He leaned against the cabin wall, thinking of Ginnie and Lowry, cold and frightened, confined on the other side of these stones.

It seemed a lifetime, but at last they heard the crunch of footsteps approach. He raised the pistol over his head and focused as he waited in the dark.

The guard came around the edge of the cabin.

Alex called to him in a husky voice. "How 'bout a hot date, big boy?"

He stood dumbfounded. John clubbed him with the pistol. The guard fell to the ground, and they dragged his inert body into the brush. Alex pulled off the guard's hat and jacket and gave them to John.

"Put these on and move to the front of the cabin." She drew a cutting tool from her pack. "Stay there, until I knock on the inside of the front door. If it takes me more than an hour, circle—but let's hope not."

John walked to the front of the cabin and stood at the door. He hoped no one would bother to check a lone guard in the middle of the night. He watched the compound, now that the sun had set. Interesting that there were more shapes moving in the gloom than during the day. *Perhaps the chains of religious hypocrisy loosened in the shadows?*

He turned toward the sound of clanging metal. Someone shuffling along the row of cabins. As the shape moved into the dim light of a street lamp, he realized it was an old woman. She looked around furtively, then dug into the dumpster. His stomach lurched as she pulled out a piece of garbage, sniffed it and put it in a bag. Only a human on the edge of starvation would do such a thing.

She moved to a can closer to the cabin.

John reached into his pocket and lifted out the gold Bitcoin his neighbor, Bill Taylor, had handed him on the day of his inauguration. "For luck—you'll need it."

He cast his eyes left and right to see if anyone was watching and then tossed the coin to the old woman. The coin struck the side of the can with a clink and fell to the ground. She started at the noise and looked at the money. She glanced toward John, bent down, and clutched it in her fingers.

With her head twisted at an angle, she limped over to him and held out the coin. "Sir, I think you dropped this."

John strained to see her face in the dimness of the streetlight. He looked into her eyes and whispered, "No, ma'am, I saw it fall out of your coat pocket. Please keep moving. This is a restricted area."

Tears came to the woman's eyes as she looked at him. "Thank you, sir. How can I ever repay you?"

"No need. I just wish I had more. Please, you'll have to leave now."

John watched her disappear into the darkness and hoped it was enough for her to eat for a few days.

He listened to the sounds of cutting on the back door and flinched as Noelle called out, "Who's there?"

He heard Alex's faint voice. "A friend. You must be quiet and do exactly as I say."

"I understand. And thank you."

The cutting continued for several minutes. At last, he heard the rear door open and murmuring voices. John glanced around the compound to see if anyone had noticed the sounds.

There was a slight knock on the inside of the front door, then Alex's muffled voice. "They're getting ready. Meet us at the back in ten minutes, like the guard making his round."

At the end of the longest ten minutes of his life, John looked at his watch and circled the cabin. He turned the corner, and moved toward the dark shapes at the rear of the hut.

In the dim light, Ginnie whispered, "Daddy," and gave him a quick hug.

"You're okay, baby." He pulled Lowry to him with his other arm.

Alex grabbed his shoulder. "Single file. Let's go!"

She had the only pair of night vision goggles and led them toward the plane. The snow was deep, and they didn't have enough hovershoes for everyone. They struggled to the top of the ridge. One of the students cried out as she slipped into a deep drift.

As he helped her up, John snapped under his breath, "You must be quiet!"

Halfway to the plane, shouts boomed from the camp.

"Faster!" Alex called to them. They panted, fighting to keep up with her in the deep snow.

A pale moon peeked through the gathering clouds as they reached the clearing. The moonlight glinted on the wings of the Hawkplane.

Alex handed John her hovershoes and leapt into the cockpit. He drew the hovershoe straps over his shoulder, and then pushed Ginnie and the other students into the plane.

The voices came closer.

The propellers rotated with a whirring noise as Alex started the motor. She checked the plane and shouted to John, "Ice on the wings!" She threw him a scraper. "You'll have to scrape it off!"

He and Noelle frantically worked on the wings as Lowry cleared the windshield of ice.

A shout echoed across the frozen lake. "There they are!"

"Come on, guys, get in. It's good enough!" Alex yelled. She started the plane forward.

Lowry scrambled into the cockpit while John jumped onto the step of the plane.

He waved to Noelle as she slipped on the ice, struggling to keep up with the plane. "Noelle, run!"

John grabbed Noelle's hand and jerked her onto the ski. The plane picked up speed. The door banged above John's head as he hung on to the frame. Noelle and John rode the ski as the plane sliced over the frozen lake. Lopsided with the unbalanced weight, the plane lifted for an instant and lurched over the steep shore of the lake. The freezing wind bit through John's gloves, numbing his hands.

The ski clipped the branch of a tree, jolting the plane. Noelle's foot slipped off the ski. "Help!" She clung to the frame of the wing by one hand.

He wrapped one arm around the step and stretched his hand out to her. "Noelle, grab my hand!"

The plane dipped over the next hill. Noelle turned to John, her mouth opened in a scream. She lost her grip and tumbled off the ski, disappearing into the darkness.

John gasped but dared not shout. They were too close to the compound. In front of them, the moon sparkled on a snow-covered ridge. With him unbalancing the plane, he knew it wouldn't clear the crest.

Her face twisted in fear, Lowry leaned out and reached for his hand. "John!"

He cried out, "Alex, take them home!" staring into their shocked faces. "Ginnie, Lowry—I love you!"

He let go. Their voices faded as John fell to earth.

The wind whistled in his ears as he pulled himself into a ball. John slammed into the snow and the pain of impact shot through his body. He vaguely felt himself slide down a bank and hit something buried in the snow. He lost consciousness.

CHAPTER 15

A chill morning broke. John opened his eyes, squinting against the pale sunlight glittering on the snow. He shook his head in a daze, breathing in and out as the memory of his descent came back to him. *I guess the fall didn't kill me—hell would be a lot warmer than this.*

He rolled to his side, but all he could see were blue shadows randomly draped across a white expanse of snow. Where the fuck was he? Slowly, he tested his body, avoiding sudden moves. He winced as he lifted his arms. Bruised perhaps, but functioning. Next, he tried to move his legs but felt nothing. Was he paralyzed? Frantic, he raised himself onto his elbow, and thumped his head on a rock overhang. His legs shot up out of the fresh snow and he laid back, groaning with new pain. But at least his legs were working.

"That rock you just pounded your head against may have saved your pinkies from freezing last night."

John turned toward the voice. With a moan, he rubbed his head and rolled out from beneath the ledge.

Noelle slid down the bank to where he lay.

Massaging his legs, he asked, "How did you find me?"

"After I landed, I saw you drop off the ski." She motioned toward the compound. "The bad guys ran after the plane, but apparently missed our inglorious exits. I heard them searching for a couple of hours, but they eventually left. I spent the night under the trees back there and headed this way at daybreak."

John studied her face. "Are you in pain?"

"My shoulder seems to be out of joint." She looked at John. "You fell pretty far. Do you know if you broke anything?"

He stretched forward to feel his legs and then grunted, pinching his lips against the pain as he caressed his rib cage. "I may have a bruised rib, but I'll know more after I thaw." John flicked on the emergency batteries that ran to his boots and gloves to ward off frostbite but set the power to transition off once his skin had warmed. Without knowing when they might reach civilization, he needed the batteries to last.

Noelle rubbed her shoulder. "When you're able, I'm afraid I'll have to trouble you to put my shoulder back into its correct position."

He struggled over to her. She pointed to the bad arm. John could see the odd angle, despite the heavy coat she was wearing. John grasped her arm and wrenched it sharply. "This is going to hurt." With a pop, it slid back into the joint.

Noelle gasped in pain. "Thanks for the warning."

John chuckled. "You're welcome. I figured you tensing up would have been worse than just doing it."

They watched the sun fade as gray clouds drifted overhead. A brilliant pain rose in his hands and lower extremities as they thawed. Gentle snowflakes began to wander through the air, threatening to bury the contents of the nearby backpack, spewed from a rip in the fabric. His and Alex's hovershoes stuck out of the snow at odd angles, like palette knives in a white frosted cake.

"No rest for the wounded," John muttered. They collected the scattered items and crawled under the rock ledge for shelter.

John dug in the pack and pulled out an energy bar and ibuprofen.

He split the bar and gave half to Noelle. "We'd better conserve our food."

"Good plan," she said, between chews.

He scooped snow into the Insta-Hot coffee cup, twisted the cap closed to the Hot Coffee position, and the snow instantly turned into a steaming cup of coffee. He handed it to Noelle, and she gulped half of the coffee while he ate his breakfast. She handed him the cup. He popped the ibuprofen into his mouth and gulped it down with the hot liquid.

Fortified with food, a hot drink, and pain relief, John scooted out from under the ledge, and located their position with the GPS. He grimaced. The agreed upon emergency pickup point meant days of hiking through the wilderness, assuming they evaded Zoric's people.

"With the short days, we'd better get going," John said. He stood and gritted his teeth against the prickles in his legs as the muscles warmed. *Pain was better than paralyzed.*

Using bandaging from the first-aid kit, John rigged a sling for Noelle's arm. They packed their gear and put on the hovershoes. "The fresh snow will cover our tracks in case Zoric realizes that not everyone made the plane."

He handed Noelle one of the ski poles. "Today, I'd only use one ski pole. You should rest your shoulder."

With a nod, she grabbed the pole.

John shouldered the pack, clenching his jaw against the pain. They extended the ski poles and started off across the snow. The numbness in his legs eased with the cross-country-skiing motion of the hovershoes, but at every stride, the rest of his body ached. A snowflake landed on his face, and smiling, he took a deep breath of cold air. No matter what happened next, his daughter, Lowry, and the students were safe.

They came to a lowland of dense brush and low evergreens. The snow was soft and they struggled through the drifts despite the hovershoes.

Voices echoed across the valley and John signaled with his hand. They dropped on their bellies and crawled beneath the boughs of a spruce tree. John's heart thumped against the snow.

Two men appeared, traversing along the hillside toward them.

He struggled to calm his breath, afraid the frosty wisps might betray their position. He glanced at Noelle. She met his eyes, her lips pinched in fear.

The voices came closer. Without moving a muscle, he studied the pair as they approached. They carried axes, and John hoped they hunted fuel rather than humans. They spoke in an unfamiliar Slavic dialect. *Serbian?*

Hidden under the branches, they lay motionless, the cold of the frigid ground creeping into their bodies. The men seemed unaware of their presence as they passed their hiding spot. They disappeared over the next ridge, but John and Noelle remained until the birds began to sing again, signaling all was clear. He nodded his head, and they inched out from under the tree.

Silently, they stood, listening for voices of the men, but heard only the sounds of the forest. John inclined his head, and they started off, quickly leaving the valley. The snow stopped, and the sun re-emerged as they climbed a low hill, then scooted down the other side.

They kept a fast pace until midday, when John pointed to a small cubbyhole beneath an overhang. Noelle nodded, and they stopped for a short break. They sank in the snow and caught their breath. John opened his pack and brought out much-needed food and drink. They split an energy bar and drank more hot coffee.

John leaned back against the rock and slipped into a weary daze. Noelle nodded forward in exhaustion. He shook his head to clear the cobwebs. They had to keep going—the days were short and they were deep in Zoric's territory. If they found their tracks, they would start searching for them. Besides, they had enough supplies for only three days.

Like a sinking vessel, Noelle crumpled halfway onto the ground.

He leaned over and whispered to her, "We must get as far as we can today."

She opened one eye, and then frowned. "You interrupted a lovely dream. I was snuggled in a luxurious bed in front of a roaring fire."

"I'll grab the marshmallows and join you," he grunted, struggling to his feet. He stretched a hand to Noelle, and with a groan, she stood. She swept the snow from her pants, dubiously watching him hide their tracks with a branch.

John shrugged. "I saw it in a movie. Who knows, maybe it will make it a little harder to find our trail."

He slung the pack over his shoulders. Weariness fogged his mind as they hovered over the snow. The light faded, and they searched for a campsite. Noelle pointed to a grove of short evergreens and they pushed under the branches. They split another energy bar, then leaned against the trunk of the largest tree. Lying under the boughs, they listened to the sounds of the forest at twilight as the day animals gave way to the night creatures.

"Such a brilliant, efficient plan, isn't it?" Noelle whispered.

"What plan is that?"

"That Mother Nature has a day and night shift, always in full utilization. Just amazing!"

The sun faded behind the trees and John said, "This day creature is going to bed." He dug the sleeping bag out of his pack, then looked at Noelle. "Um, we only have one sleeping bag. I hope you're not shy."

Noelle grinned. "The more the merrier, I always say."

They stared at the bag between them, contemplating the sleeping arrangements.

He cleared his throat. "Spoons, I would say."

"Spoons?" She glanced at him.

"You know, spoons versus . . ." He gestured with his hands.

"Oh, I understand." Noelle shrugged. "Yes, I believe spoons would be best."

John took off his shoes, set them near the tree, and crawled into the back of the bag. Noelle pulled off her boots and placed them next to his. He opened the bag for Noelle and she scooted in with him. Awkwardly, he struggled to zip the sleeping bag around both of their bodies.

"Ow! Watch it, mon ami!" Noelle cried softly as he accidentally hit her with an elbow.

"Sorry."

He closed the top of the bag around their heads as best he could. The heat from their bodies warmed them. Exhausted, he fell into a deep sleep.

CHAPTER 16

John awoke to Noelle's voice in the pale light of dawn.

"You have quite an alarm clock nudging me."

John's face turned red. "Oops—early-morning reflex." He squirmed away from her, hurriedly drew his arm out, and began to unzip the bag. As he opened the zipper, his body shifted, and he unceremoniously propelled Noelle out of the bag.

"Hey—" She landed face first in the snow, with her arms stretched out and her feet floundering in the air.

Chuckling, John pushed himself onto his elbow. "Sorry, on all accounts!"

Noelle twisted her head, spitting snow out of her mouth. "That was a hell of a wake-up call—the snooze alarm might kill me."

"Please don't backhand it." John pulled on his boots. "I'll get your boots. Keep your feet up so your socks won't get wet." He crawled around her and lifted her onto the bag. "Nice form on your snow dive—I'd give it an eight."

With a grin, Noelle wiped the snow from her face. "Thanks. Next time I'll try for a ten, but I'm hoping I won't have another opportunity."

He raised an eyebrow. "No guarantees on the alarm clock, but maybe we should switch positions on the spoons."

John crawled under the branches and drug the pack out. He threw a handful of snow into the Insta-Hot cup and twisted the top. He drank his half of the coffee, and then dug out a breakfast bar and handed it to Noelle. "Would you be so kind as to fix breakfast?"

"Certainly, gentle sir." Noelle opened the package and broke the bar in two.

John pulled the sleeping bag into the sun. They sat next to each other facing the valley ahead and Noelle handed him half of the bar.

She said, "Cheers," tapping his half with hers.

After the meager breakfast, he packed their gear while she drank the rest of the coffee. John hefted the pack onto his back and they returned to the trail. He breathed in the crisp air, thankful that Zoric's compound was far behind them.

The sun was at its highest point of the day as they traversed a meadow packed with snow. The anemic rays warmed his face as they floated over the white carpet of snow, crossing tracks of snowshoe rabbit, ermine, and arctic fox. Near a low line of brush, a shrill *kraa* sound hit their ears, and a pair of ravens burst out of the thin branches above them, snow sparkling as it drifted in the air. The birds retreated into a lone evergreen at the edge of the meadow.

Noelle chuckled. "What beauties they are, but they're not happy with us." She pointed to the highest part of the tree. "I see a nest up there."

The large male bobbed its head, preening its glossy black wings. As they neared the tree, a deep rasping sound came from the birds, warning them away from the nest.

She shook her head. "Humans can be pompous and think animals are unintelligent, but if they understood the silent—" The male's full-throated croaks boomed from the branches overhead. "—and not-so-silent, communication of animals around them, they would realize how intelligent they are. It's hubris to think that animals are stupid because you don't understand their language."

The black beady eyes of the ravens followed them past the tree. With a nod, John raised his ski pole in salute to the birds. "We yield the meadow to you."

Noelle laughed. "And nevermore return!"

They left the meadow and climbed a hill. At an outcrop of rocks, they removed their hovershoes and scrambled to the top of a ridge. They peered down the steep slope and stopped to catch their breath. Noelle sat on a boulder while John scooped snow into the heating cup and twisted the cap. He joined her on the rock and they drank the warm liquid, admiring the view of the small valley spread before them.

Like petrified gnomes, frozen patches of tussock grass bordered a narrow stream slicing through the lowlands. Spots of bare earth dotted the water's edge where the spring sun had melted the snow. A small flock of pintail ducks circled over a patch of shallow water where the surface ice had thawed.

Noelle broke into his reverie. "Are you still in love with Lowry?"

Startled, John turned to her. "What?"

"I sense a lingering relationship between you two?"

In confusion, he looked away. He cleared his throat and stowed the cup, feeling her eyes studying him. But what could he say?

He stood and shouldered the pack. "Once we get off the hill, we need to watch for permafrost—that valley looks like prime territory." He pointed to the undulating stream.

They climbed down the slope, sliding in mushy snow, softened with the afternoon sun. At the bottom, John brushed the wet snow from his pants.

With his hand, he gestured to the crease where the hillside met the flat terrain. "It's brambly, but safer than crossing the valley floor."

They continued along the edge of the valley, fighting their way through ice-laden brush and brambles.

John's thoughts became as tangled as the bare vines grasping his legs, wrestling with the question of raising another child. Did he have the energy and fortitude? He had to deal with that issue, because Lowry would not agree to marriage without that element, nor would he ask it of her.

Finally, they left the gauntlet of brush. John checked their location. "Yep, still going east. We're close to the Concordia Refuge." Then he added off-handedly, "We might be getting married."

"Who? Oh, yes, you and Lowry."

After a quick drink, they knelt and strapped on the hovershoes. Noelle came up beside him as they hovered over a section of thin snow.

John picked up the conversation again. "Lowry wants a child."

Noelle nodded. "She should. Lowry would be a great mother."

Eyebrows raised, John turned to her with a huff. "For someone who preaches population control, that seems an odd statement."

She smiled. "Life is not a bad thing. It is life *out of balance* that's the problem." With a slight shake of her head, she continued. "The rich nations gorge themselves on the raw products of the poorer countries. The poorer countries look at the industrialized nations and cry for a chance to be like them. And it's natural to want children, and fine to have one or two, but more than that overloads the eco-system." She mimed a check mark in the air with her good arm. "We propagated the Earth, so we can check that off the list. We need simple replacement, not growth, for our population."

The wind rose across the plain, swirling dead grass from last season into the air. They pulled their hoods up against the chill breeze until they reached a protective screen of branches along a knoll. The shrubs thinned as they climbed to the far side of the crest, facing a narrow valley.

John pointed to a bare slab of granite warming in the sun. "Let's rest and hydrate." He lifted out the Insta-Hot cup from his pack, filled it with snow, and twisted the lid. He handed Noelle the cup.

She sipped the warm water. "Not much coffee flavor left."

He grinned. "Imagine it's a cup of rich cappuccino."

She stuck her tongue out and gave it back to him. "I don't have that good an imagination."

John emptied the cup and grimaced. "Me neither."

He cleared his throat and glanced at her. "Um, we were discussing Lowry."

Noelle turned to him with a questioning look. "Yes?"

"Our relationship is complicated." He shrugged. "Besides, I'm almost fifty, with a daughter ready to go out in the world."

She chuckled. "Whose relationships aren't complicated?"

"I guess the bottom line is that I'm not sure about having another child."

A look of pain crossed Noelle's face. "My late husband and I didn't have children." She dropped her gaze, plucking randomly at a strap on her pants. "We traveled across the world for our work and various conferences. There was no time to raise a child." She sighed. "We discussed adopting, but our lives were so crazy." In a voice thin with emotion, she whispered, "Then he died suddenly—a plane crash. In my grief, I threw myself into promoting the HOME foundation."

"Ginnie mentioned it to me."

"It's global now, and I hope taking root, so to speak."

Silently, she stared at the empty landscape, her jaw clenching and unclenching. She looked at John, her eyes searching his, and laid her hand on his arm. "You and Lowry can have the child we never had."

John glanced away for a second, and then turned back to Noelle, placing his hand over hers. "I know how much that means to you—it's a beautiful gift."

"You have my blessing, but never forget that love is a sacrifice of self for another being. If your decision is to not have a child, then you cannot marry Lowry."

"I know." He withdrew his hand, and stared into the pale blue sky, thin clouds stretched like frayed rubber bands across the horizon. "This situation with Lowry has hit me hard." He rubbed the side of his face. "You think you know where you're going and then you're thrown onto a completely different path." With a shake of his head, he glanced at Noelle. "Lowry has a talent for that."

"Most strong women do."

John nodded. "She's a person to be reckoned with for sure."

Noelle inclined her head. "Perhaps this journey was meant to be, John. A vision quest to reveal your fate."

He grunted. "Fasting and exhaustion—perfect conditions for reaching a decision."

She smiled. "It's not a decision of the head, but of the heart."

He shot her a crooked grin. "Empty belly, full heart?" He rose and placed the cup into his pack. "We should get going."

With measured strides, they floated slowly downhill across a slope of glazed ice, hardened by freezing and thawing into a thick shell. John squinted against the brilliance of the sun reflecting on the mirrored surface, listening to the cadence of the ski poles cracking the ice.

When they reached the bottom of the hill, John stopped to check the GPS readings. At the sound of crashes through the underbrush, they froze, and then stared at one other. If it were Zoric's men, the only direction they could go was across an open snowfield, with nowhere to hide.

Grunting, a huge brown bear broke through the undergrowth and stumbled into sight.

Noelle whispered to John, "Stay completely still. It's a Kodiak emerging from hibernation. He may be too groggy to see us."

John whispered back, "Isn't this the time they're grumpy?"

"We'll find out."

The bear walked closer and caught their scent. He looked puzzled and turned in circles, sniffing the air. He fixed his eyes upon them and roared.

"Whatever you do, if he charges, and you can't escape, fall down and play dead—with a Kodiak, he might leave you alone."

His heart in his throat, John stared as the bear wandered closer.

The bear kept coming. Without warning, the bear charged. Noelle and John split apart, running in different directions. Noelle dived under a tangle of brush.

John sprinted toward a granite boulder and glanced over his shoulder. The bear was narrowing the gap, the sound of his breaths louder with each stride. John knew he couldn't reach the rock before the bear overtook him. He clutched his hands behind his neck and collapsed into a fetal position in the snow. He tried to calm his labored breath and willed himself to relax completely.

Rumbling, the bear circled his body, its smell hitting John's nostrils. The bear came closer and nudged him. John hoped the bear couldn't hear the wild beating of his heart. He bit his lip to keep from twitching, the bear's whiskers tickling his neck. He held his breath, emptying his mind as the bear panted across his face.

The bear roared. John grunted as the bear's paw hit the side of his head, the huge claws ripping into his left ear and cheek. A searing pain burned his face. He was lifted, suspended in air for a second, and flipped like a steak on a grill. Face first, he slammed onto the snow-covered ground. The snow cushioned his impact, and he clenched his teeth against crying out. He willed himself to remain limp and eased his gashed skin into the snow to conceal the scent of his blood and dull the aching wound.

The bear sniffed him again, pushing John with his snout. He snorted, and then ambled off, his grunts fading into the distance.

The side of John's face was on fire, but he lay still for what seemed to be an eternity. He heard a rustling of branches, and felt a tug on his arm.

Noelle whispered, "John, it's me. Are you okay?"

He opened his eyes. Noelle was kneeling beside him. He blinked, focusing on her worried eyes.

"Well, I'm alive." John shifted onto his back, staring at the blue sky arched above them. Noelle clasped his hand and pulled him into a sitting position.

"I must say, you did a fine job as dead meat."

He grimaced and then winced in pain. "You flatterer, you." He pointed to the left side of his face. "Tell me how bad he got me."

Noelle gently turned his head, and with a frown, sucked in her breath. "You might have a beautiful set of scars to impress the ladies." She patted his arm. "I'll get the first-aid kit." She rose and retrieved his pack, and then knelt beside him. "Let's hope the bear is really gone." She unzipped the pack, lifted the first-aid kit, and pulled out cleaning wipes and a tube of antibiotic/painkiller gel. She brushed back his hair and cleaned the gashes. "John, you are lucky he was only playing with you."

"I'll be more elated when my face stops throbbing."

She applied the antibiotic medicine over the gashes, holding his hair away from his scalp while it hardened into a flexible bandage.

With a smile, she repacked the medicines and stuffed the first-aid kit into the bag. "You'll feel better when the painkiller kicks in." Noelle stood and stretched out her hand to him. "It's my turn to say that we need to get going."

John took her hand and staggered to his feet. "Thanks, Noelle." Light-headed, he swayed for a second. He put his hands on his knees, breathing in and out to clear his dizziness.

Noelle squeezed his shoulder. "Don't pass out on me, John."

With a slight shake of his head, he whispered, "I'm fine, I just need oxygen." He stood and inhaled deeply. He lifted the backpack and eased it over his shoulders. "But I'm getting too old for all of this fun."

His entire body ached as they crossed the plain. John focused on the rhythmic shush-shush of the hovershoes until the medicine reduced his pain. *I could have died just now, but providence spared me—why?*

They left the open snowfield and wove through a grove of anemic spruce trees. The trees thinned, and they followed a faint animal trail down a bluff, listening to the sound of running water. They rounded a corner and stopped, gasping in wonder at a massive cliff of pink granite standing before them, neatly swept of snow by the wind. A huge glacier had carved its way down the valley during the Melt, polishing the rock face, but all that remained of the glacier was a half-frozen stream, meandering along the bottom of the gorge. Interspersed in the pink granite, quartz crystals sparkled in the sun.

"It's gorgeous," Noelle breathed.

With his hand, John shielded his eyes from the sunlight, studying a narrow rock shelf along the rock-face. Water tumbled out of a fissure above the cliff edge, steam rising as it showered down the cliff. "We can cross that ledge, but we need to take off the hovershoes."

Noelle's mouth dropped open. "Are you thinking of crossing on that skinny shelf?"

John shrugged. "It's either go forward or circle back through Zoric's territory." He pointed beyond the gorge. "We're almost out of the Grace Region and this is the shortest route." Gingerly, he eased his hood over his head, avoiding the gashes on his face. "You'd better pull up your hood. That water looks to be geothermally hot."

They descended to the ledge. John swallowed hard at the pink granite shimmering in the steaming cascade. He glanced into the gorge below and, with a grin, turned to Noelle. "Ladies first?"

She shook her head. "Not on your life."

He faced the pink stone, shuffling sideways along the ledge. Noelle followed behind him. John's muscles cramped as they crept along, until they reached the center of the scorching waterfall. Boiling water splashed his back as he pressed tightly against the granite, arching away from the geothermal shower thundering between the stone and the gorge. Out of the main torrent, he looked at Noelle, her face haggard in fear, but keeping up with him.

Past the waterfall, he exhaled in relief, but with a gust of wind, the mist enveloped him. His foot slipped and he glanced at the sheen of ice on the rocks below his feet. The spray from the waterfall had frozen on the downwind side of the ledge.

Noelle reached him. He pointed at their feet. "Ice on the rock on this side of the falls," he shouted over the rush of water.

She nodded. John studied each step, picking his way across the ice-incrusted rock.

With a scream, Noelle slipped on an icy patch. John caught her arm and pulled her back onto the ledge. Breathless, they stopped, and leaned against the face of the rock.

"Are you okay?" John asked.

"My legs are shaking," Noelle panted.

"Only a bit to go."

They shuffled along the rock shelf and stepped onto a narrow path on the far side of the cliff. They reached a bend in the gorge and climbed onto a broken slab of granite.

"Let's rest our legs."

On the side of the stone, John knelt and scooped snow into the coffee cup. He stood, twisted the cap to heat the liquid, and then handed her the cup. His legs quivered in fatigue, and he slumped next to Noelle. His stomach gnawed in hunger, protesting the unfed exertions of the day.

With a tired smile, she lifted the cup in salute. "We made it!"

They sipped the hot beverage, gazing at the steaming water cascading into the half-frozen stream. Algae lined the stone in the rocks beneath the waterfall.

Noelle pointed at a flock of birds darting over a calm pool downstream from the cascade. "Those might be killdeers. They eat insects that propagate near thermal ponds."

"It's amazing that life exists in an environment of such extremes." John inhaled deeply. The crisp breeze carried a slight mineral scent from the cascades. The surreal landscape was like seeing into the dawn of time. "Noelle, with all of your philosophy, what is your take on this thing we call life?"

She glanced at him and gestured to the beauty surrounding them.

"This *is* life, mon ami. Just being."

John sighed. "I've found that 'just being' is one of the most difficult things to do. I feel a big hand at my back, pushing me."

"The hand of God?"

"No, I'm pretty sure it's Lowry's."

Noelle laughed. "Ah, you're speaking of one's Mission in Life, from wherever the impetus may spring. I think the most important thing you can do in life is to become the person you wish to be. It's also the most difficult. As simple as it sounds, doing what you want in life is the most challenging task you'll ever undertake. You must overcome the worn adages you've been taught and climb alone to your destiny."

"I thought my destiny was to come to Antarctica and become a simple farmer."

Noelle's eyes twinkled. "Perhaps it was, mon ami, perhaps it was."

John shot a puzzled look at her, but Noelle had turned away, gazing at the veil of mist, bursting into a rainbow as the sunlight peeked over the cliff.

He repacked the cup, they put on their hovershoes and followed the stream downhill. The path widened and they walked side by side. They hovered over a snow bank, with puffs of ice crystals effervescing around their legs.

Noelle pointed to a flock of seedsnipes flying in the evergreens on the far bank of the stream, calling *pu, pu, pu.* The air shimmered with snowflakes as they darted from branch to branch. "Intelligence is our strength in the animal kingdom, but it can be a double-edged sword. Sometimes we humans think too much. The beasts of the Earth live simply, but with grandeur and passion." She gestured to the flock. "Listen to the birds. They are the true voices of the Earth."

The calls of the birds faded as they floated across an open field of snow.

Noelle glanced at John. "Why did you homestead in Antarctica?"

"Disgust with civilization, I guess." He jabbed his ski poles deep into the snow. "After my wife was killed, there was no reason to stay." He sighed. "But it wasn't only that. I didn't fit into 'normal' society. I've always been a lone wolf. Antarctica, for me, was an opportunity to breathe."

The clouds began to thicken and the wind bit their faces. They moved into a shaded patch of deep snow, tightening their hoods against the chill air.

John glanced at her. "Everyone has something that scratches their itch. Something made you become Noelle, savior of the Earth—what was it?"

Noelle smiled thinly. "My mother was a wildlife photographer, primarily working in the rain forests of South America. I spent my youth tagging behind her on her photo shoots in the jungles." She shrugged. "I was lucky that my parents never pushed me into a career. As a child, my mother always taught me that true love is allowing someone to bloom fully in their own way. I remember her telling me that life, in whatever form it exists, is a gift from God." Her voice softened. "She's an amazing woman, still has incredible joie de vivre, thrilled at the sight of the tiniest flower or insect."

A haunted look came over her face. "The bell tolled for me when, after several years, we returned to a rainforest in Peru to follow up the original photo shoot. The entire forest was gone—only the burned stumps of once-giant trees." She shook her head. "All the animals we had seen and photographed before had vanished."

She paused and John glanced at her stricken face. Noelle murmured, "I can't forget the image of my mother, falling to her knees, sobbing."

John exhaled. "Humans destroy nature by a thousand cuts and karma bites us with every slice."

"We must teach love and reverence of the Earth to our young children, so they will care for her from deep within their hearts." Noelle glanced at him. "Are you a religious man?"

"I'm a spiritual person. But I'm not interested in organized religion. Too many people with hidden agendas, for my taste. I want my God straight-up."

"I agree, sometimes religion can become more about the leader than God."

"Case in point: Mr. Ivan Zoric."

She huffed. "He twists religion into a lethal weapon."

The sun broke through the clouds and the snow shimmered like a carpet of diamonds.

Noelle stopped and rested on her ski poles. "As shepherds of the Earth, we have a responsibility to not kill without reason, neither beast nor man. Every cell in every living being is a part of God and the great circle of love." With a smile, she turned to John. "Everyone wants to know the meaning of life. I believe it is love. Love is life and life is God."

John and Noelle drank some water, and he reflected on the simple words from a complicated woman. He breathed in the crisp air and, in Noelle's words, the abundance of love.

As they continued on, exhaustion dragged at him. The side of his face throbbed, and he was thankful when the sun began to fall and he could rest.

They found a narrow grotto, dug out by the glacier's path, and stopped to make camp. They burrowed themselves under the rock overhang and mounded snow on the outside, making a snug den.

John pulled off his boots and placed them on a stone ledge at the back of the cavern. "Even has a shelf."

"If we had a bureau, we'd be set." Noelle chuckled.

She changed John's bandage, and the refreshed medicine eased the discomfort of his wounds. He dug out one of the last two energy bars, broke it in half and passed the other piece to Noelle. His stomach twisted with hunger, but they had two more days until they reached the pickup point.

After they finished the meager dinner, John dumped snow into the cup and twisted the lid. He handed it to her. "An Irish Coffee for a digestif?"

"Perfect." Noelle sipped the hot liquid and raised the cup to John. "A toast to love."

John smiled, took the cup, and lifted it to her. "To love." He drank the hot water with a bare taint of coffee flavor left and raised the cup again. "And to this being our last night in Grace Region."

"Tomorrow we are out of Zoric's grasp?"

"Yes, we should reach the river tomorrow, and once across, we're in the Concordia Refuge."

They snuggled into the sleeping bag and packed the snow around them for extra warmth. John's stomach growled. *With luck, maybe one more night after this?* He closed his eyes and sank into a forgetful sleep.

CHAPTER 17

Lowry felt nauseous. It had been three long days without news of John and Noelle. Today, she had gone to Amundsen for an update and moral support. She sat next to Ginnie in the living room of the presidential apartments.

Tears in her eyes, Ginnie looked at her. "Dad might be dead for all we know."

She placed her hand on Ginnie's shoulder and managed a facsimile of a smile. "We must hope for the best." She clenched her fist. *No choice but to hope.* John and Noelle might be lost in a snowy wilderness—or in the hands of a madman.

She tapped the arm of the sofa and re-crossed her legs. *I need to move around before my nerves explode.* "Ginnie, I'll get you a cup of tea." She rose and walked into the kitchen, calling out, "Hot black tea." With a faint chime the brewer started.

She slumped at the counter and dropped her head into her hands. Since she and John had met, they'd been friends, lovers, and adversaries, but regardless of their relationship du jour, he had been a constant in her life over these last years. The specter of life without him hit her in the gut. With a moan, her shoulders convulsed, tears streaming down her face. She was in love with him, not as a means to a child, but as a human being. *What will I do if he's gone?*

Lowry wiped her cheeks with her sleeve. If she hadn't pushed him into the candidacy years ago, he wouldn't be president. They might be married and at the house, doing chores, perhaps caring for their child. Now, it might be too late.

Another chime signaled that the tea was ready. Lowry raked her hair back, went to the counter and set the tea, two cups and a jar of honey on a tray. She asked the frig, "Any cream?" The door opened and a carafe of cream slid to the front. She grabbed it and set it next to the tea. Her stomach growled—she'd forgotten to eat breakfast. She found a covered plate of chocolate-chip cookies on the counter, placed a couple on the tray and walked to the dining room.

"Why don't you have tea and a little snack, Ginnie?" Lowry placed the tray on the table. She poured herself a cup of tea, added a bit of cream, and stirred. The white liquid blended with the dark tea, the hypnotic sound of the spoon striking the side of the cup like the metronome. She shook her head to clear the haze, and then grabbed a cookie and nibbled it. *If you don't eat, you might pass out.*

Ginnie ambled into the dining room and sat across from Lowry. Her lips trembled. "It's my fault; Dad wouldn't be out there if it weren't for the expedition."

Lowry poured her a cup and handed it to her. "Drink some hot tea, Ginnie." She raised her half-eaten cookie. "And you need something on your stomach."

She gazed at Ginnie's pale face. From Lowry's childhood, her pseudo-father, Duff, had been an expert in pointing the finger in every direction except toward himself. The game of 'Fault' was a pastime that nobody won. But in this case, she knew exactly who was to blame. Her unsteady hands lifted the cup to her lips. "If it's anyone's fault, it's mine."

As Ginnie spooned honey into her tea, she gave Lowry a puzzled look. "You?"

"If your father hadn't been elected president, all this wouldn't have happened."

"Dad always said there's a chicken and egg to everything." Ginnie shrugged. "I guess we can't worry about who laid the egg."

Lowry chuckled, and began to laugh. She dropped her cookie, and set her cup on the table to avoid spilling the hot liquid.

Blinking, Ginnie stared at her. Her face quivered, and with a twitch of her shoulders, she guffawed, spilling tea into the saucer. She scooted her cup onto the tray and shoved it to the middle of the table. She crumpled onto her folded arms, giggling uncontrollably.

Lowry threw her head back, laughing and crying until her sides hurt. Between the exhaustion of the events of the last days and the inability to sleep, the anxiety had been overwhelming for them both. She grabbed her aching stomach, and in self-defense, finally stopped laughing. "I think we needed that." She breathed deeply and gave Ginnie's hand a quick squeeze. Exhaling, she lifted her cup and sipped her tea.

Ginnie shook her head. "I hope Dad and Noelle are having a few laughs." She brushed back her hair, and picked up a cookie. With a heavy sigh, she bit into it, then glanced at her. "You realize, that despite everything, he still loves you?"

Lowry's throat tightened as she swallowed the tea. With a cough, she set down the cup and tapped the porcelain edge, gazing across the table at her.

"I told Dad that he should reconnect with you." Ginnie grimaced. "When I was sixteen, I wasn't totally in favor of him remarrying, at least so soon after Mom's death, but now. . ." She held out her hand to Lowry. "I think he needs you."

"Perhaps."

Henry-dog padded into the room. He sat near Ginnie's chair, looking expectantly at her.

Ginnie looked at him with a raised brow. "You smelled food, didn't you, boy?" She stood and waved her hand. "Okay, buddy, let's get you a treat, too." They walked to the kitchen, and she smiled. "Everybody wants something."

Lowry tilted her head. "If there ever was a truth, that's it." She picked up the cup and swirled the dregs of tea, staring at the spinning liquid. Just as Henry-dog's reality was different from Ginnie's, truth reflected images from each person's prospective.

Ginnie returned and pushed the chair back from the table. As soon as she sat, Henry jumped into her lap. "Ugh, you're kind of big for a lap dog."

"His brother Leo is as bad."

As she petted Henry's head, tears welled in her eyes. "What will happen to Henry if Dad is . . . gone?"

"We can't worry about that now." With a smile, Lowry picked up the honey jar. "As a young girl in Texas, I remember catching fireflies in a jar. Trapped inside the glass, we watched the insects turn from bright to dark. My mother told me to release them back into the night air. 'Like letting go of your worries, Lowry.'"

Lowry chewed the inside of her cheek. Her early life had been flipped topsy-turvy after the death of her mother. The man she considered her father, Duff, had his own abusive past. A petulant man, he was an alcoholic and emotionally unavailable during her adolescent years.

She turned the jar back and forth, watching the viscous honey flow from one side to the other. The litany of mistakes and stupidity of her early adult life drifted into her mind. A short-lived marriage to an abusive husband, then a divorce— the internal wounds had taken longer to heal than her physical bruises—PTSD from an emotional bomb blast. Her vulnerability had led her into a rebound with someone bent on betrayal. She exhaled and set the jar on the table and the honey leveled into balance. *But I made it out.*

Lowry squinted at the jar, imagining opening the lid, her worries scattering to the wind. *Just let go.* She closed her eyes for a second, breathing in and out, and then opened them. Did she feel any better? *A glass of wine might help.*

Ginnie wrapped her arm around Henry. "I know, it doesn't help to worry."

Lowry looked at her. "As far as reconnecting with your father—" She drew in a breath. "—I do still love him. I've asked him to reconsider our marriage." She leaned forward.

"I'll be straight with you, I want a child with him, but he will need to agree to it before we marry."

"Yes, Dad talked to me the other day." Ginnie pursed her lips. "You and he are the ones to make the decision as to marriage and baby, not me." With a faint smile, she whispered, "You'd be a great mom, Lowry." Her smile faded as she stared at the table.

Lowry's brow furrowed. The unspoken words of *if he's alive* echoed in the room. She cleared her throat. "Thanks, that means a lot to me." With a smile, she whispered, "Your father loves you very much. He thinks you hung the moon."

Her face brightened. "And vice versa."

Lowry glanced at her, sweetly nuzzling Henry. Ginnie's life not been easy but the love from John and her mother had given her strength to mature into a beautiful person inside and out.

She gathered the snack items together, placing them on the tray. Marriage was a challenge at best, and ghosts of her childhood might pop up at inconvenient times. She and John had never lived together, and they both were stubborn souls. If they conceived a baby, the child must be wanted by both parents. Lowry gritted her teeth. But manipulating him any more than she had already could not be a part of their relationship—if they had one.

*   *   *

A virtual image of Lin standing in front of the apartment materialized near the table. "Miss Barrous, may I come in?"

Ginnie bolted upright. "Yes—do you have news?"

The exterior door opened and Lin, followed by a small man in uniform, came into the dining room. The man halted and stood at attention in the entryway while Lin walked to Ginnie.

Lin nodded to Lowry. "Ah, good morning, Ms. Walker. I'm glad you're here. Yes, we finally have some news. Before it was neutralized by Zoric's protective web, one of our drones transmitted a video indicating traces from hovershoes near the Grace River. We can't tell for sure if it's the President and Dr. Clavet, but the direction was away from Zoric's land. We'll take it as a positive indication that they're alive. If so, they should reach Resolution Rock by tomorrow. In case of combatants, we have a SWAT team in place at the rendezvous site. John's personal physician will lead the medical unit."

Tilting her head, Lowry tapped her knuckle on her chin. "If you have the coordinates of the tracks and roughly estimate their path to the rendezvous, you might be able to find them near the river. That's closer than Resolution Rock."

Lin blinked slowly, then with a fleeting smile, said, "The president said the rendezvous was at Resolution Rock, and I took that as an order from my Commander-in-Chief. And strategically, if we spread out our team, they might be vulnerable to attack."

Lowry clenched her jaw. *You bastard.* She narrowed her eyes at him. "I understand that it could increase the risk to your team, but John and Noelle may be out of provisions and *they* are vulnerable to exposure and death. Frankly, saving them is more important than orders . . . or misplaced strategy."

He pursed his lips and faced her.

To keep from grinning, she bit her lip. *That got under his skin.*

With a shrug, he turned away and said flatly, "We are doing everything necessary and prudent."

A knot formed in Lowry's brow as she studied Lin's expressionless profile. *Perhaps you'd benefit if John didn't make it back.* Rumor had it that Lin was hot to run for president. What better way to get a leg up on the next election than become de facto president? Patel was weak—a puppet whose strings Lin would delight in pulling.

They turned at the sound of a cough. The small man stood shuffling his feet. Lin walked to him and leaned over while the man whispered into his ear. Lowry caught a few words in Chinese.

Nodding, Lin replied in Chinese. The man bowed quickly, shot a glance at Lowry, then left.

Lin smiled. "While John is out of pocket, I needed assistance coordinating a response to Zoric." He cocked his head to the exit. "A distant cousin of a cousin has taken a position as my adjunct." A smile grazed his face, then he turned away.

She knew enough Chinese to know that they'd been discussing John and Zoric. But there was something else, the way Lin had avoided her eyes, that made the hair on her neck rise.

Lin cleared his throat. With a brief bow to Ginnie, he pivoted toward the door. "I must get back."

Ginnie waved. "Thanks for the good news!"

Half-turned away, he smiled. "Yes, wonderful news. With luck, your father may be home tomorrow." His mouth jerked, and with a bob of his head, he hurried from the room.

As elated as she was to hear the news of a possible sighting of John and Noelle, Lowry had a twist in her stomach. Could Lin be brewing something devious? He had always given her the heebie-jeebies, but now her alarm bells were ringing.

Lowry watched him leave, his rapid footsteps matching the beat of her heart. Perhaps she'd caged her inner demons, at least until the next wrestling match, but the external ones were alive and well.

CHAPTER 18

John awoke to hunger pains gnawing his hunger pains. With a yawn, he blinked against a sun already high in the sky. Noelle sat on a corner of the sleeping bag, drinking hot water.

He grunted. "You let me sleep late."

Noelle grinned at him. "You were dead asleep; I didn't want to disturb you."

He crawled out of the bag and sat cross-legged, facing her. "I guess I needed it." He stretched his arms upwards, and winced.

"Your ribs still sore?"

"Yeah, a little." He pointed to her shoulder. "How's the shoulder?"

"It's healing." She handed him the rest of the hot water and a half of the last energy bar. "I fixed expresso this morning, but I'm afraid that's it on the food—better enjoy it."

John sipped the warm water. "I think you forgot to add coffee to the expresso." He forced himself to chew the breakfast slowly.

Noelle crawled to his side. She pushed back his hair and examined the bear wound under the clear bandage. "Hmm, looks good. We were lucky to find such an excellent doctor in the hinterlands."

A twinkle in his eye, he replied, "Yes, thank you. Don't make me laugh and I'll be fine."

She packed the sleeping bag and Insta-Hot cup, while John erased the evidence of the campsite. They climbed the stone ledge and John checked their position with his watch. He scanned the terrain of sporadic brush and leftover mounds of glacial till and rock. They were near the Grace River at the edge of Zoric's region and should reach it around midday. Adrenaline pumped energy into him at the thought of lounging on the far bank of the river—and out of Zoric's territory.

They made quick time across the flat landscape. The sun was at its height as they neared the river. They glided to the ridge that marked the edge of the river's flood zone and paused to view the mighty Grace River in frozen slumber. Downriver, an otter poked its head above a hole in the ice.

John glanced behind them. On this exposed ridge, they would be easy to spot by Zoric or one of his drones.

"I don't want to come this far and then be caught by that son of a bitch." He cocked his head toward the far bank. "Let's get across and out of Zoric's domain."

As they descended down an animal trail, a small herd of Andean deer burst out of the brush along the riverbank. They leapt high into the air, running upriver, and then stopped. The largest deer turned toward them, flanked by the smaller ones.

"That's the buck." Noelle whispered, pointing to the one closest to them. The deer's eyes watched them intently. "See the black pattern on his face?"

"Yeah," John whispered. "No antlers?"

"He must have just shed them."

The buck stomped the ground and snorted, his vaporous breath curling around his nostrils.

Noelle smiled. "He's saying, 'Go away, humans.'"

Another snort and the buck turned, and with his does, bounded away, disappearing over the ridge.

At the edge of the river, they stopped for a moment, gazing at the mighty river stilled by winter. Random snowdrifts, molded by the sun into bulbous sculptures, dotted the riverbank. In front of them, the flat ice glistened dully in the slanting rays of the sun, broken by a snarl of branches in the middle of the river, frozen into place like a macramé sculpture. Sunny patches of muddy ground near the riverbank hinted of uneven melting, and a faint gurgle beneath the ice warned of the growing rage under the surface. Spring melt was the most dangerous time to be on the ice.

John shielded his eyes from the glare, surveying the ice for weaknesses.

Noelle pointed upriver. "I see steam rising along the river bank. It must be a geothermal vent."

Grimacing, he said, "Hopefully it's only localized melting."

The wind rose along the ridge, rustling the brush they had passed. John shot a glance back, but the only movement were the frozen branches scraping each other like the legs of a cricket.

He knelt and unstrapped his hovershoes. "We can't risk losing our hovershoes or them pulling us under if the ice cracks. We'd better take them off and walk." He shouldered the hovershoes.

Noelle removed her hovershoes and slung them over her back.

John exhaled. *I guess it's now or never.* He moved onto the ice, stabbing his ski pole into the crust to test its integrity, while the river murmured below him. He tilted his head to Noelle and whispered, "It looks solid, but go slow. Follow exactly in my footsteps."

Noelle nodded, stepping into John's tracks across the marble-like surface.

They approached the middle of the river. He halted, studying the depth of the ice. Upriver, puddles of water shimmered in the sun. The ice trembled from the raging currents hungrily nibbling beneath his feet.

In a low voice, John said, "We'd better cross one at a time. The ice may be too thin here to support us both."

He removed his watch and stowed it in a pocket of his pack. With a glance at Noelle, he said, "If I fall and get swept away, don't try to save me. Continue on to the meeting point.

My watch has the coordinates of the rendezvous." With a grunt, he flung the backpack toward the opposite bank of the river.

John held his breath, edging across a patch of clear ice. The river percolated angrily beneath his feet, its raging water aching to snatch him. Another step and he clutched one of the gnarled branches of a twisted dead tree, solidly encased in ice. He exhaled in relief, and turned, beckoning to Noelle.

Noelle nodded and with careful steps, followed his trail. She approached the thinnest spot in the ice and John stretched his ski pole to her. Then her front foot slipped on the glassy ice, and she fell forward, with her entire weight on the thinnest patch of ice. John heard a crack. Noelle shrieked as the ice splintered under her feet.

John thrust his ski pole out, yelling, "Grab the pole!"

With one hand, Noelle clutched the shaft.

"Hurry, step to me," he shouted.

With a loud pop, the chunk of ice disappeared from beneath her like a trap door. Arms flailing, Noelle lost her grip on the pole and dropped halfway into the rushing water.

"John!" Noelle slid under the frigid water in mid-scream.

The enraged current snagged her body in its powerful grip. John leapt flat onto the ice and caught her hand. The river whipped Noelle's body and dragged him toward the hole. With a yell, he stretched the toe of his boot out behind him, curling his foot around the snarl of wood. The current twisted him to the side, but he held on to her.

Terrified, she stared into John's eyes. The water billowed up through the hole and slammed the hovershoes into the back her head. With a gasp, her eyes closed and her body went limp.

The river was eating at the ice underneath him. With his other hand, he clutched her arm. "God, help me!" he moaned, and with a grunt, he jerked Noelle half out of the water. "Come on!" His muscles burned as he heaved her onto the ice.

Breathing heavily, John lay beside Noelle's body, but he knew he couldn't rest. The ice might crack at any second.

With a kick, he freed his boot from the branch. Panting, he rose to his knees and crawled away from the hole, dragging Noelle's inert body across the ice. Near the river's edge, he stopped and pulled the hovershoes off of her back.

He cast his eyes for a shelter along the bank. Facing him was a shallow cavern eroded under a sandstone ledge. He swept her into his arms and struggled up a slope of snow softened in the afternoon sun. He stumbled to the narrow cavity, and with a groan, fell to his knees in the slush. Under the rock, he laid Noelle on a strip of bare earth sheltered from the snowfall. John peeled off his jacket and draped it over her.

John brushed the matted hair out of her face, whispering, "Stay with me, Noelle." Then he slid back to the river, and with his heart pounding, crept across the ice to retrieve his pack and their hovershoes. He grabbed the backpack, swung the hovershoes over his shoulder, and shuffled across the ice to the bank.

His legs shook in exhaustion as he scrambled to where Noelle lay. He dropped the gear, knelt and caressed Noelle's face, her skin cool to his touch. If he didn't get her warm and dry, she would die from hypothermia. He pulled out the sleeping bag, opened it, and shoved it underneath the ledge behind her. He yanked off her wet clothes and dried her skin with a small towel from his pack. She moaned and began to shiver. He rolled her into the bag and gently eased on the hand and foot warmers.

But he knew it wouldn't be enough to warm Noelle to a sustainable temperature. The warmest thing John had was his own body. He sucked in his breath as he peeled off his clothes in the frigid air, and slipped into the bag, gasping at the touch of her cold skin. He zipped the bag and struggled to rub her dry in the tight quarters. He wrapped his arms around her trembling body, her heart beating rapidly against his chest.

John gazed across the frozen river. The last rays of the sun caressed the ice, burnishing it into a mirror of gold. But the muted roar belied its elegance. He laid his head onto the hard ground and shifted against her warming skin.

At least Noelle was alive.

*   *   *

When he woke the next morning, Noelle was asleep, her breath rising and falling evenly, and her skin as warm as his.

John crawled out of the sleeping bag, gasping as the icy wind seared his nude body. He threw on his clothes, drew the Insta-Hot cup from the pack and scooped snow into it. With a twist of the cap, he crawled on top of the rock ledge and sat in the anemic sun. He sipped the hot liquid and rubbed his bruised ribs, throbbing in pain from pulling Noelle from the water.

He listened to the muffled sound of the river battling its way out of winter. It had nearly taken both their lives. Mother Nature is neutral to the individual—a death in one place springs into a life elsewhere.

John scanned the horizon across the far bank and breathed a sigh of relief. *The sun was shining and we survived the crossing.*

He staggered up, his legs trembling. The ordeal of the ice had used up his energy reserves—he had to get something to eat. He unsnapped the sheath of his knife and moved quietly through the trees. His hunger made his mind sharp. He heard a chirping sound, and froze, searching the forest floor around him. A flock of ptarmigans nested under a nearby spruce.

John spied an outcrop of rocks. He eased to it, gathered a handful of stones, and moved toward the birds. He would have one chance for a kill. He knelt. They picked at seeds laying in the snow. He drew his arm back and flung the stones at them.

The birds exploded into flight, except two. One lay still in the snow. The other ran, dragging a wing. He dove at the bird as it struggled into the air, seized a wing and pulled it to the ground. It screeched, pecking his hand viciously. He gripped its head with his other hand and snapped its neck with a brutal twist. The bird went limp.

John struggled to catch his breath, watching the blood stain the white snow. He had never been a hunter, but now he was.

He brought the birds back to where Noelle slept. He opened his pack and got out the fire kit and a cooking pot. Now that they were out of Zoric's land, they could finally light a fire. He set up three stones to hold the pot, broke open the fire chips and arranged them in the center of the fire pit. Exposed to the air, the chips started blazing, and he scooped snow into the pot and placed it over the flames. He skinned the birds and threw them in the boiling water. His stomach rumbling, he cooked them for as long as he could stand, and then pulled them out.

He nudged Noelle awake.

"Ptarmigan," he whispered, wafting the cooked meat under her nose.

She mumbled, "No thanks, I'm a vegetarian."

John blinked, then shook his head, and slowly dragged the sleeping bag out from under the ledge. He pulled her into a sitting position.

"Hey, what are you doing?" Noelle cried.

"Don't you remember falling through the ice?"

Noelle yawned. "Oh yes."

John handed her a cup of hot water and she drank thirstily. Groggy, she stared at the bird.

"I know you're a vegetarian, but I brought down a couple of ptarmigans. Just like chicken?" He frowned as she ignored him. "You have to eat something—this is called survival."

She turned away and stared at the river.

Shrugging, John searched through the backpack. In the bottom, he found broken bits from the energy bars, and gathered them into a small handful. He offered them to her. "Sorry, only crumbs left."

She smiled and carefully brushed them into her hand. Methodically, she licked the crumbs from her palm.

John split open one of the birds and tore at the hot meat, still bloody at the bone, devouring it in a few moments. When he finished, he leaned back against a rock. He felt energy flow into his body and turned to Noelle.

"Do you think you can hike a little farther?" John gestured over his shoulder. "We need to keep moving."

Noelle nodded. "I'd like an ibuprofen for my splitting headache." She rubbed her head and shivered in the cold. She glanced at her bare arm and looked in the bag at her nude body. With a cough, she glanced at John.

"Um, your clothes were soaked—I had to get you warm and dry as fast as I could." He gestured to her clothes hanging, frozen stiff, on the rocks. "Until your clothes thaw and dry, you can wear the extra set of clothes from my pack." He dug a pair of pants and a shirt from the pack, set it on the bag, and turned away.

She eased from the bag, and teeth chattering, jerked on the dry clothes. With a smile, she wiggled her arms, hidden in the long sleeves.

"Good to see you smile, Noelle." He grinned.

"I have you to thank for the privilege."

John peeled her frozen clothes from the rock. He sang "Me and my shadow" as he tied the stiff clothes onto her back.

Noelle did a little soft-shoe in the snow. She tilted her head in a bow and then swayed in exhaustion.

"Don't overdo it." He handed her the ibuprofen gel pain and water.

She gulped the medicine with a long drink, then murmured, "A big bowl of steaming rice would hit the spot." She knelt and packed her gear, while he rolled up the sleeping bag.

John kicked a hole in the snow and buried the ptarmigan bones. He sliced one leg of the second bird and threaded the other leg through to make a loop, and attached it to his backpack. Through the pale morning light, they left the riverbank and hiked up a small hill through a dense patch of stumpy evergreens.

Noelle stopped, and with a grin, gestured to the trees. "Hurray, a grove of Scotch pine! I'm starving and pine nuts would make a great breakfast."

They gathered pine cones from the branches and those that had fallen to the ground. Noelle piled them into John's arms.

"Let's take them to that boulder, and we can knock the seeds out."

They sat cross-legged on either side of the rock, pounding seeds from the cones. Noelle took a pile of them, peeled the husks from the seeds, and stuffed a handful of pine nuts into her mouth. With a deep sigh, she chewed the nuts.

He swept the rest of the seeds into his palm and handed them to her. She popped them into her mouth with the rest, and pointed to the trees. Her mouth full of food, she mumbled, "John, can you peel some bark for me? If we can boil it, I'll eat them for dinner."

John stared at her. "Is that safe?"

"Yeah. Not super tasty, but better than nothing."

With his knife, he popped off small chunks of the pine bark and shoved them into a pouch in the pack.

She tore apart the last of the dried pinecones, picked out the nuts and dropped them into her pocket. "I'll save the rest for desert. I'm lucky that the animals didn't completely raid the pantry."

"Good. I can tell your energy level is better."

"I needed that protein." She smiled. "Onward we go!"

They reached a clearing, and John stopped as they crossed the tracks of a big cat.

Noelle knelt and studied them closely. "Fresh tracks. Only two cats are of that size, a snow leopard or a Siberian tiger. Either one could be trouble." Noelle stood up and brushed the snow from her pants. "Snow leopard, I believe. Not large enough paws for a Siberian tiger." She rubbed her jaw. "Of course, it could be a cub."

"And a mother with hungry little ones—that's a pleasant thought." John looked over his shoulder. "What were we talking about during the dinner on the eve of the expedition? Fear of large animals?"

"Neither of those cats usually hunt humans, but perhaps in a pinch? The best thing is to move out of the cat's territory."

They quickened their pace along the trail and hovered into open snowfields scattered with low brush.

Twilight came upon them and they searched for a campsite. With the complication of a big predator, they scaled an isolated boulder and made their camp on the top of the rock. It wouldn't be cozy, but with no large trees to climb, this was the safest spot in the area. Though they were out of Zoric's land, John brushed their tracks from where they'd left the open field to the boulder as a precaution.

They scrambled up the rock, dusted the thin snow from the surface, and spread out the sleeping bag. He set up the fire and pot, and when the water began to boil, Noelle dropped in the pine-bark pieces.

John handed her a slotted spoon. "Dig in when you think they're done." He cut the second bird from the loop on his pack and offered Noelle half. "Sure you don't want any?"

She shook her head.

With a shrug, he asked, "I hope you don't mind if I eat?"

Noelle looked away. "No that's fine, I'll just sit here and meditate—or pass out waiting for the bark." She sipped warm water from the cup.

John ripped the cold meat from the bones.

"Did you know that the Cro-Magnon were more carnivore than omnivore?" Noelle stirred the bark in the pot.

Half the ptarmigan was gone. He swallowed a mouthful and muttered, "Interesting."

"They had a different digestive system and could efficiently assimilate meat. They also learned that the act of cooking enhances the digestibility of meat and kills off harmful bacteria."

He pivoted the bird and bit into the second breast. "How fascinating." He finished the breast and started devouring the thigh and leg.

She lifted a piece of bark up and pressed it with her finger. "Of course, the real difference between Cro-Magnon and homo sapiens was intelligence." She dropped the bark chunk back into the boiling water. "Not quite ready."

With a nod, he pointed at her with the leg bone, broke it open and sucked out the marrow. "At least that's what we tell ourselves."

After the ptarmigan was gone, John leapt from the boulder and walked into the brush behind the outcrop, throwing the bones underneath the thick branches. He scaled the rock and sat next to her with a satisfied sigh. Nothing like a full belly to perk up the spirits.

Noelle pulled several pieces of bark from the pot. "Finally, soft enough to eat." She sat them on the rock to cool. In a few minutes, she popped a couple in her mouth, and slowly chewed.

With a guilty shrug, he said, "I wish we had something for you to eat besides boiled bark." He looked at his watch and took a reading on their location. "If we have a good day tomorrow, this should be our last night." He coughed. *Assuming someone was waiting for them.*

She shrugged. "Great, because that backpack is starting to look mighty tasty."

The sunlight faded and Noelle pointed out the moon, rising above the horizon. As the stars appeared in their glory, they gazed up at the brilliant canvas of the sky. The forest was quiet, but in the distance, they heard the wind rustle in the trees. The whirring sound came closer and a chill gust hit them on the exposed rock. They huddled together for warmth.

With sadness in her voice, Noelle whispered, "Antarctica is the last wild place. Lowry is right. The prey instinct of humans drives us to protect our surroundings, dooming the wilderness."

John glanced at her. Even in the dim moonlight, he could see the worry in her face. "We are more predator than prey. Civilized humans have simply shifted the drive to 'catch and kill' to the corporate coup of the day. To those people, nature is something to be conquered."

Noelle drummed her fingers on her knee. "Is it possible that humans can evolve intellectually?"

He shook his head. "We're the same animals who fought the Neanderthals to extinction. Now, we hang the enemy sign on whoever doesn't look or act like members of our tribe."

She exhaled. "Self-preservation is instinctual as well. People fear nuclear war or a world-wide pandemic, but can't understand how the health of the planet affects them. For most, 'just being' doesn't mean living in the moment, it means irresponsible gluttony."

John shrugged. "I've tried to do what makes sense here in Antarctica and you've seen the backlash from some people. When you're hungry, or think you might go hungry, all the talk of 'nature' and 'conservation' isn't even on the scope. Sanity needs economic stability."

With a stick, he jabbed an ice-filled crack in the boulder. He wasn't a natural politician. His constant fights over his policies of ecological balance in Antarctica had been grueling. To others, politics boiled down to turf wars.

His face pensive, John murmured, "The battle wears on you. Sometimes, I imagine going off into the wilderness, like we are now, and never coming back. I dream of building a small cabin where no one can find me."

Noelle smiled. "They might find your carcass at spring thaw. But I appreciate your wish to simplify. There are times I feel the same. But then I remember that every creature, every plant, needs to be heard. Mother Nature needs our voices."

"Perhaps so, Noelle, but my fear is that my work will be destroyed as soon as the opposition gets into office."

"Change is the nature of time." She touched his hand. "But you've created a sustainable system that is also the path of least resistance. All we can do with our short lives is to make a difference. An act of love never goes unnoticed."

They eased into the sleeping bag, shifting back and forth to get comfortable on the jagged rock face.

John said, more to himself than Noelle, "Tomorrow, we return to civilization."

He hoped.

*   *   *

John twitched in his sleep as a strange dream came to him. He was alone, deep in the forest. He turned toward a sound and saw a snow leopard crouched in the trees. The leopard sprang toward him, but he didn't move. He wasn't afraid.

When the cat was almost upon him, John raised his arms and roared. Startled, the cat stopped in his tracks. He began to circle him warily, his yellow eyes watching for an opening. John pivoted, facing the cat as it moved around him.

The leopard turned to John, his lip curled in a snarl. He growled, "Why are you here? You humans destroy all you touch. Leave—you are not welcome in the kingdom of animals."

"But we are of the Earth, too."

"You do not act like it. We only eat what we need, taking out the weak. No one species dominates an area. Everything is in equilibrium. We have a state of balance in the animal kingdom."

The cat nodded at John. "The creatures who are out of balance are humans. It is written, 'Ask the beasts, and they will teach you; the birds of the air, and they will tell you,' but you cannot hear us. The sounds of you human animals drown out our cries of death. You have sentenced us to die and you aren't even aware of it. And you call yourself the most intelligent animal?"

The snow leopard glared at him with contempt. "Humans believe they are superior to animals—arrogance is intoxicating, isn't it?" His lip curled into a bitter smile. "But it's only the potent flower of stupidity." The cat swiped the air with his paw. "When the cubs of Man have all died, we will still be here." The beast turned and padded away.

* * *

John woke in the dim light of morning at the low yip of a snow leopard. His heart thumping, he searched for the cat, not moving an inch. A scratching sound in the snow drew his eyes to the low brush where he had thrown the remains of the ptarmigan from his dinner last night.

He sucked in his breath as a ray of sun broke through the branches, illuminating the cat's gray and white fur, dappled with black rosettes. The cat brought his paw to his mouth, and with his head to the side, crunched the bones, then licked his paw.

The leopard turned, his amber eyes staring at him. John's dream flashed into his mind. Unthinking humans had pushed this magnificent creature to near extinction. The cat froze in his tracks and then leapt away, disappearing into the forest.

He clenched his fist. This creature had no voice, but he did.

CHAPTER 19

After she returned home from seeing Ginnie, Lowry sat at the table picking at her dinner. With a final jab at her pasta, she set her fork down and shook her head. Finding John and Noelle alive was apparently not high on Lin's priority list. *I may not know what's going on in Lin's mind, but I do know the area of Concordia Refuge near the Grace River.*

With a screech, Lowry shoved her chair back. *Fuck it, I'm going after them.* She put her dishes in the dishwasher and started packing provisions.

Lowry rang Chuy. "I'm taking the new hoverbike and finding John and Noelle."

There was a pause, then he replied, "I know you're too pig-headed to argue with—how can I help?"

"Please have the bike ready at five a.m. I'd like to reach the river by daybreak."

In a flat voice, Chuy said, "I'll pack the survival kit in the hoverbike side case." He cleared his throat. "Don't get yourself killed, Lowry."

She shrugged. "This cat has a few more lives to go."

Lowry packed a bag of nuts and fruit, with a sack of beef jerky for John. She set up delayed messages to Ginnie and Lin to be delivered at daybreak, hopefully at the same time she had found John and Noelle. *That should twist Lin off.*

She grabbed her insulated coveralls, draped them over a chair, then walked to the bedroom. In front of the closet, she said, "Open." As the doors glided apart, she moved to the rear of the closet and shoved the clothes aside, revealing a locked drawer. With the touch of her fingers, the drawer unlocked and slid open, and she pulled out a pistol. With a pop, she snapped a full magazine into the handle, shoved the pistol into its holster, and set it in a nearby chair. *I hope I don't have to use it—again.*

After a quick shower, she threw on a night shirt. "Please wake me at four a.m."

"Yes, Lowry, all set," her virtual assistant said. "I hope you sleep well."

"That would be a miracle." She laid on the bed and stared at the ceiling, going over the journey ahead, until she drifted into a fitful sleep.

*　　*　　*

With a gentle chime, the lights glowed in the room. "Wake up, Lowry."

Lowry opened her eyes and rose from the bed. She pulled on the coveralls and marched into the kitchen. A traveling coffee mug was ready for her and a bagel. "Can you get two more coffees and more water bottles to go?"

"Certainly."

She ate the bagel and then placed the drinks in the pack. With a grunt, she slung the pack over her shoulder and walked to the barn.

Chuy waited for her under the shed. "All ready." He took the pack from her, and with a raised eyebrow, lifted it with a grimace. "I'll split this between the two side cases so the bike will be balanced." He stowed the supplies, clicked the cases shut, then patted the bike. "Unlike the old models, these new hoverbikes are great on hills. You shouldn't have any troubles . . . at least with the bike." He glanced at her. "Are you sure you want to take this risk—alone? I could go with you."

"The cattle and horses need to be tended." Lowry touched the holster on her belt. "I have a partner right here." She waved the directions over the hoverbike's computer screen, then pulled on the helmet, shivering as the cold metal hit her neck. She straddled the seat. "I have to try. If something happened to John and Noelle that I could have prevented, I'll never forgive myself." She closed the face-shield, and with a thumbs-up, headed into the darkness.

The hoverbike floated smoothly along the plotted course through the homestead lands. Lowry dozed off until the bike jerked and she woke. The bike had bumped into a knot of tussock grass near the border of the homesteads and the eastern side of the Concordia Refuge. The hoverbike shifted into climbing gear and the bike's low drone dropped an octave.

At the top of the ridge, the bike slowed, and fingers of sunlight crept over the horizon, revealing a blanket of fog nestled in the valley. They began to drift downhill as the rays of light edged along the valley walls. Lowry gasped. The sunlight burst across the cloudbank, and like alchemy, transformed the gray haze into a cocoon of spun gold.

The hoverbike swept down the hill. She inhaled the cold, moist air as they entered the fog. The dawn broke, but in the mist, Lowry could only see a short distance in front of her. The hoverbike veered around an arctic fox that yelped in fear at the sudden appearance of the bike. She felt the bike ascend and they popped through the fog near the top of a hill. As the sun rose, the sky lightened, revealing a terrain of rolling hills and rock formations.

Lowry's mind returned to yesterday's conversation with Ginnie. Lowry wanted marriage and a family, but what did John want? Conceiving a baby was one of the deepest needs of a human being, especially for a woman. With every cell of her body, she needed to love and nurture an infant, and raise that child to adulthood.

She clenched her jaw. In loving someone, you must allow their spirit to thrive and not "bonsai" it into the shape you desire. But could she deny her urge for a child? She had betrayed John once with her machinations, she'd not do it again. Lowry sighed deeply. At least she hoped.

They entered a broad valley peppered with glacial gravels and boulders. Random thickets of stunted evergreens broke the sight-line, and where the sun had shone, patches of brown Antarctic grasses peeked through the blanket of snow. Like a silver chain carelessly tossed onto the land, the shimmering Grace River lay frozen, waiting for spring to awaken.

Lowry stopped the hoverbike, flipped up her shield, and put on a pair of binoc-glasses. She scanned the open field of snow sloping to the river. Nothing moved. She removed the binoc-glasses and chewed her lip. *Where are they?*

She stared into the white emptiness before her. The reflecting sun on the vast ashen field of nothingness pounded fear into her head. What if Antarctica had taken another life or two? There was no guarantee that the tracks seen by the drone were from John and Noelle.

Lowry clenched her fist. Over the years since the Land Rush, so many had died of exposure, suicide, murder, or just left, not able to take the fatigue of chaos and death. She personally had been touched by the suicide of Duff, the assassination of Durant by her father, and now the murder of Hank. She blinked away the tears. Had John joined the ranks of the dead?

Antarctica was a cruel mistress—both physically and mentally—her harsh winters and long months of darkness barely dented by the reflected sunlight from the grid of satellites. But living in a land on a knife's edge invigorated the soul. In Antarctica, life was precious in its tragic drama.

She looked up at the sounds of honking. Vast areas had begun to thaw, and the geese had started to arrive with the spring melt. Her heart lightened gazing at the V-shape of hundreds of birds migrating to a continent on the verge of life. Perhaps the birds brought an omen that John and Noelle were safe.

She adjusted the setting of the binoc-glasses to include heat sensing and re-swept the landscape. Nothing in view except a few geese that had landed near a warm spring. Odd to see the infrared images of birds landing near the glowing springs. She put away the binoc-glasses and took control of the hoverbike, floating parallel along the riverbank. The mapping software had given her the most likely route from the position of the tracks to the river, so they should be somewhere close.

Lowry rounded a bend in the river and approached a grove of spruce trees near the bank. On the point of the tallest tree, a ringed kingfisher, with scarlet belly and tufted head, preened its wings, waiting patiently near an open hole in the ice.

Between the spruce grove and the river, she stopped the bike and put on the binoc-glasses to peruse both sides of the river, in case the integrity of the ice hadn't allowed them to cross. With a rattling scream, the kingfisher flew from the tree, and she turned to see what had frightened it. A flash of motion in the sky drew her attention. Two Drots scanned the landscape, drifting back and forth in a diamond pattern.

Her heart beat a staccato. Had Lin sent the Drots out to find John and Noelle?

Lowry stayed still, not wanting to pull them off course. Methodically, the Drots continued weaving along the riverbank.

She put away the binoc-glasses and hovered after the Drots. They'd find John and Noelle before she could with her crude search method. She accelerated, keeping pace just behind the Drots.

The Drots shifted away from the river and farther into the refuge.

Had they spotted something?

Lowry followed the Drots up an incline. In front of her, a trail of hovershoe impressions led her across a flat snowfield. The Drots now hovered above an outcrop of boulders.

She heard a shout. A man stood waving at the Drots. *Was it John?*

The Drots descended, and she lost sight of them. Lowry sped across the field, then slowed as she approached the boulders.

John turned toward her as she shouted, "Hello!"

With a surprised look, he asked, "Lowry, why are *you* here?"

Noelle yelled, "Who cares, she's here!"

In a flash, the Drots zipped to Lowry, blocking her way. She halted while they buzzed around her like wasps defending a nest. She shivered as one of them came at her, then stopped in front of her. Three lights beamed onto her, scanning her face. A green light blinked as they recognized her. She exhaled as the Drots returned to benignly hovering above their heads.

Lowry swung off the bike, removed her helmet and set it on the seat. She pushed her tangled hair back as John approached, a happy smile on his face.

Facing him, her lips trembled, her fears of him dying in the wilderness swept away. She squeezed his arm, tears welling in her eyes. In a thin voice, she said, "Thank God you're alive."

He drew her into his arms and smoothed her hair. "Don't cry, honey."

With a smile, she looked at him. "They're tears of pure joy. Ginnie and I have spent days worrying about you two."

John kissed her forehead and wiped her cheeks.

Noelle cleared her throat. "I'll pack our things." She gathered the camp items, keeping her face turned away.

He held her close. "Is Ginnie okay and the rest of the students?"

"Yes, besides being emotional basket cases."

He looked behind her. "Is Lin nearby?"

Lowry shrugged. "He's waiting at Resolution Rock." With a grin, she said, "I decided to bring you breakfast." She opened a side case and lifted out the food.

"Some vegetarian items." She handed the bags of fruit and nuts to Noelle and then waved the sack of jerky in front of John. "And some homemade beef jerky for you."

"Fantastic!" He grabbed the bag and opened it, smelling the smoked meat.

While they ate, Lowry brought out the water and two coffee cups. "French-roast coffee—hot and strong." She handed each a mug.

Laughing, Noelle and John looked at each. "Coffee!"

Between chews, Noelle mumbled, "Merci, we were starving."

They sat on the scattered rocks, finishing breakfast and their coffee. Lowry took the packaging and shredded them into mulch with her hands.

John stood and patted his belly. "That hit the spot." He grabbed the pack, turning in profile to her.

Lowry grimaced at the red slashes on the side of his face. "What happened to your face?" She stepped closer and pushed his hair back.

"Bear; emerging from hibernation and pissed off at the world. But, lucky for me, more grumpy than hungry." He tilted his head toward Noelle. "Dr. Clavet patched me up."

She touched his chin. "You're a lucky man."

A teasing look in his eye, he said, "Hey, you didn't ask how the bear came out in the fight."

"No scars on that dude." Noelle chuckled.

Lowry laughed and stepped back, pretending to wind up a punch to throw at him.

A grin crossed his face, then he grabbed his ribs, gesturing *stop* with his hand. "Careful of the old war wound."

Her brow furrowed, Lowry asked, "Are you hurt?"

"A bruised rib, I think, from my inglorious fall from the plane."

She tilted her head. "Let's get going. Lin has a medical tent at the rendezvous."

A humming noise drew their attention toward the river.

"Maybe the Drots sent a message to Lin and he's sending in the cavalry," Lowry whispered.

John waved his hand for them to hide behind the rock. "In the wild chance that Zoric was bold enough to cross the border, let's be prudent."

Lowry moved the hoverbike behind the boulder. She grabbed her binoc-glasses, unsnapped the holster of her pistol, then hid. John clambered up the boulder and flattened himself on top.

A young man glided over the snowfield on a hoverbike.

The Drots sped away to challenge him.

Lowry whispered, "One guy on a hoverbike. Not in uniform, so I doubt he's a part of Lin's team." She glanced up at John. "He might be from Zoric's group. What do you think the Drots will do?"

John crouched on top of the rock. "I'm not sure. Hopefully, just capture and not shoot to kill."

The Drots buzzed around the bike, their limbs partially lowered, aiming at the man. The rider accelerated away from them, yelling, "Help me!"

In an instant, they reached him. Strobe flashes exploded from the two Drots simultaneously, the light waves merging as they struck him. With a cry, he jerked as if shocked with electricity, his arms flailing upward. The hoverbike died and slumped forward with a lurch. Already unconscious, he flipped over the handlebars and onto the ground.

"Damn!" John leapt from the boulder and ran to him. Lowry drew her pistol and raced after him.

The young man lay face down in the snow.

John squatted, reached out and gently turned him onto his back. He glanced at Lowry. "He's just a kid."

She lowered her gun, but kept it in her hand.

He felt his pulse. "He's alive—just stunned for a moment."

With a loud gasp, the boy woke. His eyes filled with terror, he stared at the Drots circling above, their weapons trained on him.

"Stay still," John said to the young man. "And they won't hurt you." He frowned at the boy. "Are you from Ivan Zoric's gang?"

"No, my mother wanted me to help you."

"Your mother?"

The young man snapped, "Yes, my mother. You gave her money—or have you forgotten?"

John blinked. "That's your mother? Sorry, no offense, I just assumed your mother would be younger."

"Well, she's really my grandmother. My mom died when I was a baby."

"Okay. But *why* did she send you?"

"A drone intruded into Grace Region. After it was neutralized, a search party went out and found your tracks. My mother sent me after you when she overheard Zoric order a group to find you. They're tracking you right now." He pointed to the river. "They might slow down crossing the river. It took my bike a while to find a solid path over the ice. But they're only minutes behind me."

John got up, waved the Drots away, and helped the young man to his feet. "Let's go."

They righted the bike and John asked, "What's your name, son?"

"Marko."

"How did you come across a vehicle such as this?"

"Hard to believe a beggar's son could afford such a toy? You're right—I stole it."

"That's what I get for asking."

Lowry brought her bike from around the boulder. John grabbed his backpack and stuffed it into one of the side cases on Lowry's bike, while Noelle and Lowry loaded the rest of the food and gear.

Marko nodded to Lowry's bike. "Good thing we have another hoverbike. One bike couldn't carry three people."

John squeezed Lowry's shoulder. "If you and Lowry hadn't shown up this morning, we'd be in Zoric's hands." He pointed to Marko's bike. "Noelle, you ride with Marko and I'll ride behind Lowry. With luck, we should have an armed party waiting for us at the foot of Resolution Rock."

They mounted the bikes. Lowry checked the direction of the rendezvous and then accelerated forward with Marko on her heels. Overhead, the Drots followed as they flew across the valley floor. They topped a low hill, and in the distance a tall outcrop of granite came into view: Resolution Rock.

John leaned over her shoulder. "Almost there!"

A vast snowfield lay between them and the rendezvous. The low-angle rays of the spring sun reflected off the glaze, blinding them as they raced over the snow.

A whirring noise drew Lowry's attention to the west. With a yell, John pointed at a set of hovers leaping from the shadows and over the ridgeline. Slush spraying from under the bikes, the rugged crew rode breakneck toward them.

"Zoric's men coming up on our left!" John shouted.

Lowry pushed the hoverbike as fast as it would go. Marko zoomed beside her, fear in his eyes. They neared Resolution Rock. Shouts echoed off the rock face. Someone, possibly Lin, waved his arm. Like disturbed bees, the SWAT team mounted the hoverbikes and sprang forward to meet the enemy.

Zoric's men had the angle. The gap between them narrowed. Lowry glanced at the brutal faces, anxious to do the bidding of their master.

The Drots broke away from above them and zoomed to the oncoming combatants. Like a pair of predatory birds, they circled, darting and diving in front of Zoric's men. A *pop, pop, pop* echoed across the field as the men fired at them.

A bullet whizzed over their heads. Lowry crouched over the handlebars. *Shit!*

The Drots spun away from the gunfire, but twisted in mid-air, their armatures descending as they dived toward the attackers. In an instant, they halted, aimed their limbs and a flash of light enveloped the two leaders. As if lightning struck them, the men jolted up and over the bike's handlebars. Now riderless, the first bike veered wildly into the other's path. The following hoverbike T-boned into it, then flipped and spun, end over end, across the snow.

John pumped his fist. "Score for team Drot!"

Frightened, the next wave of Zoric's men slowed, staring at the Drots zipping toward them, weapons poised. With a shout, one of Zoric's men waved his arm. The group turned and retreated at full speed toward the border, abandoning their unconscious leaders laying on the snow amid the wrecked hoverbikes.

The Drots returned, hovering above the stunned men as the SWAT team raced across the open field, chasing the rest of Zoric's group. The SWAT leader screamed through a bullhorn for them to surrender, but they did not stop. The leader waved her arm and the SWAT team broke off the pursuit at the border. When they reached the downed men, they circled, jumped off the bikes and handcuffed them.

The immediate danger past, Lowry and Marko slowed their bikes as Lin and his second-in-command approached. Lin narrowed his eyes at her, his lips thin. He was fuming that she'd gone after John and Noelle. She turned away, and with a cough, adjusted her helmet.

With a nod to John, he said, "Mr. President, I trust the Drots found you okay?"

John nodded. "Zoric's men might have captured us if the Drots hadn't been here."

Lin's mouth tightened. "I'm sure my team would have engaged the enemy and prevented your capture, sir," he said with a shrug. "But no doubt the Drots are an engineering marvel." He gestured toward the rendezvous. "In case Zoric's men return, we'd better get to a safer spot, sir."

Marko glanced at John and cleared his throat. "You're President Barrous?"

"Sometimes I ask myself the same question." John smiled. "But, yes, I am."

"Sir, I had no idea."

John chuckled. "I want to thank you and Lowry for saving our lives. And please thank your mother."

While John spoke with Marko, Lowry sensed a presence on her other side. Lin had eased his hoverbike parallel to Lowry's. At the annoyed look on Lin's face, Lowry gripped the handlebars and swallowed hard.

His mouth twitched. "Nice to see you this morning, Ms. Walker."

She shot a glance at him. In a clipped voice, she replied, "Funny, that's just what John and Noelle said."

CHAPTER 20

Lin followed them to the hospital tent. Lowry glanced at him. His jaw clenched, Lin watched her like a wolf stalking his prey. He was pissed.

After they parked, several medics jogged out to help Noelle and John off of the bikes. One medic took Noelle's arm and led her to the field hospital.

As John dismounted, Ginnie shouted, "Daddy!" and grabbed him into a hug.

John grunted in pain, and then tears sprang to his eyes. "Ginnie!"

One of the medics placed a hand on Ginnie's shoulder. "Careful, Miss, we need to check your dad and make sure he's okay."

John kissed Ginnie's cheek. "This is the best medicine." He turned toward the others gathered around him. With one arm still around Ginnie, he smiled at the group. "I want to thank you all for saving our lives."

The medic took his arm. "Sir, we should go. The doctor wants to examine you."

Lowry turned away from Lin and followed John to the front of the medic tent. The back of her neck prickled as Lin trailed behind her.

John's personal physician, Dr. Oduva, was standing, arms crossed, at the entrance.

He grinned. "Dr. Oduva, so good of you to visit me in the hinterlands."

She raised her hands and flexed her fingers. "After you scared us to death, you deserve a bit of poking and prodding."

Lowry waved at John. "I'll meet you back here in a few minutes."

As they disappeared into the tent, Lin called out to Lowry, "Ms. Walker, can I speak with you for a moment?"

She glanced at him and turned to Ginnie, "Sweetie, would you mind bringing water and something to eat for Noelle and your dad?"

"Sure, right away."

With teeth clenched, she strolled over to Lin, ready for war. She stopped at a safe distance from him. Lowry inhaled, balling her fists. She had jumped into Lin's yard and now he was on the attack. She didn't relish a fight, but both of them would be bloody by the end of this battle.

He stood tall, his back straight and his jaw shoved out, glaring at her. "I got your message this morning." His voice dropped to a low growl, emphasizing each word with a karate chop of his hand. "What do you mean taking off in the night to find them?" His tone was that of a man who demanded obedience.

Lowry's lip curled into a snarl. *Don't treat me like a dog, asshole.* She leaned forward, jabbing a finger at him. "Lin, I will tell you straight up—nobody talks to me that way. If I *hadn't* found them, while you were *relaxing* at Resolution Rock, Zoric would have John and Noelle in his clutches." She tilted her head. "Perhaps that scenario would be fine with you?"

He stepped closer, his chest heaving in and out in fury.

She could almost hear her Uncle Duff say, "'Way to go, Lowry, you've made another enemy.'" *As the saying sort of goes, I'd rather die a lion than live a sheep.*

Lin studied her, his eyes flitting back and forth. With a razor-sharp grin, he shifted his weight onto one leg. "Ms.

Walker, you have a somewhat, shall we say, checkered past? John may find a few of your 'details' interesting to hear."

Lowry sucked in her breath at his blatant allusion to blackmail. She stared at his impassive face, blinking as she digested Lin's threat. She shook her head. "John is aware of my past. We hide nothing from each other."

His smile broadened as he stepped within a hair's breadth of her face. In a chill voice, he whispered, "Is he aware that you were a key witness over a decade ago, in the trial stemming from the attack on the ISS?" His eyes narrowed. "Perhaps bribed by the notorious capitalist pig, Elliot Halder, to twist evidence?" Lin's lip curled, baring his teeth, keen on her capitulation. "Maybe perjured yourself in testifying against a man ultimately convicted of a crime that he didn't commit?" Eyes in brilliant ecstasy, he leaned into her. "Does he know *that*, Ms. Walker?"

She blinked as his exhalation touched her face, her stomach twisting in revulsion. Apparently, Lin had sniffed through the details of her past, to the point of reading her testimony in that infamous trial. *But why?* Unconsciously, she stepped back.

"By your silence, I'll take that as a *no*." As if he had delivered the punch line of a joke, he leaned back and laughed. "Let's hope that doesn't become inconvenient." Lin pivoted away and strolled behind the SWAT team shelter.

Shaken, Lowry turned and stumbled to the medic tent. Why did it seem to be her luck to spar with evil? Elliot Halder had desired power and money, but had no interest or energy to spend on cruelty. Lin enjoyed it.

In front of the tent, Ginnie had set a tray of sandwiches and waters on a table. She turned to Lowry, nodding her head toward the back of Lin. "That looked nasty even from a distance."

She frowned. "Fun and games with Lin, the louse."

Ginnie furrowed her brow. "He's a weird one."

"That's an understatement." Lowry slumped into a chair, staring vacantly at the tabletop.

"I got your message this morning." With a thumb, she pointed over her shoulder. "And I spoke with Marko." Smiling, Ginnie touched her hand. "Both of you saved Dad and Noelle."

Lowry turned to her, forcing her lips into a smile. "A bit of providence and the Drots."

"Are you okay? You look pale."

She clenched her eyes shut and pressed her fingers into her temple. "My day started at four a.m., so I guess my brain's a bit scrambled. I need a cup of coffee."

"I'll get one for you." Ginnie rose and squeezed her shoulder. "You're exhausted."

After she left, Lowry placed her hands on the top of the table, gazing at her trembling fingers. For an unknown reason, Lin had thrown down the gauntlet. She had to figure out why and formulate a defense.

John and Noelle appeared at the door of the tent, squinting in the sunlight.

With a wan smile, Lowry lifted her hand. "Over here."

They joined her at the table and Lowry gestured to the tray.

"Ginnie brought lunch. What'd Dr. Oduva say?"

John handed Noelle a vegetarian sandwich and water, and grabbed a turkey sandwich for himself. "She assures me that women love scarred men. Besides that, I have a couple of bruised ribs and am suffering from exposure. She shot me up with extra vitamins and orders to eat, hydrate, and rest. She scheduled a follow-up in Amundsen."

"And you?" Lowry asked Noelle.

"The same prescription, except a dislocated shoulder instead of bruised ribs." Noelle bit into the sandwich and, with a hum, chewed slowly. "I'll never take avocados for granted again." She sipped her water and pointed the end of the sandwich at John. "What are the next steps in arresting Zoric and his gang?"

John swallowed a mouthful and cleared his throat. "We now can levy charges of kidnapping and murder." He shook his head. "Poor Hank. I feel sick about his death." He set down his sandwich. "But any raid on the compound will have to be carefully planned. Over a hundred years ago, there was an assault by the authorities in the States on a religious cult. During the attack, a fire broke out, burning nearly everyone alive in the group—mostly women and children." He tapped the table. "I don't want that to happen on my watch. Most of the members are innocent."

Noelle frowned. "What about the trapping?"

"Unfortunately, we have only circumstantial evidence at this time, but I'm hopeful we can gather more."

"Even if Zoric and a few others are convicted of kidnapping and murder, the rest will still trap for fur. It's a part of their livelihood."

He shrugged. "Noelle, we'll try our best." He jabbed the air with his finger. "I don't want a slaughter to occur at Zoric's camp."

She narrowed her eyes, and with a snort, rose. "John, you're putting humans over the animals." She walked off in a huff.

He watched her leave. "She's right, but I don't think she understands that this has to be done strategically."

Lowry glanced around for listening ears, and then leaned forward. "John, just to add to your troubles, you may want to watch Lin. I'm not sure he's for you or against you."

He looked at her. "What happened?"

"I tried to force his hand to meet you closer to Zoric's border, but he insisted that you'd ordered him to stay at the rendezvous."

With a shrug, John said, "Well, I suppose technically that was true, and for the same reasons that I was explaining to Noelle."

"Yeah, I get it." Her voice dropped to a whisper. "He just upbraided me while you and Noelle were being treated by Dr. Oduva." At his grin, she gestured with her hand. "I know I stepped in his shit, and a chewing-out I would expect." She leaned closer, her brows furrowed. "Instead, he threatened to tell you details of my testimony in the ISS trial from years ago. But with his spin applied."

"Testimony?"

"Yes, I'll explain it later, but he's trying to twist my words against me." She bit her lip, shaking her head. "What's so unsettling is that he investigated *me*. Why?" She looked at John. "Is he simply positioning himself for president, or is it something nefarious?"

"I feel it too, Lowry. When Lin joined the cabinet, he was solid as a rock. Now subtle cracks have appeared—like vibrations before an earthquake."

They quieted as Ginnie returned with coffee. "Dad, what did the doctor say?"

"I've checked off two of the three items Dr. Oduva prescribed."

She handed out coffees, and asked, "Where's Noelle?"

John raised a brow. "She left rather pissed, I'm afraid. She thinks we'll forget about the animals and arrest Zoric and a few henchmen for the attack on the expedition without going after the fur trapping."

"Well, as I said, she's focused on her passions." Ginnie glanced toward the parked hovercars, now loading with passengers to return to Amundsen. "She's leaving with the other group. Dad, do you mind if I go back with her? I can talk to her."

"That's a good idea, and try to assure her that we'll do our best. Lowry can ride with me."

She kissed his cheek. "I love you so much, Dad."

He squeezed her arm. "I love you too."

Ginnie looked at Lowry. "If it wasn't for Lowry, you might not be sitting here."

John reached over and covered Lowry's hand with his. "You're right—she saved both Noelle and me."

With a wave, Ginnie left.

Lowry wagged her finger at John. "You need to go home and get onto that third item: rest."

"I'm more than ready to sleep on a nice, soft mattress." With a yawn, John rubbed his chin. "I can't wait to take a hot bath and get rid of this hairy face."

Lin's second in command walked to the table and nodded to John. "Mr. President, we have a hovercar ready for you."

They rose and went to the car. Marko stood nearby looking lost. John waved to him. "Marko, come to Amundsen with us; you can ride in our vehicle."

He smiled broadly and jumped in beside John.

As they hovered back to the Amundsen, John asked Marko, "How old are you, son?"

"Fifteen, but I turn sixteen next month."

"Almost sixteen. I vaguely remember being that age once." John smiled. "Son, I want to ask you a few questions."

"Yes, sir."

"What was the real reason you rescued us?"

"I told you, my mother asked me to help you."

John faced the young man. "There has to be more to it. No mother would send her son on a dangerous undertaking, just to pay me back for a bitcoin. Tell me. There's something else, I know it."

Marko hesitated. "Ivan Zoric is my uncle; my father's brother. My father opposed him and tried to get the people of the region to oust him." Tears welled in Marko's eyes. "Last year, my father disappeared. We believe he was 'eliminated.' The only way my mother has kept out of his hands is by playing a crazy woman. He thinks I'm too young to bother with."

The young man swallowed hard. "My mother says Ivan Zoric is crazy. He destroyed most of our food, and then blamed my father."

"Hungry, frightened people are easier to dominate, especially if you control the food."

Marko turned to John. "My uncle says you believe in animals more than humans. He says God gave the world to Man for our use. He says it's sacrilege for them to be raised above Man." He chewed his lips and exhaled. "He had five wives. Two were younger than me."

With a faint groan, Lowry closed her eyes. *Child abuse. Zoric is a sick bastard.*

John slipped his hand into hers. Lowry glanced at him, pain evident in his eyes. With a slight shake of her head, she squeezed his hand.

He looked at Marko. "Don't worry, son, we'll figure out how to apprehend Zoric."

Brows furrowed, he stared at John. "If you attack the compound, they'll use the women and children as shields. They'll fight you to the death." He grabbed John's arm. "I don't want my mother hurt."

"I know." John nodded. "This operation will take finesse, intelligence, and staying one step ahead of Zoric."

Lowry bit the inside of her cheek. In this deadly game of chess, the pawns would be the most vulnerable.

CHAPTER 21

The day after the rescue, John awoke late in his apartment and gazed at the ceiling—it seemed odd to be sleeping in a bed. He yawned, stretching his arms out, then winced, his bruised ribs reminding him to not do that. With a sigh, he threw back the covers, swung his legs over the side and sat on the edge of the mattress. He scratched his head, avoiding the side the bear had tattooed. Finally, he rose, willing his sore body to walk to the bathroom.

Half-asleep, he washed his face, and swept his wet fingers through his hair to tame the wayward strands. He grimaced at the mirror, then stumbled to the dining room and slumped into one of the chairs. "Coffee, please, P."

"I started it after I saw you were awake. Just a minute more and I'll send you a cup."

"Great, thanks." His mind foggy with exhaustion, he stared vaguely at the wall. He breathed in the aroma as the fresh mug of coffee floated to him. With a grin, he picked up the mug and sipped the hot, and thankfully, strong coffee, and then closed his eyes as he leaned back in the chair.

P said, "Sorry, John, but Kisho's at the door."

With a grunt, he opened his eyes. "Yeah, I forgot that he was coming by this morning to get me up to speed."

Kisho strolled into the room. Grinning, he said, "Sir, if I was kind, I'd say that you look great, but you look like hammered shit."

"Thanks, Kisho." John chuckled. "I'll be better after breakfast."

"Eggs and toast?" P asked.

"Yes."

"If you don't mind, I'll join you for coffee while you eat." Kisho gestured to the sunroom off the kitchen. "Perhaps we can sit in the solarium?"

They moved into the solarium, brightly lit in a mix of real and artificial sun.

Kisho glanced around. "Is Ginnie home?"

"She's still asleep." John narrowed his eyes. "You're acting strange. What's up?"

He shifted from foot to foot, then coughed, staring at John. "You may need to pull Lin's teeth now that you're back."

John studied his pinched face. *First Lowry, now Kisho.* With a scowl, he asked, "Lin's been over-stepping his bounds?"

A cup of cappuccino floated to Kisho. "Thanks, you remembered my preference."

"No trouble. Breakfast up in a couple of minutes. I'll serve in here."

They sat at the table facing the exterior pocket garden. John finished his coffee, the caffeine making him feel human again.

Kisho sipped the cappuccino, then set down the cup. "He's been preparing to attack Zoric's camp with every weapon we have."

He shrugged. "As if we have any?"

"We may not have much, but he's positioned what weapons we have and has called on the UN army to be ready."

John shook his head. "Zoric understands bullying—what we have to do is outwit him." His mouth watered as the tray of food drifted in and set itself in front of him. He sprinkled a dash of salt and pepper on the fried egg, sliced a piece and chewed slowly. His first hot breakfast in days.

"Regardless, Lin showed his cards when you were lost in the wilderness, sir. A few days after you and Noelle disappeared, he called a press conference. In the midst of the reporters' questions, he took the opportunity to float his intentions to run for the president in the upcoming elections. I believe Lin's a serious political threat. He has a healthy percentage of support from the homesteaders who think the Grace Region is out of control. Add on the economic slowdown we're having and this could create a powerful backlash against your policies." With a long sigh, he stared at John. "I'll tell you honestly, sir, Lin is a political snake, not the ally we thought he was. And he's smart enough to take advantage of this situation."

With a nod, John buttered his toast. "I'm beginning to agree with you."

"Another bit of news has surfaced involving Lin." Kisho shot a look at John. "After Lin's cousin was thrown in jail a few weeks back, the police ran Tao's background check and have discovered that he was a member of the notorious Chongqing gang—a drug smuggler." He leaned forward. "Their members have deep ties to the Chinese Communist party."

He shrugged. "I would think everyone in China is connected to the Communist party in some way. But the gang connection sounds alarming. I realize that Tao wasn't in our inner circle, but I assumed that Lin ran a background check on him, so why didn't we know about Tao's link to this criminal group?"

"I wondered that myself."

John bit into the toast and then rubbed the dripping butter from his chin. "As far as Lin goes, my recollection is that he was raised in the States and had a distinguished service record in the military. After his parents divorced, he moved to China with his father."

Kisho inclined his head. "Yes, that's the story. But the odd thing is that Lin seems to have a large war chest for his campaign. Who's funding him? Could it be money from the

Chongqing mafia or perhaps the Chinese government? Antarctica has billions of dollars of raw materials the world wants, and if he wins, I don't get a warm-and-fuzzy that he's pro-environmental, especially if the strings are manipulated by a foreign power. Even if there's no link to the gang or the Chinese, he has connections with the hawks in the Assembly who despise you."

"I know how popular I am with our esteemed legislators, you don't have to rub it in." John set his fork down, his insides knotted in anger. "Antarctica is the only land mass not picked clean by humanity and all the political predators are circling. Our minerals are a boon to us, and necessary for the world, *if* we can manage the environmental impacts, but with someone like Lin in charge . . ."

John frowned, tapping his fingers on the table. "But I'm still missing one piece of the puzzle. Who did the original background checks?"

"An excellent question, sir. The UN had engaged Lin as the head of a temporary security force for the Land Rush, but one would assume only a low-level check. In the craziness after the assassination, Lin rose through the security ranks. He was vetted, passed with flying colors, and you picked him as your Defense Secretary." Kisho cleared his throat. "I took the liberty of perusing those files. Guess who was in charge of the vetting?"

"Do we need a drumroll?"

"Exactly. Lin was in charge of his own background check."

"Wow. That's on my head." He picked up the fork and pointed the tines toward Kisho. "This picture ain't pretty— something's not right with that bastard."

"Perhaps we should have the police discreetly rerun Lin's background?"

"I agree completely, and the results brought only to us." Scowling, he snapped, "Let's pull back the curtains and see who Lin really is."

He turned to the window. In the garden, birds dove after insects brave enough to test the spring weather. *After his years of battling, would Lin prevail and brush all of his work away like dust?*

Arching a brow, John glanced at his half-eaten breakfast. "I guess having a nice, relaxing breakfast just wasn't on the menu."

* * *

Two days later, John watched his staff mill around the coffee and donuts. He waved to the chairs. "Please be seated." The group grappled for seats according to their political alliances.

"I called this meeting to discuss strategies for dealing with Zoric. I want this to be a frank and informal discussion."

When they were seated, John glanced around the table. "One thing I want understood. Zoric's core group is fanatical and dangerous, but the rest of the people in the camp are victims of circumstance. Most are in a difficult situation, without basic essentials. Zoric destroyed or hid much of their stockpile of food when he seized power. He doles it out on a limited basis to keep them under his thumb."

He glanced toward Patel, sitting next to him. Patel's eyes stared ahead and his mouth twitched. John gritted his teeth. The son of a bitch was playing a game or watching a video through his iBrow implants, rather than participating in the discussion. *Where had he been during Lin's press conference?*

John shifted his gaze to Lin. "Secretary Lin, please outline your plans for dealing with Zoric."

Lin nodded, and with a flick of his finger, a grainy photo of the compound appeared on the wall monitor. "Once we are in position around the compound, we storm it with light armored artillery hovers and subdue the criminals with few casualties." He smiled. "At least, few casualties on our side."

John gripped the arm of the chair. "The real challenge in this crisis is to out-strategize the man, not out-gun him. Let's see if we're smarter than Zoric." He lifted his finger. "Remember, the women and children in that camp are citizens of Antarctica and have little to do with the current madman in charge. We can't drop to his level. We must stay on the high ground."

His lips pursed, John turned to Patel. "Do we have any diplomatic strategies to deal with, or to at least contain Zoric?"

As if awakening from a dream, Patel straightened abruptly in his chair. "What?"

Kisho coughed. "If I may answer the question, sir. They're fairly independent from our government infrastructure. Despite food shortages, they've managed to survive—by hunting for food and trapping in our refuges, and then selling the furs on the black market."

John glanced at Patel, who was now listening to the conversation.

Patel nodded. "Exactly. The black market itself is almost impossible to stop, but an option is to try to barricade the region."

John shook his head. "That would hurt the people more than do any real harm to Zoric—no worries on him going hungry."

"Perhaps a trade of the two prisoners? We could lure him to what appears to be a neutral zone." Patel gestured to Lin. "And Lin's SWAT team could capture him."

"Good idea. But we need to ask for something." John scratched his cheek.

"What about their fur traps?" Patel asked.

Lin shook his head. "He'd just deny he had any."

John drummed his fingers on the table. "What about Marko's mother?"

Alex leaned forward, snapping her fingers. "We could tell Zoric that Marko and his mother want to return to Serbia. He would probably love the idea of getting rid of both of them."

"I think that's a good strategy." He looked at her. "But we need to make it believable."

Kisho grinned. "We could throw out a few social media posts to 'verify' the story, so Zoric buys it."

"The internet is down over Grace, I'm sure to control outside influences into the cult. Can we assume that Zoric himself can access social media?"

"We know that Zoric has an independent satellite phone, which uses the same orbiting satellites as your GPS, not the low-level grid that he keeps knocking out," Lin said. "As much of a control freak as he is, I'm sure he follows anything involving his flock."

"All very good points." He looked at Kisho. "Let's get with Marko and work on a couple of posts."

John gazed at the men and women around the table. "Thanks to everyone for a great brainstorming session—we have a few options to develop. This operation will be a complex game of chess. We need to develop a psychological profile on Zoric to decide how best to checkmate him."

In the quiet pause, John turned back to Lin. His lips pinched, he rapped the table with his knuckle. "But most importantly, I don't want *anyone* to use the current crisis as a springboard for political ambitions."

A hush fell over the group.

Eyes fixed on John, a thin smile crossed Lin's face. "Chess is a game of the mind. Zoric may or may not have the intellect to be a great chess player." His smile faded. "The question is, do we?"

CHAPTER 22

Lowry's dog, Leo, stood with his head cocked to the side, listening. Lowry glanced up from planting the tomato seedlings in the interior garden. He padded over, staring out of the front wall of windows.

"Is someone here, boy?" she asked.

With a whine, the dog bolted out of the room, and skittered from the house through the doggy door. She heard him barking around the front of the house. Someone was here.

"Hey buddy, where's your mom?" John's voice floated on the breeze. "No, down boy, down."

She chuckled. By now, John probably had a dozen muddy paw prints on his pants.

John's voice came through the house virtual system. "Lowry?"

"Open the front door," She said to the house.

The door opened, and Lowry called out, "In the garden!"

John appeared at the entrance of the interior garden. Lowry patted the last of the tomatoes into the beds. She turned to him, grimacing at the muddy paw prints on his trousers. *Yep, Leo was a bad dog.* With a grin, she said, "Sorry about Leo. I've tried to break him from jumping."

He shrugged. "No worries. Spring has sprung into a mud-fest."

"Yeah, 'tis the season. Luckily, the new mats at the doors absorb the mud, so the house isn't a wreck."

She rose and stretched her arms to loosen her back muscles. Panting from his run, Leo padded into the garden. She frowned at him. "Leo, you're a naughty boy."

John patted the dog on the head. "Your brother Henry is worse."

Lowry leaned on the nursery shovel and looked at John. "I see you escaped from Amundsen."

With a grin, John nodded. "Yes, I cleared the emergencies and left the rest to Kisho." He held up a bottle of Ricard Pastis. "A gift from Noelle; straight from Paris." He reached out and squeezed her shoulder. "I want to thank you for watching over Ginnie during the kidnapping. You're a real hero. She told me how you 'slew Goliath' while in Zoric's clutches. You may have saved all of your lives."

She smiled. "You're welcome. And you can be proud of Ginnie, she held up well." Lowry picked up the empty seedling tray and placed it in the compost bin. She glanced at him. "John, I did want to tell you that while you were in the wilderness, I spoke with Ginnie about us, and um, the possibility of marriage and a child."

He tilted his head. "And?"

She turned and hooked the shovel onto its hanger. "I'll quote her, 'It might be fun' to have a half-brother or sister."

"Yes, she seemed fine with it." A smile flashed, and faded as quickly as it had crossed his face. "Lowry, I want to discuss Zoric. You're one of the few people who have firsthand knowledge of him. I need every tool I can get to beat him."

She washed her hands in the utility sink, and dried them. "I had a feeling this wasn't a social visit."

"Work first, I'm afraid."

She held out her hand. "I'll put the Ricard in the kitchen." After John handed her the pastis, Lowry gestured to the small table and chairs near the window of the garden. "Why don't you sit for a moment and I'll be right back."

Her hands shook as she carried the liquor to the kitchen and set down the bottle. She stared at counter reliving the image of Zoric's raging face. She shook her head and returned to the garden.

He glanced at her face. "Are you okay?"

"I'm fine." She chewed her lip. "But Zoric is not a pleasant subject."

"I understand, but to bag the bastard, we need thoughts on his weaknesses." He tapped his chin with his knuckle. "We have to figure out the right hook for this guy."

Lowry waved her hand. "Megalomaniac, power-mad. But he's not stupid. He knows how far he can go and how to influence those around him. He's a charismatic speaker. You can tell he gets a kick out of being in front of an adoring audience. My sense is that he can be manipulated to a degree, but only if he thinks it's in his best interest."

They sat facing each other. She glanced out of the garden window, brushing back her loose strands of hair. As sunset approached, shadows crawled across muddy fields and lingering snow. Spring wrestled winter for dominance, with pale shoots of crocuses heralding the ultimate victory to spring. But deep within the soil, the earth remained frozen.

She sighed. "He's a man with no feelings. It's difficult to understand how someone becomes evil, but with no love, something will fill the void—whether that be hate, or perhaps worse, indifference." She glanced at John. "The question is: what drives his hatred?"

"From what little background we've dug up on Zoric, his mother was a drug addict absorbed in her own hell. There's nothing on the father, so he is assumed absent. His mother died of an overdose when he was ten. His grandparents shuttled him and his brother around to various schools. He 'found' religion in a Christian cult and disappeared for years, then emerged as one of the leaders of the group who settled the Grace Region, but more radical than his brother, Anton."

Lowry looked at John. "It's sad that mental weak points can be damaged by a tragic childhood." She shrugged. "I'm no psychiatrist, but I suspect he's a sociopath at least and a psychopath at worst. A dangerous man to whom life means nothing. There is no difference in killing humans or flies to him—except killing the human may be more fun. He uses religion to justify his acts and keep control over his flock."

Her mouth twisted in thought as she tapped her lips with her fingers. "He's intelligent, but power is his aphrodisiac. I think the way to trap him is with his ego."

John raised an eyebrow. "Sound like the job for a woman."

"Or an intelligent man—is that an oxymoron?" Lowry laughed.

"You're so humorous." Then John frowned, and he mumbled something under his breath.

"What did you say?"

"I said, 'I should have caught this, before it got out of hand.'" He scratched his head. "I blew it on Zoric. I failed to do my job."

"It's hell to be human. . . and I should know." She glanced at him. "While we're on the subject of foibles, I need to talk to you about my situation with Lin. I don't want him to beat me to the punchline on my testimony that 'helped' convict an innocent Inuit man in the trial of the ISS—"

John shook his head. "You have nothing to explain to me."

Lowry touched his arm. "I want you to know everything about me. The hidden scars that make me who I am."

She turned away, gazing out of the window at the rolling hills of her farm. Those terrible times seemed like someone else's past. Now she had to dig them out of the dark crevice in her mind, and into the bright light of day.

She cleared her throat. "I was young and fresh out of an abusive marriage. In my stupidity, I fell prey to a young lawyer more interested in the material he could use in court than my love. During a private conversation, and frankly, in a compromised position, this young lawyer gleaned innocuous material on Nick from me, and gave it to the prosecution. They bundled it with a package of circumstantial 'evidence' against the Inuit leader, manipulating the public's anger over the attack on the space station, and derived a guilty verdict purely for political reasons."

He slid his hand over hers. "Sounds like a nightmare."

"A nightmare you never quite shake, especially with the guilt over Jean-Luc's conviction."

"What happened to him?"

"He went to prison, and of course, was disbarred from practicing law. I assume he's still serving his term." She pressed her lips together. In a thin voice, she whispered, "Most of the Inuit territory was taken by the government for mines and lumber. The tribe was forced onto a tiny slice of what had been their original lands."

"A terrible end to the story. Political corruption at its worst." John squeezed her hand. "I'll make sure that Lin won't be able to start a fire from old ashes."

Lowry had shared a vile part of her life, and John had not judged her, he had simply held her hand. She blinked back tears. "You've always been there for me."

He smiled. "And despite my words to the contrary, I know that you believed in me."

She chuckled. "And I was right—you've been the best president Antarctica's ever had."

John stuck his tongue out. "Thanks, Lowry, you always know how to trim a man's sails."

"I was raised in a mining camp, what can I say?" She glanced at the clock. "Let's celebrate—it's almost five o'clock—would you like an apéritif, courtesy of Noelle?"

"Sounds good to me." He rose from the chair, and jerked up his trousers that had slipped over his hips.

A twinkle in her eye, she glanced at his exposed boxers. "You lost weight on your journey."

"I needed to lose a little." He smiled, patting his stomach.

"I'll meet you in the living room. I'm going to change my clothes." Lowry walked to her bedroom and peeled out of her gardening gear. She opened the closet and zipped through the rack until she found a pair of silky yoga pants and a crop top. She slipped them on and winked at her image in the mirror. *Looking good, girlfriend.*

When she returned, John was sitting on the sofa. He did a double-take and whistled in approval.

With a grin, Lowry nodded her thanks as she walked into the kitchen. She pulled out two highball glasses from the cabinet, set them on a tray, and popped open the bottle of pastis. She poured a serving of the liquor into each glass. With a carafe of chilled water, she carried the tray into the living room and set it on the coffee table in front of the sofa.

She sat next to him. With a smile, she lifted the carafe. "I love this part." And filled the glasses with chilled water, the liquor and water mixing into a beautiful milky color. She handed one to John, and clinked his glass. "Cheers."

After he clinked hers, he took a sip. "Wonderful. It's been ages since I had a pastis."

They sipped the cocktails, gazing out of the large windows facing the river, watching the landscape vanish as dusk turned to night.

Lowry called out to the house. "Mood atmosphere."

On the edges of the room, soft lights began to glow, and a fire blazed up in the hearth.

John held up his glass and rotated it, staring at the cloudy remnants spinning at the bottom of the glass. He cleared his throat, and with knitted brow, touched her arm. "I did a lot of thinking and talking to Noelle on the trek out of Zoric's land." He drained the pastis and set the glass on the coffee table.

Lowry studied his stoic face, no hint revealed of his next words. Words that might decide the rest of her life.

He turned and gazed at her, leaned closer and caressed her cheek with his fingers. With a smile, he lifted her hand and kissed it. "I came to the conclusion that *I'm* the one who's nuts if I don't marry you."

Like a cool breeze on a warm day, her heart lightened. She saw in his eyes the depth of his love. In all the trials of their relationship, no matter how far apart they had drifted, no matter how worn the thread between them, their love had endured.

Her lips trembled as she drew his head toward her and kissed his brows. She whispered, "I love you, John."

"I love you, too, Lowry." He cupped her face in his hand, and then eased off of the sofa onto one knee. He lifted a small silk bag from his pocket, opened it, and shook a diamond ring into the palm of his hand. He took her hand and kissed her fingers. "Lowry, our journey has been a bit, up and down, shall we say, but will you marry me?"

Lowry blinked. The resentment and pain between them had dissipated like the mist on a warm day. She squeezed his hand. "Absolutely."

A broad smile on his face, John gently pushed the ring onto her finger. "This ring has a story. Years ago, during one of the first Antarctic geologic surveys, Nick found this diamond. Before the disastrous election with Durant, I had confided to him of my wish to marry you. To my surprise, he gave me the raw diamond." A look of pain crossed his face. "I had it cut and mounted, but, as we know, that didn't work out. I threw it into a drawer, and since then, it's been gathering dust."

Lowry dropped her gaze. "I'm sorry. I had no right to put your name on the ballot. When you won, your life was hijacked. It was totally my fault."

John shook his head. "Not totally, Lowry. My ego had as much to do with it as your persuasion."

He drew her into a long kiss. Lowry slipped her hand to his chest and broke the kiss. She searched his eyes in the dim light. "John, I want you to know that I won't force you to have a child." She touched his cheek with her hand. "I'm done manipulating you."

He smiled and caressed her nose. "Somehow, I doubt that second part." He gazed at her. "During the trek, overpopulation was one of the subjects Noelle and I discussed."

She held her breath.

John turned over her hand and kissed the palm. "But she and her late husband didn't have children. Noelle wants us to have the child they never had." He tugged a lock of her hair. "I had an epiphany in the wilderness—let's make a baby, Lowry."

His pants fell to his knees as he scooted back onto the sofa. "Oops," he chuckled, not pulling them up.

She wrapped her arms around him and drew him to her lips.

He winced in pain.

In mid-kiss, Lowry pulled away from him. She glanced into his eyes. "Are you all right?"

With a grunt, he patted his ribs. "I'm okay, but still recovering from my 'vacation.'"

Lowry stroked his face, then sat up and gently pushed him back on the cushions. "Let me see." She unbuttoned his shirt, eased it off, and dropped it over the back of the sofa. She touched the faded bruising on the side of his chest, and massaged his shoulders. With a sigh, he closed his eyes, and relaxed under her hands.

John opened one eye and pulled her on top of him. "You'd better come up here—you're in an awkward position." He kicked off his shoes and the rest of his pants. "I wouldn't want you to strain yourself."

Laughing, she said, "I don't want to hurt you."

He shifted her legs strategically onto either side of his hips. "Trust me, you're not hurting me."

With raised brows, Lowry grinned. "Are you sure? I distinctly feel some swelling."

He chuckled. "Well, it's been a long time."

She leaned forward and massaged his neck. The strands of her hair tickled his chest, and he glanced at her breasts in front of his face. His hands slipped beneath the crop top and eased it over her head. "Just like a woman to take advantage of a wounded man." He threw it across the room.

Her breath quickened. "Just like a woman."

John's hands shifted downward, slipping his thumbs under the waistband of her pants. She gasped as he jerked them over her hips. He threaded his fingers through her hair. "Please, do it just like a woman." And he drew her into a deep kiss.

CHAPTER 23

The next morning, John sat in his office, with his back to the desk. Brow furrowed, he stared out of the window. With a scowl, he ruminated on the battle of egos, playing itself out between Zoric, Lin and, frankly, even himself. He ran his fingers through his hair. *Gamesmanship must not win over statesmanship.*

He turned his chair around and asked his com-secretary, "Any messages?"

A shimmering ball formed above his desk. "Most recent to past?"

"Yes, please."

His com-secretary droned through his usual mundane messages. Noelle's face appeared. "From Dr. Noelle Clavet, yesterday evening at four p.m."

She smiled. "The voice of Nature calls, John. I'm going to save the animals. I have special video drones for animal studies. I'm returning to the trapping sites we found and setup the drones to video the cult's illegal trapping. If we capture Zoric's abuses, you can charge him with a crime, and maybe pressure the UN to kick the entire group off the continent." Her eyes were bright with excitement. "I hope to see you again. If not, carry the torch, John."

Noelle had gone back to Zoric's territory. John hit the desk with his fist. *They'll kill her this time.*

John forwarded Noelle's message to Kisho, telling him to discuss with Lin as necessary. Then he called Alex. "We're flying over the Concordia again, please ready the Hawkplane."

He sent a delayed message to Lowry and Ginnie, then jumped into the presidential car, flanked by the Drots.

With a feeling of déjà vu, he and the Drots slipped into the Hawkplane once again.

Alex glanced at his ashen face. "What's up?"

He stared at her. "Noelle went back to the Concordia Refuge area near the Grace border."

"Is she crazy?"

"I'm afraid so, to a certain extent. She wants to document Zoric's trapping activities and gather enough proof to charge and convict him. Perhaps she thinks she could sneak in and out before they know she's there."

Alex taxied the plane down the runway. "If she falls into Zoric's hand again—"

"Yeah." John bit his lip. A feeling of dread hung in the air. He didn't have many friends and Noelle had become one of the few.

They cruised over a land awakening to the spring. Only stubborn bits of snow remained and where the sun had lingered, tentative grass struggled up through the water-soaked earth. John scrutinized the ground as they approached where the research group had last camped.

Alex clicked to glide mode. "We'd better go silent."

His heart pounded at the sight of smoke swirling near the horizon. They came over a ridge. John gritted his teeth. Scattered around a pole, smoldering carcasses of animals were strewn upon the ground. The stench wafted into the plane as they flew through tendrils of smoke.

Alex gasped. "My God!"

John examined the site as they passed overhead. "The bodies seem to spell out something. Go back over again."

They circled again over the smoking carcasses.

His hand over his nose, John read aloud what the bodies spelled. *"Don't Tread On Me."* Grimly, he signaled her to land.

"We'll be vulnerable on the ground, sir."

"We need to see if Noelle is alive or dead."

Alex steadied the plane and landed in a mushy field near the carnage.

John yelled to Alex, "Stay here. Keep the engine running." And jumped out of the plane.

He ran toward the smoking remains. The pungent smell of burning flesh hit his nostrils, and he almost retched, then dragged out a handkerchief to cover his nose. He gagged at the sight of once-beautiful animals, burned beyond recognition, and stumbled to the pole in the middle of the massacre. The acrid smoke blinded him for an instant, but he could see something on top of the shaft. He shielded his eyes, then stared at a misshapen head. A shock jolted him as he recognized Noelle's face. His knees buckled. "No! No!"

Noelle's gray lifeless eyes gazed out over the killing field. John crawled to the pole and stared at the ashen face above him, shuddering as Noelle's hair gyrated in the wind as if endeavoring to carry it away.

John whispered, "I'm so sorry, my friend."

He turned angrily as Alex approached. "I told you to stay in the plane!"

"I had to come and see. Mr. President, we have to document everything." Tears came to her eyes. "That bastard will pay for this."

John slumped back to the ground and shook his head. "Noelle was a person who truly loved life, to the point of sacrificing her own." He struck the pole with his fist, his face twisted with rage. "And she was killed by a man who hates life itself." He staggered onto his feet and looked up into Noelle's face. "I swear to you, with my last breath, that I'm going to get Ivan Zoric."

CHAPTER 24

A week later, John, along with Lin's SWAT team, headed out to meet Zoric. He had agreed to trade Marko's mother for his two men, but only if John himself oversaw the exchange. Yesterday, in deep camouflage, key members of the SWAT team had crept into position behind the rendezvous site. The neutral location was on the border of Zoric's region, at the Grace River, near the place where he and Noelle had crossed. He swallowed hard. Though he had saved her from the river, death would not yield. Her voice was silenced.

He took a sip of water and reviewed the plan again. John's role was to engage and distract Zoric while the rest of Lin's team surrounded Zoric's group. But John knew that these fanatics wouldn't go down without a fight. In the midst of battle, he didn't want Marko or his mother in the crossfire.

For moral support, he had agreed to Lowry's request to join them, but on the condition that during the exchange, she stayed at the medic tent positioned away from the site.

"Lowry, I want you to ride with Marko and me, and we'll drop you at the medic tent."

With a glance, she nodded.

The Drots flanked the military hovercraft as they flew across the plains awakening from their long winter slumber. Vast muddy fields stretched before them, sparsely covered with dead grass, matted like wet hair in the rain. Only a few patches of snow remained with tiny streams flowing from them in a downhill race to the river.

John stared out the window, shielding his eyes from the sunlight reflecting on standing pools of water, his mind clouded with the memories of Noelle's death. Tragic to lose such a beautiful person. Gentle and loving, she had been a woman who believed that evil was an aberration. But on the day she died, evil had won. Zoric's ephemeral dominance had destroyed a life. He clenched his jaw. But power shifts with the wind, and today, they were the storm.

After John and Alex had left the horrible scene and returned to Amundsen, Lin had organized a detail, armed to the teeth, to remove Noelle and the dead animals. Zoric had left them alone. It had been a gruesome task, transporting Noelle's head and the remains of her charred body back to Amundsen to ship home.

John shivered and breathed deep, trying to shake off his despair. He had to concentrate on his encounter with Zoric. Once the bell rang in this chess game, he had to be ready— lives were at stake.

Lowry broke the silence, speaking in a low voice to John, "I hope our boy Lin is under control?"

He grimaced. "Lin will join us at the meeting site; we need to keep an eye on him. One of his lieutenants, a fellow named Nemechek, is in charge of surrounding the camp. I gave him direct orders to only contain the camp. I don't want the women and children to come into harm's way."

Marko sat up in the back seat. "Are you talking about my uncle? Has something happened in the camp?"

Lowry raised a brow, mumbling under her breath, "Sometimes it's hard to keep track of the bad guys. . ."

John replied to Marko, "No, son, I'm discussing making sure the meeting goes off without a hitch."

Marko leaned forward, gripping the back of the seat. "I'm glad my uncle agreed to the trade, but I'm terrified she'll be hurt."

"We're doing everything possible to make sure this goes as planned." John looked at Marko. "Your sole duty today is to protect your mother without putting yourself in harm's way."

"Yes, sir."

They stopped at the medic tent. John followed Lowry out of the hovercraft. "The Drots will video the exchange. I've set it up so you can watch it on the monitor," he said, pointing inside the tent.

Her face pale, she touched his cheek. A thin smile crossed her face. "Break a leg."

With a nod, John pulled her into his arms and kissed her. "I love you." They held each other.

Lowry leaned back, searching his eyes. "Promise to be careful."

"Don't worry, I'll be fine," he whispered. He slipped back into the vehicle and they continued toward the river.

As they neared the meeting place, John said to Marko, "Now, remember our plan. For everyone's safety, it must go as we rehearsed."

Marko's face was grim. "I remember."

The rest of their group stood along the riverbank, next to a large hovercraft brought in yesterday. Zoric had refused to cross the river, saying they had no way of making it across now that the river was at spring melt. They parked and sloshed through the mud to the makeshift command center.

John approached Kisho and quipped, "A lovely day for fishing, isn't it?" He said under his breath, "Any sign of Zoric?"

"No, sir. I think they're playing us for fools."

"He'll be here." Then John shrugged. "Unless he smells the trap." He tilted his head toward an armored vehicle parked nearby, surrounded by soldiers in full protective gear, resembling robots more than men. "I assume the prisoners are in there?"

"Yes, sir."

He glanced at Kisho. "Where's Lin?"

Kisho shrugged. "I don't know. He should be here by now."

John left Kisho and paced along the shore, Drots in tow. He gazed at the river and listened to the thrum of churning water. The warmth of spring had awakened Antarctica. The raging current had flushed a tangle of branches and brush, tenuously sandwiched between blocks of ice. A pulse of water freed the snarl and it escaped into the bubbling flow.

He watched the mat flow down river until a motion caught his eye. A kingfisher dove into a sheltered pool, then lifted an unlucky fish in her talons and flew over the river. Mother Nature was an ambivalent hostess. One bad step and you're fertilizer.

With a sigh, John chewed his lip. He and Noelle would never have made it across the Grace River now.

He returned to the group and stood next to Kisho. He clenched his fist behind his back. *Where is Zoric?*

John's breath quickened as hovers appeared over the horizon. They paused for a moment at the ridgeline overlooking the river, then continued down the slope to the bank. When the hovers stopped, Zoric got out. He stared at them from across the river with his head thrown back and dark brown hair blowing in the wind. His men assembled behind him, surrounding a petite figure—Marko's mother.

"Get ready," John mumbled, as much to himself as Kisho.

Zoric sneered and waved for them to cross the river.

The four soldiers escorted the prisoners to the front of the hovercraft, holding their arms with robotic pinchers. John and the rest of their party got into the rear.

The pilot turned to him with a pinched face. In a hushed voice, he said, "Mr. President, this is dangerous. We don't usually try to cross a river during spring break-up."

"I know." John looked at him. "We'll be fine—until we're not." He squeezed the pilot's shoulder. "Don't worry, we'll make it."

The hovercraft floated across the ice-laced river with the Drots following overhead. John squinted against the glare from the drifting blocks of ice, crashing into one another like bumper boats at a kiddie ride.

The pilot called out "Hold on!" as they navigated around a giant slab of ice rushing in the current, an entire evergreen tree trapped in its icy clutches.

With a final lurch, the pilot spun the hovercraft parallel to the shore, and they landed on the far bank. The prisoners were hustled onto the riverbank and positioned near the front of the hovercraft, the guards containing them in a de facto cell with their robotic armature.

John stepped out onto the gravel beach and nodded to the pilot. He turned and walked toward Zoric, breathing deeply to calm his thundering heart and steady himself for the contest ahead.

With his jaw thrust forward, Zoric stood erect, his chest puffed up and his feet planted broadly—primed for a fight.

Drots flanking him, John stopped in front of Zoric, chewing the inside of his lip until he tasted blood. Though he wanted to punch Zoric, he pasted a thin smile on his face, reached out and shook his hand. He had to play this as straight as he could. Zoric might be an egotist, but he was no idiot.

A scowl crossed Zoric's face. In a curt voice, he said, "The only reason I'm here is to get my men."

Grimacing, John shot back. "They're here." He turned to the captain of the guard. "Let's go." The soldiers slowly marched forward with the prisoners.

"Start Marko's mother coming this way."

Zoric waved and several men ushered her down the riverbank.

No one spoke as the opposing groups inched closer to one another on the flat stretch of land and halted. The captain tilted his head. Two soldiers escorted the prisoners to Zoric's men. Marko's mother stepped from behind the men and walked to the soldiers, and each group turned, retreating into their fold.

John clenched his fist. *The rest of the plan better work.*

Zoric flicked a glance at John and abruptly pivoted to follow his men up the slope.

He took a deep breath. "Zoric! We still have another issue to discuss."

With knitted brows, he stopped and glanced back at John.

"You've never told us what happened to Professor Clavet."

Zoric's lip curled and he snickered. "I heard she got a little ahead of herself."

John sucked in his breath. Leave it to Zoric to make light of killing another human being. He jabbed his finger at him, his mouth twisted in rage. "Murderer!"

Furious, Zoric turned to John. He wasn't used to being confronted. Zoric's men tightened into a knot behind him.

John counted on his anger to throw him off guard. With a step forward, he pressed his attack. "You killed her, you bastard!"

Zoric stared at him with eyes glittering in rage. His mouth convulsed as he growled, "The woman, Clavet, put the beasts above Man. She, like the blasphemers of old, idolized the Golden Calf." He pounded his fist into his other hand. "We must rule the earth as God intended."

With their hands in the air, several of his entourage shouted, "Amen!"

Zoric darted a smug look at John. Then he raised his hands to the sky. "It is written, 'The Lord made humans in His own image. He placed the fear of them in all living beings and granted them dominion over beasts and birds.'"

The soldiers escorting Marko's mother were now behind John.

John pointed at Zoric. "The Bible also tells us, 'For the fate of the sons of men and the fate of beasts is the same; as one dies, so dies the other. They all have the same breath, and man has no advantage over the beasts; for all is vanity.'"

Dramatically, Zoric stretched a hand toward John. "When the choice is the hunger of my people, versus a few wild animals, I choose my people."

His men shouted, "Alleluia!"

John felt his stomach turn. The poor souls surrounding Zoric were themselves hostages—minds bound tightly by their past and their present—now controlled by a man who would sacrifice them on the altar of his ego.

He scanned the faces of his disciples. "Your leader created the crisis, by destroying the food you'd stored for the winter. We offered resources to help, but he refused it."

Behind Zoric, his men stood, confused glances telling more than their silence.

With his lips curled like a rabid dog, Zoric threw his hands in the air. "Lies!"

John faced Zoric. "You're against life itself. And to hate life, is to hate God. You cloak yourself in the apparel of religion, but you are a *religionist* who uses God for the sake of power!"

The veins throbbed in his neck and Zoric's face flushed red, blotches pulsing across his skin. In the deathly quiet, his eyes bored into John's, but John didn't blink.

Zoric's hair blew in the wind, veiling his face for a second. Then the preacher returned to his role and he wrapped himself in his piety, turning in a circle to impress the gathering. Arms stretched to the sky, he gazed at the heavens. "We live for God and that is *all* we live for."

The captain nodded to John. Marko and his mother were halfway across the river in the hovercraft.

Zoric dropped his arms. "Enough of this nonsense." He waved his hand. "We must go." He stalked toward the hovers, closely followed by his men.

Like a tiny hummingbird, a combird appeared before John. It opened its beak and said, "Checkmate," then dissolved into a mist, disappearing on the breeze.

The trap was set—the SWAT team and police had completed the noose, cutting off Zoric's flank. The SWAT team stormed out of the forest. They confronted Zoric's group, waving their rifles. "Get down! Get down!"

"Shoot them!" Zoric screamed. Three of his men drew pistols from under their jackets, knelt in a protective band, then fired toward the rushing officers.

The SWAT team returned fire. A rat-tat-tat of gunfire echoed across the river valley. With a groan, one of Zoric's men hit the ground. Zoric and the rest of his entourage ran to the hovers, but officers rushed to cut them off. The Zoric follower who had stayed with the hovers leapt onto a hoverbike and accelerated toward Zoric. As he neared Zoric, a torrent of bullets hit him, and he screamed, falling backwards onto the bike. Out of control, the hoverbike careened into a boulder and flipped over, crushing the man into the rock.

The Drots had descended into fighting mode, circling John defensively. A bright light flashed behind him. He felt a blow like a giant's kick, throwing him onto the ground, smashing his face into the gravel. He twisted to his side, staring at the crashed bike now ablaze—its hydrogen fuel cell had exploded. Trapped beneath the wreckage, the man shrieked as the flames engulfed him.

John scrambled up, gazing with horror at the inferno, but there was no hope for the man. The blast had blown the Drots away from him, their light metallic limbs akimbo. In an instant, they righted themselves and returned to his side.

Yells drew his attention upriver. The police converged on Zoric, cutting him off from the hovers. He faced them, his teeth bared as he backed up slowly. Like a trapped beast, he eyes searched for an opening, but there was no escape by land. He pivoted and darted for the river.

"Shit!" John cursed. *What if Zoric slipped from their hands?*

Zoric raced along the shore. Like a cat, he leapt onto a huge slab of ice floating in the river. He fell on his side, sliding to the edge, then grabbed a branch sticking up through the ice. Zoric twisted around, laughing at the shocked faces of the police as he drifted down the river. He crouched low on the gyrating block.

Two SWAT team members jumped on Zoric's hovers and raced along the riverbank.

The remaining SWAT members ran to the river's edge and futilely shot at Zoric. John shook his head. The disciples were in custody, spread-eagled on the ground. He turned back just as Marko scrambled onto a piece of ice from the opposite bank. *Dammit, he was supposed to stay with his mother.*

"Marko, no!" John yelled, waving his arm.

Marko wobbled on the slab as it bucked in the current. John jumped onto a hoverbike and sped along the bank, paralleling the seething river.

Sporadic gunfire reverberated over the water. Zoric's block of ice had slammed into a mat of grass. The police were taking shots at him from the bank, but he kicked away from the obstruction and twirled into the current.

John glanced at Marko, kneeling on the jagged ice as it pivoted around a boulder, his face pinched in terror as the block spun into the center of the surging river. But he was gaining on Zoric. He crouched over a small swell in the river, then jumped to a large block of ice behind Zoric.

Zoric turned, and with a vicious grin, pulled something out of his boot.

John sucked in his breath at the flash of a knife.

Facing each other, Marko and Zoric floated down the river. A dull roar of a waterfall beyond the dam drifted on the breeze. A ridge of ice had smashed into a dam against a submerged line of rocks.

Like a slow-motion train wreck, Zoric's slab of ice rotated in the swirling water and crashed into the ice dam. The impact propelled Zoric forward onto the jammed blocks of ice. His feet landed on the slippery surface, and scrambling for his footing, he slid to the brink of the waterfall. He threw his arms into the air, flailing for balance.

A pop-pop-pop echoed across the river. Zoric jerked as the bullets hit his body. For a second, he stood motionless, his arms outstretched to the sky, his hair whipping in the wind. Then a red ooze of blood stained his shirt, and he slowly tumbled over the waterfall.

John stopped the bike and scanned the river bank past the waterfall. He gasped at the sight of Lin, holding an automatic rifle to his shoulder. Lin lowered it as Zoric's body disappeared under the frothing waves and ice.

Marko's block of ice careened into the ice jam and flipped him onto his side.

John turned back, cupped his hands around his mouth, and shouted to him, "Marko, come across the ice dam."

Marko scrambled to the shore and jumped onto John's hover. They moved past the waterfall and stopped at the bottom of the cliff to look for Zoric.

"There he is!" John pointed to the limp body caught in the vortex at the base of the cascade. Zoric twisted like a rag doll, swirling in the pounding force, and then disappeared. A log popped from under the spray and his body surfaced for an instant, eyes closed and hair matted. He rolled under the foam again and vanished. They got off and moved to the edge of the water, a freezing mist enveloping them. Zoric's body reappeared, then drifted in the slow current beyond the falls.

John put his arm on Marko's shoulder. "Zoric's dead. Even if he survived the bullets, the cold would kill him."

Marko clenched his teeth. "He'd better be dead."

"Forget about him."

"I'll never forget that he killed my father."

"No, you can never forget that. But don't let hate be a part of your life."

Marko's lip quivered, then he nodded his head. "My mother said the same thing."

John glanced at the sky. "We'll send a search team down river tomorrow. It's going to be dark soon." He exhaled and knelt on the pebbly shore. "The animals might save us the trouble of mulching him. Whatever's left of Zoric will fit into a shoebox." He picked up a stone and threw it into the water. "A fitting end to the bastard."

John rose and placed his hand on Marko's shoulder. "Come on, Marko, I need to see Lin."

K.E. Lanning

They mounted the bike and hovered to the sandy point bar from where Lin had shot Zoric. *No sign of him.* John pointed to footprints in the wet sand. "Tracks—two people." He cupped his hand around his mouth and shouted, "Lin!"

A startled crow flew from the brush behind them and across the rushing river.

He shrugged. "Maybe they've gone to the exchange location."

They hovered upriver.

John stopped as they neared the crashed hoverbike. A SWAT officer sprayed foam onto the contorted vehicle. The flames died then flared as she swept the extinguisher nozzle back and forth over the wreckage. Two medics carried the deceased man in a body bag to the hovercraft. The nauseating smell of burned flesh drifted on the breeze.

His stomach twisting, John parked the bike, and they dismounted. He slumped onto a rock as the images of Noelle's head and the smoldering carcasses flooded his mind. Too many nights, he had awoken to that odor—the brain haunts you with tiny details. He closed his eyes. *So much death, for no reason.*

Kisho brought waters out to them. "It's over, sir."

The hovercraft returned. Lowry and Marko's mother came ashore.

"Mother!" Marko dashed to her.

"Over here, Lowry." John waved.

She ran to him. "Are you okay?"

He pushed back his hair and pointed to an abrasion on his forehead. "A little scrape after the blowback of the hydrogen cell blast, but I'm fine."

Lowry examined the wound, then shook her head. "It was terrifying watching the monitor and seeing the whole thing through the eyes of the Drots."

The SWAT team loaded the remaining members of Zoric's group into the hovercraft.

John took a long drink. "Yeah, Zoric's dead. Almost like a scene from a thriller, Lin appeared out of nowhere and shot the fucker."

Lowry sat on a stone next to him, a scowl on her face. "Now God can deal with that bastard."

He gingerly touched the knot rising on his forehead. "Or the devil."

Kisho walked over and stood for a moment, then cleared his throat. "Mr. President, you're not going to believe this, but Lin has already posted his dramatic kill shot online—his adjunct videoed the whole thing." He swept his finger across his watch and the video clip materialized in front of them.

After the final scene, John snorted. "It's a perfect highlight reel for his upcoming presidential campaign."

A puzzled look on her face, Lowry gestured with her finger. "Wait, go back to the inset video in the corner."

Kisho backed up the video and expanded the inset piece.

Lowry pointed. "That's the same video I saw on the monitor in the medic tent." She looked back and forth between John and Kisho. "How did he snag the feed from the Drots?"

With a glance at John, Kisho whispered, "That's encrypted video and we only transmitted it to the one monitor—and Lin did it in real time."

CHAPTER 25

The captain of the guard approached John and snapped to attention. He cleared his throat. "Um, Mr. President, we've just received a report that Secretary Lin's forces have engaged the compound."

"What?" John stood, staring at him.

He pointed to a wisp of black smoke drifting over the horizon. "I'm afraid I don't have any details, sir." With a slight bow, he said, "I must return to the prisoners. We'll be taking them to a holding tank at the prison in Amundsen until they can be charged." With a salute, he pivoted and returned to the hovercraft.

Marko screamed, "Alexi!" He ran past them, leapt on a hover and sped toward the compound.

"Marko, wait!" John shouted, but he didn't stop. *Shit—he overheard the captain.* He turned to Kisho. "What the hell is going on?"

He shook his head. "I don't know. My guess is that Lin and his troops are mopping up the compound."

"God help them!" John ran to the hoverbike and mounted.

Tears on her face, his mother approached. "Alexi is his girlfriend—she's still in the compound. We must follow him!"

John turned the hoverbike around and the Drots zoomed into position behind him.

"Marko is all I have left, I have to come with you!" his mother cried.

Lowry ran to him. "And I want to go."

"Lowry, take—" John glanced at Marko's mother, realizing he didn't know her name.

"Mrs. Petrov."

"Mrs. Petrov behind you and follow me. But stay under the Drots."

They raced after Marko up the riverbank, around piles of glacial till and tangles of brush. Away from the river, the terrain flattened. Side by side, they flew across a marshland, scattered with shallow pools of water, a veil of mist rising in the wake of the hovers.

They climbed a ridgeline and paused at the crest. The spring sun lit the village below, shrouded in black smoke. They flinched at the rat-tat-tat of gunfire.

Mrs. Petrov moaned. "We must hurry!"

Shouts echoed across the valley floor as they descended. They slowed at the edge of the village. Flames shot skyward from several cabins.

John coughed as the acrid stench hit his lungs.

Weapons drawn, soldiers ran to them, then stopped as the Drots zoomed in front of their hoverbikes. A commander recognized John and shouted for the troops to disengage. They split into two lines at attention. The commander saluted John. The Drots descended into fighting mode, circling the two hoverbikes as they proceeded into the compound.

Bedlam reigned in the village: loud crashes of doors being knocked in, punctuated with sporadic screams. They passed a group of children huddled near a burning cabin.

Lowry gasped. "Stop! I see a child lying over there. We may need to help."

They parked the bikes and dismounted. The children shrieked at the Drots.

John gestured with his hand. "The Drots are scaring them. I'll stay here."

The children encircling the child edged back as Lowry and Mrs. Petrov walked to the little girl. The child sat still, petting a small dog. The dog's fur had been burned off—only tufts remained on its head. The dead animal's tongue lolled out of its mouth.

They knelt beside the girl. Deep scarlet blisters speckled her arms and legs—she must have tried to save the dog.

Lowry whispered, "Baby, you need some medicine for your burns."

The little girl stared at her with a vacant look of resignation. She shook her head, lifting the paw of the dead animal. In broken English, she said, "Bojan—no more."

John slumped on the bike as Mrs. Petrov stroked the girl's tangled hair. Between Zoric and now the government, what horrors had this little girl suffered?

"I'm so sorry about Bojan." Lowry gently lifted the little girl.

He looked at his watch. *One bar of satellite connection.* "P? We need a medic."

"John, a field medic is nearby, at the church."

"Okay, we'll head that way."

Mrs. Petrov clutched John's arm. "I have to find Marko," she whispered and disappeared behind the cabins.

With the little girl in Lowry's arms, they walked toward the center of the camp.

In the open square, Lin's armed guards surrounded a group of sullen men, zip-tied, sitting on the ground. Women and children sat clustered nearby. An officer barked orders through a bullhorn.

One of the women cried out and ran to Lowry. The officer screamed at her to stop, but John waved him back.

The woman desperately pulled at the girl in Lowry's arms. "Jana!"

Her arms stretched out, the little girl burst into tears. "Mati!"

"You must be her mother?"

The woman nodded.

"Be careful, she's been burned." Lowry passed the girl to her. "She needs medical attention right away."

The mother wrapped her arms around her gently, tears streaming down her face. "We have no medicines left," she cried.

John turned to the mother. "The soldiers have set up a medic station in the church."

With a nod, she hurried away with the child.

He gazed at the women holding sobbing children, their eyes filled with terror, their faces grimy with smoke and dust. He stepped closer, spread out his arms, gesturing with his hands. "This was not supposed to happen. We'll take care of all of you."

A woman, face bruised and bloody, screamed, "Haven't you done enough?" She spat on the ground and turned away.

Behind him, John heard Lin's voice. His jaw set, he turned and made his way, with Lowry and the Drots following, to where Lin was holding a press conference.

Aloof and imposing, Lin stood in front of a burning building surrounded by an entourage of staff and reporters. In his crisp uniform, Lin turned and placed his boot on a pile of fur traps, smiling at the reporters interviewing him. His adjunct stood to the side, videoing Lin's triumph.

"Don't strangle him in front of the cameras," Lowry whispered.

"I'll see you after the disemboweling."

Drots in his wake, he strode toward Lin. The crowd parted as they recognized who he was. John snapped at the reporter. "The interview is over."

John gestured for Lin to follow him. They walked behind one of the cabins, away from prying eyes and ears. He pivoted to face Lin. "What the hell do you think you're doing? Are you mad? We were supposed to contain the camp, not destroy it. Where's Lieutenant Nemechek?"

"I ordered Nemechek to patrol the perimeter of the compound."

John leaned forward, jabbing his finger at Lin. "You fail to show up during the exchange of prisoners, and then you ride in like a gun-toting hero and shoot Zoric. Not that I'm complaining—that son of a bitch deserved to die." He shook his head. "But it's a different kettle of fish if you're using the video for your presidential campaign."

Lin's eye twitched, and with a veiled sneer, folded his arms across his chest.

John chopped the air with his hand. "I thought we'd agreed that the compound, full of women and children, should not be attacked. Why did you do it?"

His lips thinned. "In killing Zoric, I cut the head off the beast, but we had to make sure the body stopped twitching."

John snapped, "So as I read this, executing Zoric wasn't enough glory, you had to come bloody women and children."

"We did no harm to the children. Our main objective was to neutralize the threat from hostile men—or women—in the encampment." Lin sniffed at him disdainfully. "However, there's an old saying in the American military: 'Nits make fleas.'"

John hands shook in fury at Lin's arrogant disregard for human life. Lin had always been hard-boiled and difficult to read, but how had he missed these weaknesses? Or had Lin carefully hidden his flaws, but now felt powerful enough to reveal them?

With his thumb, he gestured to the church where the little girl had been taken. "Like the little girl with third-degree burns?" John stared at Lin. "You are responsible for this! You directly countermanded my orders."

"Sir, Lieutenant Nemechek reported he heard transmissions from one of the cabins. After I arrived, I knew something had to be done before they attacked us."

He leaned forward, his face close to Lin's. "And to burnish your war record." In a razor-thin voice, he snapped, "Nemechek is taking over this operation. Return to Amundsen and we'll finish this later."

Lin's mouth curled into a snarl. For a moment, their eyes locked, then with fists clenched, Lin turned on his heel and stalked away.

Exhaling, John watched him leave, then returned to the village center. As the sun fell below the ridge, the light from the flames glimmered on the metal cross atop the church.

Nemechek halted his hoverbike near the group of soldiers and dismounted.

John walked to him. "Lieutenant Nemechek, I'm promoting you to the rank of captain. You are now in charge of this operation. These are Antarctic citizens; let's treat them as such."

He saluted. "Yes, sir." Nemechek turned to the armed soldiers surrounding the women. "I'm now in charge. We need to help these people." He turned to one of the women standing nearby. "Can you take us to where you store firefighting equipment?"

She nodded.

He waved his arms. "Break into three fire brigades and follow this woman. Let's get these fires out—now!" The troops jogged behind the woman.

John waved the Drots back, and knelt in front of the huddled woman and children, gazing at him with frightened faces. "I'm sorry for what happened today. We'll help you rebuild your lives. It's getting late—if you can take in someone who's lost their home, please do." Their faces haggard, they rose, and with their children, drifted into the night.

One woman approached John. "I'm the aunt of the little girl who was burned. Please let me go into the church."

"Yes, of course." She moved past him toward the door. "Ma'am, wait—do you know a young man by the name of Marko?"

A look of fear came into her eyes. "No! I don't know anyone by that name."

He touched her arm. "I'm just trying to find out if he's all right."

The woman studied his face in the light from the church window. She tilted her head to the edge of the compound. "Their cabin is second from the end," she whispered.

John walked to a small, decrepit cabin. The door was off-kilter and old clothing had been stuffed into holes where stones had once blocked the cold winds. The residence of an outcast.

He spoke softly to the Drots, "Stay outside." He knocked on the door. "Hello?"

He heard a rustling, then silence. The door ajar, he pushed it open and stepped into the stone hut. In the dim light of a single lamp, Marko sat on the ground, rocking a young woman in his arms.

Her eyes swollen from tears, Mrs. Petrov knelt beside Marko. "Alexi was standing near her cabin when the soldiers launched the rocket attack." She drew in a sharp breath and then pressed her lips together. "The cabin was hit." Her hand shaking, she motioned downward. "A piece of the rock wall fell on her. It is God's will whether she lives or dies."

John crouched next to Marko. "I'm so sorry, Marko."

He turned toward John, staring at him with red-rimmed eyes. "You may not have shot the rocket, but you share the blame."

"I ordered Lin to not attack the compound." John sighed. "But I am ultimately responsible." With a bowed head, he squeezed Marko's shoulder.

Scowling, Marko jerked from his touch. "I believed in you." He turned away, caressing the young woman's hair.

He glanced at Mrs. Petrov, but she refused to meet his eyes. There was nothing for him, the leader who had sworn to protect all the citizens of the nation, to say in comforting those in Zoric's group whose only crime was credulity.

In a daze, John staggered to his feet. "I'll get a medic."

P whispered in his ear, "A medic's on the way, John."

A knot in his stomach, he pushed open the broken door, and left the cabin.

The Drots leapt forward as a medic scurried to him.

The medic stopped and threw up her hands. "Hey, I'm just trying to help!"

John called out, "She's okay, she's a medic."

The Drots fell back to his side.

"Help the girl, please, she's been injured," he said, pointing to their cabin. "And let me know how she is."

Captain Nemechek approached with a quick salute. "The fires are almost out, sir, and the hostiles we encountered in the camp have been interned in a barn overnight." He pointed to a large rock building at the far end of the compound. "We'll sort out their status tomorrow."

"Thank you, Captain." He shook his hand. "I want you to report to me in Amundsen. You've done a great service to Antarctica."

A smile crossed his smudged face. "Thank you, Mr. President."

John stumbled to the church, brightly lit as the medics cared for the wounded. In silhouette, Lowry stood outside, talking to women waiting for their loved ones inside the field hospital.

Exhausted, he slumped on the ground, leaning his head against its rough stone walls, the taste of smoke clinging to his lips. Children sobbed in a nearby cabin, then quieted. In the village, figures scuttled between shadow and light—broken humans driven mad by one of the most dangerous creatures on Earth—the charismatic leader, twisting them into religious zombies. And now, without their false prophet, they drifted on a sea of uncertainty.

The lights dimmed in the church. The medics had sent most of the patients home and were settling in to sleep.

Lowry came to John and sat beside him, slipping her arm around his shoulders. "The medics are keeping the little girl overnight for observation." Her voice broke and John reached for her hand. "Jana will survive, but she'll be scarred for life."

John closed his eyes for a second. In a bitter voice, he said, "Whether visible or not, won't they all be scarred?" He glanced at her. "I saw Marko and Mrs. Petrov. Alexi was badly injured when Lin's forces assaulted the village."

She groaned. "What happened? Is she okay?"

"A rocket hit one of the cabins and part of the wall collapsed onto her. I sent a medic to their cabin, but when I left, it was touch and go."

Lowry shook her head. "I guess it's amazing that more people weren't killed today. What's sad is that Lin will get votes in the upcoming election for taking out Zoric and the cult." She squeezed his shoulder. "But, thank God, it's over."

"Over?" Tears rolled down John's face. "When people feel desperate, they'll grab any crazy idea, especially ones shouted with conviction. The cycle of fear turns and where it lands, nobody knows. . ."

CHAPTER 26

"He's trying to kill me," Tao whispered, clutching Nick's arm as he laid in one of the clinic beds.

Nick looked at him. His face, tense and pale, revealed his abject terror. Tao had been brought into the infirmary last night. He'd thrown up in his cell and demanded to come to the clinic. He was an addict and Nick assumed he was going through withdrawal—surprising with the robust pipeline of drugs into the prison.

He liberated his arm from Tao's grip. "Who?" he asked, placing a cool cloth on his forehead.

Tao glanced back and forth, then his voice dropped so low that Nick could barely hear him. "If I die, it will be by the hand of my cousin, Peter Liu. I've been warned that he's sending an assassin."

A smile grazed Nick's face as he tucked the sheets around Tao's neck. "I doubt an assassin could saunter into the pen."

His eyes bulged in fear. "They told me he will send a drone disguised as an insect."

Blinking, Nick stared at him. He had heard of assassin drones, but the high-end ones were pricey. Why would a low-level drug addict like Tao call for an expensive execution? He patted Tao's shoulder. *Maybe they laced LSD into his opioids.*

Tao grabbed his arm again, pulling him close to his mouth.

Nick grimaced against the stale smell of sweat and vomit.

"But you may know him by his other name—Peter Lin, the Secretary of Defense."

With a shudder, Nick gasped. "What are you saying?"

"Lin's real last name is Liu, a member of the Neo Green Gang in China. Since I was busted on drug charges, he's been trying to get me deported to China, but they don't want me back in the country."

He straightened up, gaping at Tao.

Tao grasped his hand. "I can't go back to my cell. He won't dare send the drone in here with witnesses. You've got to help me or I'm toast."

With a shrug, Nick squeezed his arm. "I'll see if the head nurse will let you stay longer, but it's not my call."

He stared at Nick intensely. "Don't you have connections?"

Nick tensed up and started to shake his head.

"Don't try to deny it. Everyone knows who you are."

*   *   *

The next day, Nick returned for his shift at the clinic. As he neared the entrance, a man with **CORONER'S OFFICE** on his coat accompanied a robo-gurney out of the clinic.

"What happened?" he asked the coroner's assistant.

"A prisoner OD'd."

"Who was it?"

The gurney rolled by Nick with a sheet covering the body.

The man looked at the name on the report. "Uh, some guy named Tao."

Nick's mouth dropped open. "Jesus."

"Did you know him?" He glanced at Nick.

He shook his head. "No, I just met him yesterday during my shift."

The night physician's assistant strolled from the doors at the end of her shift. She stopped abruptly as Nick moved in front of her.

He snapped, "I thought Tao was supposed to remain in the clinic for a couple of days?"

With a frown, she waved her hand. "There was nothing wrong with him."

"He confided in me that he was afraid that someone might make an attempt on his life if he went back to his cell."

"All the inmates would love to lounge in the infirmary. Besides, addicts are renown for being paranoid." She shook her head. "He died of a self-induced drug overdose, not murder."

"Are you sure?" Nick pointed to the gurney disappearing around the corner. "You may have signed his death warrant."

CHAPTER 27

A few days after Zoric's death, Lowry left the farm, hovering toward the penitentiary in Amundsen. Nick had sent a cryptic message asking her to visit. She floated across rolling hills of spring flowers and pale green shoots reaching for the sun. Tussock grasses waved in a breeze filled with the scent of thawing earth.

She hadn't seen John since the battle with Zoric. He had sent short messages of angst and worry as he scrambled to handle the demise of the cult. Zoric's body had been recovered and sent back to Serbia for burial. Both John and the UN had decided that if his remains stayed on Antarctica, the cult might reawaken in his memory. With the UN's aid, the cult members were dispersed and treated for psychological post-cult trauma. An agreement had been negotiated with the UN to extend the boundary of the refuge to include the Grace Region. The compound had been razed to the ground, except for the church building, set to be converted into the Noelle Clavet Nature Center.

The hover stopped at the entrance. Lowry got out and sent it to park. She moved through the check-in process, then walked to the visiting booth. With a smile, she sat and scooted her chair to the table. Gone was the gaunt face and mottled bruises. "You look great, Nick."

"Yes, thanks to a little bird, I have more freedom now and spend most of my days working in the clinic or the garden."

Her smile brightened. "Fantastic. I was worried sick after my last visit."

She felt Nick's eyes studying her.

His brow furrowed. "You, however, look worn out."

Lowry touched her forehead, and with a slight nod, muttered, "Yeah, I'm exhausted. It's been a rough couple of weeks."

"Take care of yourself, Lowry." He leaned forward. "I've been following the news. How's the young woman—Alexi, I think?"

"Yes, Alexi. She's out of critical condition and should fully recover. John arranged for the little girl who was burned to be treated at the Mayo Clinic." Lowry sighed. "She and her mother are still in Chicago."

A twinge of pain washed across his face. "All the carnage and anguish because of a megalomaniac." His shoulders dropped in resignation. "There is a plaque on the wall of the penitentiary psyche ward that reads:

Humans—a seed of madness lies within our beautiful minds.

If the seed propagates, the insanity touches all within reach.

Nick shook his head, staring at the table. "A sad truth of our human condition."

Lowry glanced at him. In their own family, mental illness had changed the course of a nation. Her paternal grandfather had been a raging alcoholic, beating her uncle Duff into a shell of a man. His father had crushed the little boy within, never allowing his spirit to blossom into a healthy person. And that broken man had wreaked havoc not only on her life, but that of Nick, John, and Antarctica herself.

Nick met her eyes and touched his hand to the pane. Lowry placed her hand over his, biting her lip at the coolness of the glass between them.

His voice thin with emotion, he said, "But you and I survived, didn't we, Lowry?" He turned away, clasping his hand into a fist.

Lowry studied his pensive face as he stared at the wall. Here was a man who, by the forces of fear and love, had been driven onto his path in life. As a young man, Nick had fallen in love with her mother, unknowingly conceiving a baby girl, but fate had cut off their chance for a relationship. But he rose past the darkness of his childhood and chose life with its myriad of forms: intensely loving the natural world and a lonely little girl who had lost her mother.

Tears welled in her eyes. "We held each other up, believing in each other despite the odds against us. You were my champion when I needed you most . . . and I was yours."

Nick sucked in a breath, and gazed at her, blinking against his emotions. "You have the gracious soul of your mother."

Lowry smiled. "She was a very special person. I miss her." She dried her eyes with a tissue and looked at her father. His fingers trembled as he brushed the white hair from his wrinkled face. In these last dreadful years, he had aged.

"Enough of the past, let's look to the future." His eyes brightened and, with a grin, pointed to her hand. "Do I see a ring on your finger?"

Lowry threw back her head with a laugh. "Yes. A bit of good news rises from the ashes." She lifted her hand, showing Nick the diamond ring John had given her. "After the battles between us, John and I are finally tying the knot."

With a broad smile, he said, "I'm so glad for you, Lowry."

"Thanks, Nick." She shrugged. "It's been an up-and-down relationship, to say the least."

A smile grazed his face, then disappeared. "Best of luck to you both."

She chewed her lip. Nick had never married, and in her own life, a committed love had been elusive. Perhaps collateral damage from the familial wounds or just old-fashioned bad luck? She crossed her fingers. *Yeah, I hope this one works.*

"Thanks, I can use all the luck I can get." She leaned forward with a smile. "I want to thank you for the diamond. John told me the story of how you found it."

Nick cleared his throat. "When I landed on Antarctica, there wasn't much to do for a young man. On one of the expeditions, we discovered the small vein of diamonds, but it wasn't a commercial find. In my loneliness, I returned to the site and dug with my pick, searching for a diamond fit for your mother. I knew it was just therapy, and one day I was angry with the world and whaled away at the earth, and suddenly, a raw diamond rolled to my feet. I picked it up, staring at the rough crystal in my palm."

With a sad smile, he met her eyes. "If Margaret hadn't died, who knows how the story might have ended? But she'd be happy to know that I gave the diamond to our daughter."

"It's such a lovely story." Lowry looked at the ring. "And an exquisite stone. Thanks for giving it to John to use for my ring."

"You're welcome, my daughter." He glanced at the clock and his smile faded.

"What's wrong, Nick?"

"I need to tell you the real reason I asked you to visit." Nick looked back and forth, then his voice dropped to a whisper. "Two days ago, an inmate came into the clinic, possibly suffering from an opiate withdrawal. He was hysterical and told me that Secretary of Defense, Peter Lin, was going to kill him. From his story, he'd pissed Lin off by getting thrown into jail."

She furrowed her brow. "Do you think he was out of his mind?"

He shrugged. "He had faked being sick to get to the infirmary and was terrified to return to his cell. From an ally, he'd been warned of the murder weapon—an assassin drone the size of an insect. He knew that Lin wouldn't dare send the drone to kill him with witnesses."

Lowry's mouth sagged open. "Who *was* this guy?"

Nick shook his head. "If you don't know, you can't tell anyone. Let's just say a guy from China. I had spoken with the nurse before I left that evening, but the next morning, when I arrived, a gurney was leaving the clinic with a sheet covering a body, heading to the coroner's office." Nick tapped the table. "It was this same guy—dead from an overdose. After the day shift left, the night staff forced him back to his cell because he wasn't sick." Nick raised an eyebrow. "Maybe it was an accidental overdose, but maybe it was murder."

"You think Lin assassinated him?" She shook her head. "He gives me the willies, but murder wasn't on my list of reasons to hate him."

"I think it needs to be investigated, though I don't know if they'll prove anything against him." Nick chewed his lip. "But the most chilling is the second bit of information this inmate gave me."

He pinched his lips together and scooted closer to the glass. He whispered in a low voice, "He told me that Peter Lin's real name is Peter Liu—a member of a notorious criminal gang in China."

Lowry inwardly shivered. They had thwarted the Russians, but was another predator circling Antarctica?

"For your safety, you shouldn't be involved any more that you have to be. All I want is for you to set up a meeting with John and myself. But it has to be secret. I was thinking that he could visit the prison gardens. I work there on Thursday afternoons."

"Okay, Nick." Blinking, she exhaled. "Sounds like someone in China read the Russian handbook: *How to Hijack Antarctica.*'"

*   *   *

On Thursday, John left his office on the pretense of touring the new prison facility. The only person he had told of his real mission was Kisho. With the security Drots following behind him, he jumped into the presidential robocar and soon arrived at the penitentiary. As he walked toward the entrance, he thought back to the conversation with Lowry that had brought him here today.

"Lowry, I know Lin has a mega-ego and would do almost anything to command the presidential suite, but it's hard for me to believe that he'd commit murder. Nick admits his accuser seemed out of his mind. And this information that his name is really Peter Liu? I'll have Kisho track it down, but Liu's a pretty common Chinese name."

Lowry had shrugged. "Yeah, but Nick knows what he heard, and best to find out if there's anything to the story."

He gritted his teeth as he approached the entrance to the pen. *After all the stress of his first years in office, why couldn't his last be a cakewalk?*

The warden looked up with a smile at John's appearance at his office door. "Mr. President!"

John smiled. "Sorry for the last-minute call, but my lunch got cancelled. I've been wanting to tour your new facilities—I've heard they are incredible."

"No problem at all! We're honored, Mr. President."

The *clip, clip* of their shoes put his teeth on edge as they marched around the building, passing cell blocks, the infirmary, the education wing, and then at last, the garden.

They entered a greenhouse built of glass, soft light filtering through the translucent panes. John breathed in the humid air and gazed at the racks of vegetables, staggered like bleachers for the plants to catch the artificial and natural sunlight. He looked up at the chirps of birds and grinned as they darted through the open rafters.

"Very nice, warden, I'm glad to see that the prisoners have a garden to augment their diet."

He nodded. "Yes, fresh fruits and vegetables for our cafeteria, and the low-security prisoners do the work. They learn a skill and it's excellent therapy."

John caught sight of Nick tying up peas. "Fantastic." He turned to the warden with a smile. "Would it be possible to get some coffee or tea brought out here?"

"Absolutely." He tilted his head. "We have limited internet within the building for the sake of security, so I'll have to leave you for a moment." With a chuckle, he swept his hand toward the Drots hovering nearby. "But I guess you're never alone."

As the warden left, John moved to where Nick lashed disheveled vines of a pea plant onto a trellis. The Drots followed closely, then zipped around the area close to Nick before they returned to John's flank.

John cleared his throat and whispered, "Hey, Nick. Lowry says you have something of interest to tell me?"

Nick blinked, but kept stringing tendrils, keeping his face turned away from the Drots. In a hushed voice, he said, "I was caring for an inmate in the infirmary. He told me a story about your Defense Secretary, Peter Lin."

He swallowed hard. *The tangled web with Lin keeps growing.* He sidled closer. "Go on, quickly, before the warden returns."

With a glance at the Drots, he turned to John, covering his mouth with his hand. "He said that he'd screwed up by being thrown in jail. He was terrified that Lin wanted him dead. He'd been tipped off that an assassin drone would be used to kill him."

John realized that Nick was worried that the Drots could read lips. He knelt, turning away from the Drots and thumped a large pumpkin in the row next to Nick. "And you're sure he was talking about Peter Lin."

With a grimace, Nick nodded. "I'm afraid so, John. Except that he told me Peter's real last name was Liu." Nick glanced up at him. "And now this inmate is dead. Murdered."

"Who was this addict?"

"Zhang Tao."

As if a fist had punched him in the stomach, John gasped. The vision of Lin's angry face when John had told him of Tao's arrest came into his head. John staggered to his feet and blinked in disbelief. He covered his mouth and coughed. In a thin voice, he whispered, "Lin's cousin."

Nick finished tying the peas and rose to his feet. "Cousin, eh?" With a grimace he shouldered his pack of tools and pivoted to leave. He scratched his nose and muttered under his breath, "Family relations can be the deadliest. Trust me, I know."

*　　*　　*

Early the next morning, John went to the coroner's office. Kisho had set up a hologram of him drinking coffee in the dining room so the Drots would remain on guard in front of the apartment.

The door to the lab slid open. As he stepped in, a cool breeze carried the faint odor of formaldehyde. Dr. Bootwala, the coroner, waved him over to the examining table, a cloth draped over Tao's body.

John balled his fists and strolled to the table. Nothing like viewing a corpse first thing in the morning to make the day a little brighter. *I guess it could be worse—I could be the one lying under the sheet.*

With a smile, the coroner glanced at him. "Good morning, Mr. President."

"Please, call me John."

"Okay, Mr. President, I mean, John. And please call me Boots, that's my nickname." He gestured to the covered body lying on the exam table. "Sorry to meet in these circumstances." With a practiced hand, he flipped the sheet back, revealing Tao's gray face, etched with an eternal grimace.

John clenched his jaw against the revolt of his stomach. *Maybe I shouldn't have eaten breakfast.*

"I've completed the autopsy on Zhang Tao. Death by overdose for sure."

He blinked, forcing himself to look at Tao's face. He cleared his throat. "Accidental?"

Boots shrugged. "The lab found a combination of drugs commonly used by addicts, but a very high dose and the location of the puncture wound by the needle is unusual." He turned Tao's head, and with a laser pointer, illuminated where the jugular vein ran along the side of his neck. A slight bruising was visible. "Usually addicts shoot up in the peripheral veins—

in the crook of the arm or sometimes between the toes, if they're trying to hide the marks."

John tilted his head. "Does that tell you something?"

"Not by itself. We asked the guard what happened that night. His story was that he heard a scream and moved to the cell. He said when he entered, Tao looked terrified, staring at a roach flying from the cell. Then he passed out. The guard called for backup, but by the time they reached the infirmary, Tao was dead."

With a cough, Boots picked up a tiny dish from a small side table and brought it into the light over Tao's body. In a whisper, he said, "But the most important discovery I made during the autopsy was a pair of those new iBrows concealed in his brows." He pointed to the minute globes, revolving around the bottom of the dish. "If there was anything nefarious, with luck, he may have videoed what occurred."

John leaned over, then blinked as he inadvertently touched Tao's cold skin. He clutched his hands behind his back, digging his nails in his hand as he fended off the nausea rising in his gut. *This is why I went into engineering and not biology.*

Inwardly he shook himself and focused his mind on the tiny spheres now trembling at the bottom of the dish. They were bionic masterpieces, solving the human need for sight and connectivity. To match his hair color, Tao's orbs were brown in color, unlike Patel's blond iBrow implants. *Would Lin have known about them?*

Boots replaced the dish onto the side cart and then pulled the sheet over Tao's body. "We've watched the prison video taken from the corridor and they match the guard's story, including the roach flying into and out of the cell." He looked at John. "The iBrows would fill in the last piece of the puzzle. If Tao had the time and presence of mind to turn on the iBrow video, then we may discover whether this is a simple overdose or a murder."

John exhaled, happy for the white cover now hiding Tao's face. "But I thought the internet was limited in the prison? Do the iBrows have enough internal memory to record and store a video?"

"That's a good question. I guess we'll need an IT person to try to read the hard drive or see if, once they reached our office, they automatically uploaded to his cloud account."

John nodded. "We need a court order to get into the hard drive and his data backup. We'd better hurry before the cloud gets 'conveniently' wiped."

Boots swept his finger across the surface of his watch. "Okay, I just sent you the final report for the judge."

P whispered, "I've got it, John."

John said, "Thanks so much," and stuck his hand out to shake Boots' hand, then pulled back at the tainted gloves.

Smiling, Boots pealed the gloves off with a quick snap and threw them into the recycling bin.

"Okay, now we can shake hands." Boots chuckled. "Don't worry, I'm used to people avoiding me."

After they shook hands, John left the building, breathing in fresh air. The warden had told him that after Tao's arrest, Lin was working with the Chinese government to get him deported to his homeland. But China didn't want him back in the country with a drug conviction on his record. Why was he murdered? Was someone worried that Tao had squealed—and if so, what were they worried had been revealed—and to whom? And most importantly, why now?

John shook his head. *Let's hope Nick isn't next on the list.*

CHAPTER 28

In a large, empty closet at the rear of his apartment, Lin sat facing a blank wall. He said softly, "Engage 'Chinese Checkers.'" The lights of the gaming unit blinked, then a virtual cave wrapped around him. The image surrounding him was that of a small office with an empty chair facing him. As he watched, a hologram of a large Chinese man solidified in front of him.

Once the image was complete, the man nodded. "Nǐ hǎo, Zhishuo."

Lin bobbed his head. "Hello, Chen."

"Are you losing your Chinese?"

"I'm getting a little rusty." Lin shrugged. "It wasn't my native language."

"Don't forget us, Peter." Chen leaned forward. "What's the status?"

"We're encrypted, right?"

He pursed his lips. "Of course."

A smile flitted onto Lin's face. "Tao has been eliminated and is no longer a threat. The leak has been plugged."

"Perfect." Chen cleared his throat. "His family will be told that he died of an overdose, but I'll make sure his family receives a nice death bonus." He shrugged. "They were aware of his addiction problem, so it won't come as a surprise, though we won't mention our part in the event."

Lin sighed. "Tao knew he'd compromised the operation with his arrest. I tried to get him back into the family's hands, but the Chinese authorities were being stubborn. I had to act before he exposed any secrets."

"Yes, it was unfortunate, but necessary." With a smile, Chen gestured with his hand. "And how is our Chinese Checkers game proceeding?"

Lin counted down on his fingers. "We have our staff hired and events planned for my campaign this summer. The Zoric situation has given us amazing footage for our ads—an unexpected gift for the campaign! Regardless, we'll be placing our ballot computers in all the districts, with a convenient virus allowing us to guarantee the outcome. Two, we've placed our people into strategic positions within the president's security, including the Drots, which have been programmed to eliminate him if the voting doesn't go our way, creating enough chaos for me to step into the leadership position of the country. Technically, the Secretary of State, Patel, would be the next in command, but he's weak. I'm sure I can box him out without a problem. And three, we have the weapons in place on the western islands in case a full-blown coup is necessary."

A broad smile lit Chen's face. "You were an excellent choice for this mission, Peter. The Chinese government will be pleased." He inclined his head. "And so will our family ties that they don't know about. We'll make a killing on the raw materials on Antarctica, just waiting to be plucked from her soil."

With a bob of his head, Lin replied, "Yes, with the massive amount of minerals under our control, and selling concessions to the Chinese government, we will make the members of the Neo Green Gang billionaires."

Lin chewed the inside of his lip to keep from giggling. Soon, he'd be one of the richest men in the world, and President of Antarctica. Who would have guessed a scruffy boy from the rough side of Chongqing would achieve these heights? He clenched his fist. But he must never forget his roots. The family ties of the Neo Green Gang would always be a tether on his future, with even tighter bounds than the Chinese government. A tether that at any time could become a noose.

Chen raised an eyebrow. "And the president doesn't have a clue?"

Grinning, Lin shook his head. "He's a good man, but myopic and trusting—an engineer by training and not a politician. He's very focused on his environment infrastructure, and to paraphrase an old saying, he doesn't see the weapons behind the trees." A scowl crossed his face. "But we may need to be careful of John's new fiancée. She's a bright, persuasive woman, but may have an unfortunate accident in her future."

CHAPTER 29

At the sound of a cough, John glanced toward the door of his office. *Patel.* His stomach had barely recovered from viewing Tao's cadaver and now he had to deal with his useless Secretary of State, Rua Patel. He forced a half-smile onto his face. "Come in, Rua."

He strolled in and sat at the chair facing John's desk. Like a child, Patel's eyes wandered around the room.

John chewed the inside of his cheek. *I'm busy here, Patel.* He tapped his thumb on the desktop. "What's up?"

Patel opened and closed his eyes as if awakening from a dream. Then, with a quick smile, Patel focused on John. He leaned back in the chair, his lips parted as if on the verge of speaking.

John clenched his teeth. *Spit it out, Patel—you can do it.*

Patel swallowed, and said in a low voice, "I know you never liked me." He cleared his throat, glancing to see if John disagreed. With pursed lips, he continued. "And I wanted to tell you that I'm planning to resign from your cabinet and return to New Zealand."

John sat back in his chair, blinking as he digested this news. True that he'd never warmed to Patel, mainly because he always seemed to be AWOL. But not enough to drive him to resign. With a sigh, he said, "I'm sorry if I'm the reason you're leaving."

Patel shrugged. "You're not the reason. I emigrated to Antarctica after a divorce from my wife of fourteen years. We had two kids." His lips quivered and twisted into a grimace. "I came here to find myself. I failed at farming and I failed as a politician. Funny, but I thought that becoming Secretary of State would change me." He dropped his gaze. "But the truth is I never fit here. Perhaps returning home will be my salvation."

He studied Patel's face. Gone was the goofy look, replaced with simple resignation.

John raised an eyebrow. "Someone close to me once said, 'You're not lost, you've just wandered onto an Under Construction detour.'" He stood, and with a grin, reached his hand out to him. Patel rose and they shook hands. "Best of luck to you, Rua, and again, I regret any anxiety that I perpetrated on you."

Patel met his eyes. "I wasn't exactly an ideal team player." He paused and tilted his head.

John studied his face. There was something else Rua wasn't saying. "Rua, is there something on your mind?"

"John, can we take a walk in the garden? I want to show you a bird I saw the other day near the feeder."

He narrowed his eyes. *What the hell?* He gestured with his hand. "Sure, let's enjoy the sunshine."

"Without the Drots?"

His throat tightened. "They're on their recharging stations."

They walked to the garden and strolled along the path. John breathed in the moist air and inclined his head toward Patel. "I assume you have something private to discuss?"

"I just scanned your office with my iBrows—it's bugged."

A chill crawled up John's back. He whispered, "Who?"

Patel replied softly, "I'm not sure, but the surveillance smacks of Chinese origin."

John blinked in acknowledgment. Were Lin and his gang at the center of this web? Without moving his lips, he breathed, "Lin?"

"It's a strong possibility." Patel coughed. "You do realize that the Drots were also made in China?"

John swallowed hard. Lin had been in charge of organizing the presidential security.

Patel waved to the feeder and they moved closer. "I'll miss the birds." He pointed to a bird sitting at the top.

It was a beauty. A long-tailed meadowlark, brownish gray, with a red belly and intense red stripes above the eyes. Hopping back and forth, it rustled its feathers, and pecked at the seeds.

Patel parted his lips and without moving them, said quietly, "That's a surveillance bird. See how it pecks like the others? But it never actually eats any seeds—it records conversations." He rubbed his nose, covering his mouth with his hand. "It also reads lips."

They moved to the corner of the garden. The meadowlark flew to a branch above them.

"Let's go outside," Patel murmured.

They strolled along the stone path through the presidential grounds. John nodded to the stoic guards at the exterior wall.

It was a lovely day, with crocuses in full bloom and green shoots of daffodils venturing above the soil. John wondered if he should tell him of the growing avalanche of worries about Lin. He glanced at him. This conversation had revealed a different side to Patel—or had it? He clenched his jaw. *I hate to be paranoid, but maybe discretion was the best path.*

"When did you discover all of this, Rua?"

"I walk in the garden regularly. A few weeks after I got the iBrow implants, the meadowlark showed up as artificial in my view." He glanced at John. "But I hadn't been to your office since the day Lin first met with us to discuss Zoric. Today, it lit up like a Christmas tree with surveillance devices."

John grunted.

"But there's another reason I needed to talk to you away from prying eyes and ears. While you and Lin were in the wilderness battling Zoric, an encrypted communique came to Lin. In his absence, the com-secretary directed it to me. We were able to un-encrypt the message. The text was ambiguous, but enough to glean that Lin may have clandestine ties with the Chinese government." Patel cleared his throat. "And more urgently, that Chinese weapons have been hidden on an island off the west coast of Antarctica."

John stopped. Heart racing, he said, "God help us. First the Russians make a grab for Antarctica, and now we have to fend off the Chinese?"

CHAPTER 30

A chill wind bit into John's face as the Antarctic Coast Guard patrol ship sliced through the blue waters of the Ross Inlet. In the distance, seabirds soared over the rocky cliffs of the western Antarctic islands.

He turned to Lin with a brittle smile. "Almost there."

His lips razor-thin, Lin snapped, "I wish you'd tell me where we are heading, sir."

John gestured to the islands. "A delightful spring tour of our westernmost provinces, Lin. And to enjoy the clean ocean waters, far from polluted coastlines, and home to our Antarctic lobster, and the best salmon fishing in the world."

With an annoyed look, Lin exhaled and stared over the bow of the ship.

John gritted his teeth, glancing at Lin's pensive face. He had trusted this man. If Patel hadn't accidentally intercepted the message, Lin could have been the next elected president, then treasonously opened the back door to China. Kisho had warned him of the risk of staging a confrontation with Lin on the ocean, but John wanted an open-and-shut case to put him away. If one more drop of proof was revealed today, so much the better. He didn't want Lin to avoid prison on circumstantial evidence.

John gripped the rail. Had he been so focused on creating a world of balance between humans and nature on

Antarctica—his work of art, and perhaps a touch of ego in the mix—and missed the signs of Lin's betrayal? Or was it just a profound naivete? He sighed. *No one expects a friend to gut-punch you.*

The ship turned and cruised to the far side of Graham Island.

John squinted as the sunlight glinted off one of the Drots hovering above him. He shot a look at the protective robots and his thoughts drifted back to yesterday afternoon. Kisho had arranged for an IT person to do a complete scan on the Drots, but nothing alarming had been discovered.

As she rebooted the units, the technician had shaken her head and said, "No detectable viruses, but I have heard of a malicious software virus being triggered using a sequence of imbedded files that individually appear to be safe." She had turned to John. "These Drots are designed to be less intelligent than humans, but they can learn. Let's hope no one has taught them naughty ideas."

John drew in a breath of cold air. *Yeah, an idea like coup d'état.*

The ship slowed as they entered a small inlet and two Coast Guard officers stepped behind them. Lin gasped at the sight before them—half a dozen UN and Antarctic Coast Guard ships faced the island—in full attack mode.

From the anchored cutter, a troop of Marines descended into a landing craft and cruised to the beach. A Stealth bot darted along the shoreline, chased by military drones. The drones fired at the bot, and in a flash, it froze in place.

One of the officers pointed to the Stealth bot. "The drones hit it with disruptors and have taken it offline, so to speak."

The marines hit the beach and ran to the camouflaged objects hidden in the rock crannies. The Coast Guard ship neared the shore as they removed tarps from three Chinese helicopters.

The officer behind John said, "Sir, those helicopters are the new Dragon class."

News drones buzzed over their heads, capturing the scene for various international channels.

John turned to face Lin. "Our lovely Graham Island, recently invaded by Chinese armaments—hidden away for a possible invasion?" He waved toward the motionless Stealth bot. "The marines spent several days surveying the Stealth bot as it monitored the site and communicated with your *buddies* in China."

Lin's eyes widened in fear as he stepped back.

"Yes, Lin—you're a *traitor.*"

With a snarl, Lin faced John. "You have no proof that I was involved with the Chinese government or with these armaments on the island."

John pointed up to a news drone buzzing over their heads. "Oh really? Wave, Lin, you're famous."

The Coast Guard officers stepped toward Lin. The lieutenant cleared his throat. "Mr. President, I've just been informed that pods of military robots and drones have been discovered in several caches along the island. Enough military might to take the city of Amundsen within a few hours."

John flicked his eyes to Lin. "Now we know the level of your betrayal."

"No!" Lin leapt to the side, twisting away from the two officers. The first officer jumped at him, snagged his ankle, and Lin crashed to the deck with a groan. His face bloodied, he spun and kicked viciously, flipping the officer onto his back.

Lin scrambled to his knees.

The second officer drew her pistol and shoved it into his temple. "If you don't stop resisting, I'll shoot," she yelled.

The first officer yanked his arms behind him and the second officer fastened cuffs on his wrists.

Lin turned his head and screamed at the Drots hovering behind John. "Engage *Chinese Checkers.* Capture the President!"

With the butt of her pistol, the officer clubbed Lin on the head. Stunned, he collapsed onto the deck.

The Drots zoomed between John and the crew, cornering him against the ship's railing. They descended into fighting mode and advanced, in lockstep, toward him.

The first officer yelled into his mike alerting the crew to rally to them. "First security unit, on the main deck now. Second security unit, ready the water cannon."

The ship's siren blared across the deck.

John turned and backed toward the railing, desperately looking for a weapon. He spied a fire ax and shifted along the rail. With a grunt, he yanked it loose from its bracket.

The first Drot rushed him. John jabbed the ax at the titanium body. The Drot pivoted like a Ninja and sprang at John, its arms wide open. The first officer tackled the Drot by the legs, but with a sharp kick, it jettisoned him across the deck.

"Get one of the drones with the disruptor!" screamed the second officer.

"They're on the UN helicopter," a sailor yelled, pointing to the gunship returning to the ship's helipad.

With a whoosh, the water-cannon crew blasted the Drots. They danced, leaping and spinning, out of its path. The second Drot dived beneath a lifeboat, shielded from the spray. The jet caught the first Drot in mid-air. Metallic arms flailing, it skidded across the wet deck and into a corner of the brass railing. With the Drot pinned against the rails, sailors rushed forward and shoved a pole into the neck of the Drot, attempting to pop the domed head away from its limbs. One sailor slipped in the water, and with a yell, slid into the Drot. With one of its pincer feet, it grabbed the sailor by the leg.

In the spray of water, Lin awoke and shook his head. He rolled out of the melee and to the pilothouse wall.

Desperately, the sailors rammed the pole, again and again, under the head of the Drot, forcing it upward, exposing the underside of the computer. The crew aimed a blast of water into the metallic oval, and like a sail in a storm, launched the Drot over the rail, still clutching the sailor's leg. Together, they somersaulted in the air and then, with a splash, hit the water.

"Man overboard, man overboard," The bullhorn shrieked. Sailors ran across the deck to rescue him.

At the sound of scuffling metal, John turned as the other Drot crawled stealthily across the deck, stalking him like a humanoid praying mantis, its titanium arms undulating as it crept closer.

Heart racing, John backed toward the deck edge. "Might need a blast of water over here," he shouted.

The Drot leapt at him. He swung the pointed end of the ax, but it dodged the blow. The Drot faked to the side, then pivoted and sprang at him again. He parried with the ax, and with a clunk, struck one of its titanium arms. The Drot whirled, its limbs spinning at a dizzying pace. John gasped as it circled its arms around him and, with a metallic click, he was caught like a rat in a trap. He grunted as the metal arms tightened around his chest and dropped the ax onto the deck with a clatter.

Lin pushed himself up the wall of the pilothouse and stood. With a scowl, he glanced at the second officer standing nearby. "If you don't release me, I'll command the Drot to crush him!"

Nestled tightly in its arms, John studied the control panel under the domed head of the Drot. In a low voice, he spoke to the Drot embracing him. "Drot, I'm President John Barrous. Peter Lin, aka Peter Liu, is a traitor. You must not follow his commands. Disengage *Chinese Checkers*." No response. John chewed his lip. The final command the IT person had said to the Drot flashed into his mind. Whispering, John ordered the Drot, "Reboot and restore settings to one hour ago." Lights blinked across a narrow panel under its head. Another flash of lights across the panel, then it went dark. *Did it work?*

The second officer waved the water-cannon crew to cease. A deathly silence fell over the deck. She nodded to Lin and glanced at John. "Release him. We must save the President." She pulled a key from her pocket and tossed it to one of the sailors.

The sailor unlocked and removed the cuffs from Lin's arms and backed away. Grimacing, Lin stood, rubbing his wrists, and then strolled over to John and the Drot.

With an arrogant smile, he faced John. "You started the battle, but we will win the war. You're coming with us as a hostage." Lin jabbed his thumb at the helicopter landing on the helipad. "We will fly to an autonomous Chinese submarine hibernating in a nearby sea cave." He chuckled. "The Antarctic invasion will commence and a new Chinese dynasty will begin."

Lights flashed across the control panel as the Drot restarted. John whispered, "Drot, release me and capture the traitor, Peter Lin."

In an instant, the Drot's titanium limbs sprang apart, releasing John. It spun and faced Lin.

"No!" Lin yelled, backing away in terror. He turned and dashed to the railing. The officer barked for the sailors to block his escape.

The Drot bounded toward Lin in two giant strides and caught him from behind, snatching him into its armature.

"Drot, release me!" Lin screamed, but the Drot did not react to his command.

The sailors surrounded the Drot with Lin wriggling in its grasp. The officer ran to John. "Are you okay, Mr. President?"

John nodded, kneading his forearm. "Yeah, especially when the feeling comes back to my arms."

He moved to the Drot holding Lin. "Looks like your dynasty will have to wait, Lin, or Liu, I suppose." John looked at the robot. "Drot, take Lin to the ship's brig." He pointed to the officer. "She'll show you the location."

Lin glared at John as the Drot lifted him and followed the officer to the stairway leading to the lower deck.

A scraping sound drew their attention to the ship's side. Metallic fingers edged over the deck. The other Drot sprang over the railing and landed, dripping wet, onto the deck. In a flash, it perused the faces of those on deck until it recognized John, and raced toward him.

An officer near John jumped in front of the Drot. From the heliport, a drone zipped overhead, a metal appendage extending from the beneath it. A strange whirring noise echoed across the deck and the Drot halted in mid-stride and stood for a second swaying drunkenly. The drone shot the disruptor again, and the Drot clattered to the deck like a felled tree.

"Finally, the disruptor shows up." John grimaced.

"Restrain the Drot!" the officer shouted.

The sailors ran over, dragged the supine metallic beast to the side of the ship, and zip-tied it to the railing.

John asked the officer, "How long does the disruption last?"

"About two hours—hopefully long enough to get its power source disengaged. Then an IT person will have to reprogram it." The officer pointed to the drone hovering overhead. "But we'll keep this handy just in case."

Several Marines surrounded the Drot carrying Lin and followed it to the lower deck.

The second officer pointed to the brig and the Drot padded in, with Lin struggling in its grip. The Drot secured him closer and Lin squealed in pain. The barred door closed, and the Drot pivoted, squatting into a chair shape, with Lin entrapped in its arms.

The officer ensured that the brig door was secure and then glanced at one of the marines. "You're on guard duty."

With a nod, the marine re-holstered his gun. He stepped back from the bars and clasped his hands behind him.

The officer gestured to the stairway. "The rest of you can return to your stations."

They saluted and trooped up the steps.

She turned to John with a stiff salute. "All secure, Mr. President."

"Thank you, Officer Aziz. I'll be recommending commendations for you and all the crew members for your bravery today. Please let me know about the status of the man who went overboard."

Officer Aziz tapped her ear bud. "Sir, I just heard that he was recovered at the stern of the ship. His only injury was a torn ACL." She saluted and then smiled. "It's been an honor to serve and protect you, Mr. President." With a nod, she returned to the main deck.

He pulled a chair in front of the brig and sank onto the hard metal seat. Beneath his feet, the engines thrummed as they cruised into the open sea. He stared at Lin, but like a naughty child, Lin refused to meet his eyes. His face, streaked with dirt and sweat, remained defiant.

In a silky voice belying his anger, John asked, "Why did you do it?"

Lin's mouth twitched into a snarl. "The UN illegally stole China's rights to their designated Antarctic lands. The Prydz Bay region was ours. Now it's the major port near Amundsen."

John shrugged. "A great many countries lost their claims granted before the Melt. After the sea levels rose, the people of the world needed the land and the UN had to adjust to the new reality."

"We *adjusted* to the UN's theft by planning our own future. The irony is that our group supported you in the presidential race because we felt, strategically, it would be better to have you as president than have the Russians in control. We feared that splitting the vote by putting up our own candidate would guarantee victory for Durant's successor."

John's mouth sagged as he blinked in disbelief. "So I can blame you for that as well."

Sighing, Lin shook his head. "It almost worked. Our vision was to establish a long-term plan for Antarctica, based on collectivism rather than corrupt capitalism. The whole of the society is more important that the individual."

John clenched his teeth. "If we were ants, communism might work—but we're not, we're human beings. We should have a lighter impact on the Earth, but communism isn't the answer. Through corruption and greed, Communist China has been one of the worst polluters in history."

"The government changed their environmental policies."

"After the horse had left the barn." John gestured toward Graham Island with his thumb. "Besides, you were ready to go to war—is that environmentally safe?"

"People around the world are desperate for raw materials."

"'Desperate' is a word I've fought against all my life. Companies complain that it costs too much to safeguard the Earth, that people need power or maybe just a new device for their convenience—*desperately*." John waved his hand. "But they don't take into account the cost of the environmental cleanup or the destruction of a wildlife area. It's more expensive to remediate than if they'd been prudent at the start."

John leaned forward, counting one, two, three with his fingers. "Our society is three legs of a stool: government, corporations, and citizenry, and if one is more powerful, the stool will topple. In a true democracy, the power lies in the citizens, so they are not subjugated by either the government, such as in communism, or by corporations via crony capitalism."

He chewed his lip, watching Lin's closed face. His words had not touched him.

"Peter." John said softly. Daily interactions within the cabinet didn't allow for true personal connections, so he had rarely used his given name. But he wanted to pry open Lin's thick facade and into his soft tissue.

Lin blinked and then looked at him.

John extended his hand toward Lin. "Man to man, human to human, without the propaganda—why did you do it? Maybe we weren't friends, but we spent nearly every day together for years, building a new government from scratch. How could you have so thoroughly betrayed us?"

Lin stared at the floor. He shifted in the arms of the Drot, and with a sigh, his shoulders slumped. He met John's eyes and cleared his throat. In a thin voice, he said, "Years ago, before America became Amerada, my mother was a prostitute of sorts. She was paid, and paid well, to get pregnant every couple of years, travel to the States, and deliver an American child." His mouth twisted into a macabre smile. "I was one of those babies. And like a package from Amazon, I was sold to a family unable to have children. As luck would have it, after a year, they conceived and a baby of their own flesh and blood came into the family." The smile faded. "I was no longer needed." With a furrowed brow, his eyes looked back and forth. "School was hell. I was bullied mercilessly. When I was sixteen, my real mother contacted me and I returned to China." He straightened his back. "I became an honored member of the Neo Green Gang. And because of my fluency in English, I was chosen for this role."

"Is there any truth on your background report?"

Lin shrugged. "Well, I *am* Asian."

With pinched brows, John stared at him. Whether a religious cult or a criminal gang, brainwashing is essential to obedience. And the leaders of these groups have a sixth sense of the weak and broken humans of society to fill their flocks. He clenched his fist. But he and Lin had worked together for years. To live day to day with someone and be perfectly willing to slip a stiletto into a colleague's back is another thing entirely.

He pointed his finger at Lin. "Regardless of your past, you betrayed me personally."

"Yes, sir, I fully accept that fact."

"Do you accept the *fact* that you are a traitor to Antarctica?"

Lin pursed his lips. "Treason to your government might be a nice label, but loyalty to a greater cause supersedes that in my mind."

John grimaced. "You trotted out a sad story of your early life. But with your ability to fabricate lies, I don't honestly know the truth of your childhood. Frankly, you're quite the performer; masquerading as a trustworthy team member, topping it off with your theatrical ruminations on the virtues of communism." His voice rose. "But what I *do* understand is that you would be in the catbird seat if you won the presidency, you and your cohorts making out like bandits selling commodities off the continent. The reality is that you don't give a *shit* about anything except power and money—your guiding spirit is greed. I'm sure the next agenda item for you would be to repeal the one-term rule."

His lips pressed thin, Lin gazed at the wall.

"Your silence speaks volumes. You'd do *anything* to seize Antarctica." John studied Lin's face for any twitch. "Even *murder*. Remember dear Cousin Zhang?"

Lin shot a glance at him, then coughed. "My understanding is that he OD'd. He was fucked up with drugs."

"Yes, sadly."

John pursed his lips. Two days ago, the judge had issued the warrant for Tao's cloud account. In the throes of a deadly overdose, Tao had activated his iBrow camera and recorded a piece of Lin's death message before he succumbed. Only a fragment of Lin's face was captured, but on the audio track, Lin accused Tao of betrayal. Enough damning evidence to indict him for murder. John hoped to fool Lin into thinking they had the entire clip, and perhaps he'd fully confess his role in Tao's execution. He wanted the bastard thrown in jail, with no chance to jump bail and flee the country. By all accounts, Lin's actions today had exposed him as a traitor, but with the legal intricacies of treason, a conviction might take months, and his ring had done an impeccable job of covering their tracks.

John leaned back, confidently folding his hands behind his head. A smile on his face, he continued. "But I'm afraid Tao was into the latest gadgetry. Ever heard of iBrow implants?" His smile broadened at Lin's bewildered look. "It might have just been one of those nasty unfortunate incidents in prison that never gets solved, except that he recorded your last touching message to him." He nodded. "I have to compliment you on the clever assassin drone, Lin. Who would blink twice at a roach?"

Lin narrowed his eyes at John. Then he spat on the floor. "He deserved to die—I figured it was he who ratted."

"And rats must be disposed of, right?" John curled his lip.

Lin's shoulders dropped in resignation. "Tao was weak. I made a mistake in bringing him here. He had to be taken out, but apparently not soon enough."

P whispered into John's ear. "We have everything recorded and being viewed in real time by the authorities. Great job!"

At her news, John chuckled. "Mr. Peter Lin, aka, Peter Liu, you'll be put away for a long, long time. And thank God, you can never run for president. After this, you wouldn't be elected for dog-catcher."

CHAPTER 31

Lowry glanced at the sky through the high windows of the room. The dreary morning cloud cover had finally burned off, clearing into a pleasant spring day. She waited in an alcove of the community room in the presidential building. With a smile, she touched the petals of the white roses in her bouquet, then brought them to her nose, inhaling the luscious scent. She closed her eyes. All so different from her first wedding years ago.

At twenty-two, she had stupidly fallen for an abusive brute, and married him right after college. The wedding arrangements had taken longer that the marriage had lasted. But the emotional scars had taken years to heal.

Voices in the hallway brought her back to the present. She bit her lip in excitement as the first notes of music drifted to her. Lowry rose and went to the tall mirror leaning against the wall, setting the bouquet on a small table. She gazed at her reflection in the mirror. The classic cream-colored dress was lovely. She smoothed her hair and turned in profile to straighten the errant baby's-breath flowers placed in her loose bun. She stepped back for a final look and grinned. This wedding felt right. Beyond their bonds of love, John was a friend.

At the sound of the door opening, Lowry turned. Nick came in dressed in a charcoal-gray tux with a broad smile on his face.

She clapped her hands. "You got a pass!"

With a twinkle in his eye, Nick replied, "Not exactly. This morning, John gave me a full pardon for my role in uncovering Lin's treason." He walked to her and smiled, clasping her hands. "And maybe a little because of his soon-to-be wife." He gazed at her and then kissed her cheek. "You look beautiful."

Tears welled in Lowry's eyes. John knew how much it meant to her that Nick gave her away. At her first wedding, Duff had taken part, but only because they scheduled the ceremony around a conference he was attending in the States. At the rehearsal dinner, he'd commented on her future husband. "Are you sure, Lowry? He acts like a prick." She shook her head. *Truth hurt—literally.*

Her friend Donna knocked on the door and peered into the room. "Everyone's ready." She smiled. "You're simply gorgeous."

Lowry swallowed hard and picked up her bouquet. Nick crooked his arm and she slipped in her hand. They walked to the entrance of the main room and stood waiting for the ceremony to begin. The large community space had been converted into a beautiful wedding chapel. Garlands lined the aisle and flower arrangements dotted the room. Silent video drones, designed to resemble floating candles, hovered to capture the wedding in 3-D.

A smile on his face, John stood at the front, next to the Justice of the Peace, Lucia Carmelo. She gazed at the friends and family seated in the white chairs on either side of her. Ginnie, Kisho, and Bill Taylor were there, along with a few others neighbors. Thank God, a small event.

The guests rose as the wedding march began and she clutched the bouquet. Her heart thumped as they walked down the aisle.

When they reached the front, Nick hugged her, whispering, "Your mother would be so proud," and then sat in one of the chairs.

John stepped to Lowry and faced her.

With her book in hand, Carmelo smiled broadly. "Are you both ready?"

Nodding, John gazed at Lowry. "Yes, I am."

Lowry smiled. "I'm ready."

*   *   *

Lowry slowed the hoverbike as they entered the gorge leading to the Oasis.

John leaned forward and kissed her neck. "With the speed you were going, I'm afraid you've lost most of the flowers in your hair."

She reached back and squeezed his leg. "I want to reach the Oasis before the sun sets."

He grinned. "Yeah, threading the needle of this gorge in the dark wouldn't be my idea of a honeymoon—especially when I'm looking forward to threading a different sort of needle."

With a laugh, she glanced at the Drots hovering above them. "With the boys watching?"

"I'll make them stay outside the entrance." He shrugged. "Unless these upgraded ones have been programmed to clap at the right times. . . ?"

"You're a piece of work." She stopped the bike and pointed into the dim chasm ahead. "With the angle of the sun, it's already dark in there. I need to see where I'm going." She drew her helmet off and handed it to John. "Can you please put my helmet in the side case?"

"Sure. I'll take mine off too." He pulled his off and stashed them both in the case.

Lowry eased the hoverbike forward, dodging protruding knobs of stone as the walls narrowed. She smiled at the gurgle of trickling water flowing along the rock walls. They crossed a small stream and gusts funneled up from the base of the hover, blowing mist into her face. It had been years since she'd been here and never during the spring melt.

Lowry navigated through the switchback entrance of the Oasis.

John waved to the Drots. "Stay outside and guard."

The air temperature rose as they entered the isolated cocoon. Lowry parked the hoverbike and they dismounted. She turned to the sound of water cascading down the cliff on the edge of the meadow. At the bottom of the falls, the frigid cascade splashed onto broken granite rocks, then bubbled along a stream, merging into the geothermal waters of the soaking pool.

"Before I start unpacking, I'm getting out of this suit." John unzipped his jumpsuit and stepped out of it.

"Yeah, it's nice and warm in here." She peeled off her suit and they draped them over the bike seat.

They pulled the camp gear from the bike and set it near the pond.

Lowry closed her eyes and took a deep breath—the air itself smelled of life. She opened her eyes, stretching her arms up to the pale sliver of sky. In a slow pirouette, she turned and stepped to the edge of the pool. She gazed into the turquoise waters, bubbling with hot currents from underground veins of magma. Emerald bog and Antarctic buttercups fringed the veined marble stones lining the pool. Vines hung over the steaming water with nascent buds catching the pale spring sun.

She had known this place since childhood. Memories of camping here with Nick; dangling her legs in the water during awkward adolescent talks. A smile on her lips, she turned to John. "I've always loved the Oasis."

Lowry ambled to the rough canopy bed near the pool, touching the silky fabric hanging over the frame. "John, it's beautiful and very special that you planned all of this."

John grinned. "I can't take all the credit; Ginnie and Nick helped with everything." He gestured to the hydrogen cell heaters around the campsite. "It's a little colder than our last couple of visits, so we brought a few heaters."

She gazed at the happy crackling heaters. "They're just like campfires."

"Yes, but we need a real fire to cook the salmon."

They unloaded the camp supplies.

Lowry grinned, clutching the bottle of Champagne. "I know where this goes." She placed it in the cold stream to chill.

She set up the camp chairs and blankets near the edge of the pool while John started a small campfire in the fire ring.

"Need help?" she called out.

John shook his head. "No, I'm done. Just sit and relax."

She sat on the rocks near the pool, pulled off her shoes, and threw them under the chair. Tentatively, she stuck a toe in the water. *Warm, but not too hot.* She scooted into the chair and, with a sigh, leaned her head onto the cushion.

John brought a bottle of red wine with two wine glasses laced in his fingers. He handed her a glass and, with a grunt, twisted open the bottle. He filled each glass, leaned the bottle against a rock, and sat next to her.

"Well, my love, I didn't think this day would ever happen." John turned to her, lifting his glass in a toast. "To my wife and true love."

"To the love of my life, my dearest husband." They clinked glasses.

John caressed her arm. "The Oasis was the starting place for our love, though I was a bit of an ass the first time."

"Just a bit." With a smile, she covered his hand with hers.

"Yeah, I know." He turned away. "I want to tell you something. After I was elected, and our relationship soured, I became a bitter man."

She lifted her hand and opened her mouth.

He shook his head. "No need to say any more than you have." His lips pinched, he stared into the water.

She waited for him to speak. The surface of the pool reflected the dancing light from the heaters. He finished his wine and set the glass on the ground.

He cleared his throat. "I've never told you why I hate politics so much. When I was a kid, my two brothers and I were shuttled off to Colorado every summer, attending various Boy Scout events or dude ranches as volunteer help. Our mother was a state representative in Pennsylvania and dad worked a lot of overtime. The wilderness was good for us, but as we got older, we came to realize that our mother wanted us out of the way so she could work or campaign." He swept his hair back. "Her political career trumped our relationship with her." John shrugged. "I'm not saying she was a bad mother, but we knew our place in her priority list."

His voice lightened. "But it was during one summer in Colorado that I found my career. On a road trip through Leadville, we saw leaching from an old mine and the contamination of the local waters. The silver-lining of my mother's political connections was that I got into the environmental engineering program at Carnegie Mellon in Pittsburgh."

With a frown, Lowry sipped her wine. "I learned a bit about 'priorities' from Duff."

"You had a tougher row as a kid than I did."

Lowry finished her wine and stared into the empty glass. "A family is a mish-mash of souls floating in a rickety boat, just hoping to survive. Parents are human beings—flawed people—trying to deal with the heartaches of their past and their fears of the future."

John kissed her hand, then held it in his. He gazed into her eyes. "Here I am, a flawed man, asking you to love me from this day forward."

Her eyes welled with tears. She squeezed his hand and whispered, "And here I am, a flawed woman, who loves you until the day I die."

He slipped his arm around her and drew her to him. Lowry laid her head on his shoulder. She closed her eyes, listening to the distant yip of a fox, her head rising and falling with John's breath. Behind them, the fire collapsed with a crunch. John nibbled her ear, then rose and threw on a handful of apple wood chips. As the fire blazed, he ambled back and tugged a lock of her hair. "Ready for a swim?" He held out his hand.

Lowry gripped his warm hand and he lifted her. She slipped off her clothes. With a smile, she yelled, "First one in doesn't do the dishes!" and dived into the pool. Warm and cool currents embraced her body as she swam through the water. The light waves from the virtual campfires penetrated the depths in spooky undulations. Clusters of thin aquatic grasses danced to the rhythm of geothermal bubbles wafting from cracks along the rock base. A school of minnows hid between the waving hornwort.

A thunderous splash hit the pond as John cannonballed in the center of the pool. She turned to watch him touch the bottom, naked as a jaybird. Desperate for oxygen, she pushed off the rocks and broke into the air with a laugh. He rose next to her, shaking the water from his hair.

With a quick snatch, he grabbed her arm. "You can't run from me," he chuckled. He pulled her close and kissed her lips. He smoothed back her wet hair and nibbled her brows, then drew her to the side of the pool. He pushed himself onto the rocks and pulled her up beside him.

John nuzzled her neck. "I'm getting hungry."

"I'll get the salmon on the fire."

He wrapped his arms around her, pulling her close. "I have my dinner right here."

John kissed her cheek and slipped his hand down her arm. With a smile, he rose, clasped her hand and led her to the blanket. Dripping wet, they lay on the cover. Lowry wrapped her arms around his neck and pulled him against her body. He laced his fingers into her hair, gently tugged back her head and kissed her deeply. The light from the fires shimmered on their naked bodies as they made love in the Oasis.

CHAPTER 32

John stared out of the window of his office. Along the edges of the sidewalk, birds darted under the hedges and bright yellow daffodils bent to the whim of the breeze. Lime-green shoots of grass ventured above the soil.

He turned at a cough behind him. Kisho stood at the door. "Come in," he said, waving his hand.

Kisho smiled. "Welcome back. I trust you had a nice honeymoon?"

"Yes, it was great." He raised a brow. "So, I'm hoping you're not going to ruin my afterglow with bad news—at least for this morning."

With a chuckle, he shook his head. "No, just updates." He flicked his finger across the shimmering tablet and threw a police report onto the monitor. "First item: the police did find a body, missing its left forearm, buried in the Grace Region. They confirmed that it was Zoric's brother. He had been shot in the back of the head."

"Is it just me or doesn't Christianity frown on murder?" He threw up his hands. "Why do humans enslave themselves in a crazy religion? Why can't people just be happy being human?"

"Sadly, that *is* being human."

Kisho threw a photo onto the monitor. "One of Noelle's wildlife video drones was discovered with an image of one of

Zoric's men setting a trap in the river. He's being charged with illegal trapping."

John said softly, "Even in death, she prevailed."

"Yes, sir." He cleared his throat. "On the Chinese issue—" With another swipe of his finger, a video taken at the formerly Chinese occupied island appeared on the screen. "—all the armaments have been removed from the island, and further sweeps along the chain haven't come up with any other depots of equipment. The UN and our government have filed complaints against China for their aggressive actions."

"What about Lin and his organization?"

"Yesterday, the police sent Lin's real background to us." Kisho tapped the screen. "I'm sending you the un-encrypted report. They'll be coming in later today to review both their own and the FBI's findings. It was shocking to learn that Chinese operatives had imbedded an avatar of a 'Peter Lin' in the Department of Defense data files, complete with a military record and a high-school transcript." He shook his head. "They even inserted a photo of Peter in the high-school yearbook, over a deceased guy's picture. But when the FBI dug deeper, they realized it was only a facade. When they interviewed the school district, besides the planted transcript, no real records existed of a Peter Lin attending the school."

John huffed. "Lin was a Chinese agent from the get-go."

"I'm afraid so." He pushed another image onto the monitor. "As to the rest of his buddies, about half a dozen of his allies have been deported or are in jail so far. It's fascinating, the roots of this gang. Some families go back to the infamous Green Gang of pre-communist China."

"Lin mentioned a Neo Green Gang. I assume a reboot?"

"Yes, the original Green Gang is the one who put Chiang Kai-shek into power during the first half of the twentieth century. Once the communists prevailed, a segment of the gang moved onto the winning side of the chess board."

"Scary, but I hope that's the end of it." John sighed. "Regardless, we'll have to increase our coast guard presence around Antarctica and I'll work with the Assembly to develop a real military. The UN will help to a certain extent, but at some point, it's our baby." He drummed his fingers on the table. "Just what the good folks want, paying to build a military."

"Yeah, that won't go over well—people are already complaining about taxes."

With a grin, John said, "Now that Alex is the Secretary of Defense, she'll have to defend the increase in the budget."

Kisho glanced at his virtual tablet. "The last item is your itinerary for the UN conference." He flicked it toward John. "I forwarded the details to you." He smiled. "That's all the updates I had for today, sir."

John leaned back in his chair. "Kisho, I don't tell you often enough, but thank you for being a great Chief of Staff."

As he stared at John, his eyes narrowed. "Sir, why do I feel like shit is blowing my way?"

"Exactly—you'd better get a raincoat. Patel is resigning and I'm planning on nominating you as my Secretary of State until the next elections."

"I have no diplomatic experience." Kisho raised a brow. "And I don't know if Antarctica is ready for an openly gay Secretary of State." He grinned. "There's a lot of testosterone in the Assembly—do you think they'll confirm me?"

"Does anyone really care anymore? After that, I'd love to see you run for president. You'd make a fantastic leader, and I'd trust you to carry on with our program."

His dark eyes twitched back and forth. "I don't want to lose the presidency, and all we've worked for, because of my lifestyle."

"You're the best person for the job and being gay is who you are."

Smiling, Kisho said, "Thank you for your confidence, sir. I'll discuss it with Douglas." He shifted from one foot to the other.

John inclined his head. "Is there something else?"

Kisho drew a small box from his pocket and set it on John's desk. "Noelle's family sent you a gift for your help with

Dr. Clavet. Apparently, she had left a message to give this to you if she didn't return."

John brushed his hair back, gazing at the present. His mouth tightened as he touched the trailing ends of the ribbon tied around it. "Noelle was a lovely person. Free, like a bird in flight." He glanced at Kisho. "Her family established the Clavet Foundation in her honor, solely dedicated to educate women and girls. Their goal is to implant birth-control chips in girls around the world to limit human population."

He pulled the bow apart and opened the box. With a gasp, he lifted out a sphere of the Earth balanced on a stand. He set it on the desk and a 3-D video appeared, demonstrating the proper hand motions to display the imagery within the globe. At the finale, a swallow, the color of the sky, flew from the center of the Earth. The bird, suspended in mid-air, spoke in Noelle's voice. "Listen to the birds and they will tell you."

He inhaled sharply, pinching his lips together as he stared at the swallow frozen in flight. Blinking back tears, he whispered, "Noelle said that to me on our trek across the wilderness."

"She made the ultimate sacrifice for her beliefs."

John clenched his fist. "They may regret inviting me to speak at the UN for the 'State of the Earth' conference—I'll be giving a speech they won't soon forget."

*   *   *

John and Ginnie boarded the presidential plane heading to the States. After they settled into their seats, he glanced at her, staring solemnly out the window. Noelle's death had been very hard on her. *Innocence lost on this adventure.*

He reached out and patted her arm. "How are you doing, sweet?"

"I can't stop thinking about Professor Clavet. She was a great person and an incredible teacher. It's such a tragedy."

"Yes, it's a real loss. She'd be happy to know that enough data was collected to carry on her research."

Tears welled in Ginnie's eyes. "If she hadn't led the research group to Antarctica, she would still be alive."

"It wasn't the expedition that led to her death, it was her decision to return to the area despite the danger." He inclined his head. "But when you believe in something as much as she did, and pursue it with passion, it's the path to truly living, even if it meant her death. Noelle regretted nothing in her life."

Her eyes searched his. "Do you have any regrets, Dad?"

"Not spending enough time with my daughter."

She smiled. "There were times I missed you, but you always called me to find out how my games went or how I did on a test. I knew you loved me. That meant more than anything. And I was proud of your accomplishments." She touched his hand. "Someone told me once, 'If you believe in something and pursue it with passion, it's the path to truly living.'"

He slipped his hand over hers. "I love you very much— you're my bit of sunshine."

They reached cruising altitude and the flight attendant brought drinks and snack. After their refreshments, Ginnie laid her head on his shoulder. Her breaths became even, and he knew she had fallen asleep. John covered her with a blanket and smiled at her peaceful face.

He gazed out of the window of the plane and watched clouds drift by against the dazzling cobalt sky. Regrets, she'd asked him. *Regrets of his failure to guard against tyrants, inside and outside of his administration.* His mistakes had led to destruction and deaths—ironic that the supposed 'authorized' military forces had caused more harm than Zoric's tyranny.

John shook his head. It still seemed unconscionable that a country like Antarctica would require a defense, but therein lay his Achilles heel in not recognizing the need. Too many nations needed raw materials, and despite a harsh climate, Antarctica was one of the few continents with large, untouched natural reserves.

The captain's voice interrupted his thoughts, "Mr. President, we are flying over Rio de Janeiro. It will be visible on the left side of the plane."

John gazed at the sprawling mass of cities and towns merged into one another, consuming the landscape. The tall buildings of a century past had disappeared under the waves, and only the tip of the once-iconic Sugarloaf Mountain peeked above the blue waters of Guanabara Bay. Christ the Redeemer had watched as the city leaders razed the slums of the poor and rebuilt a new modern city on the hills.

They flew beyond the coast and soared above the flooded Amazon Basin. A veil of smoke drifted from charred tracts of rainforest destroyed for crops and the fleeting production of cattle as the poorest were driven inland by a rising sea.

Around the world, the flora and fauna of the Earth withered against the onslaught of humans, the most destructive beasts on the planet, devouring everything in their path, not out of a mean spirit, but from living capriciously.

CHAPTER 33

John waited in the front row seats of the UN assembly room. He was one of many speakers throughout the day, filing through like lowing cattle. He turned to the scattered audience, mumbling among themselves rather than listening to the current speaker. Most of the speeches were for the home audience; bits and pieces cut and spliced for constituent consumption.

He reached into his jacket for Noelle's gift as the delegate's time allotment neared its end. His mouth twitched, chasing the globe to the back of his pocket, finally catching the smooth sphere and lifting it into the air. He gazed at the minuscule Earth and, with his finger on the Equator, shifted the image of the world, back and forth, from before The Melt to after the rise of the oceans. He sighed at the massive loss of land.

The speaker finished, and with a smile, she left the podium. The moderator gestured that it was his turn. John nodded and balled his fist around the globe. *Wish me luck, Noelle.* Then he dropped it into his pocket.

As he pushed himself from the chair, his legs buckled for a second. He straightened up and walked toward the stage, breathing deeply to calm his thumping heart. He stepped to the podium, and with trembling fingers, placed his phone on top.

P whispered, "Break a leg, John," and a virtual display of his speech appeared before him.

He scanned the sparse crowd in front of him. Delegates from every corner of the globe had assembled for the State of the Earth conference, but apparently, most of them had more important speeches to attend or hands to press.

The light turned green, signaling for him to start speaking.

John cleared his throat. As he began to speak, his voice wavered. "My fellow citizens of the world, we have gathered at this forum to discuss our future."

A few faces glanced at him, then back to their conversations.

He bit the inside of his lip as an image of Noelle's smile formed in his mind's eye. Her delight watching the birds along the trail, flitting through the branches, and the snow drifting through the air.

Adrenaline surged through him, and with a deep breath, he leaned forward. His voice rose, echoing in the half-filled room. "Humans are now the gods of old." He raised his finger. "We no longer tremble at the lightning in the sky—we create it. And like Thor, we have the means to destroy vast areas of the Earth in a sweep of the hand. But do we have the wisdom to go with that power?"

In the crowd, a nudging of elbows, and faces turning toward him.

"For millennia, humans were in balance with nature, until technology injected a sense of superiority into our veins and we felt ourselves invincible."

A quiet settled over the room. "I drew from the great minds of the world to craft a plan for the colonization of Antarctica." He swept his hand over the assembly. "A part of us is in every blade of grass, in every animal. And we pay a toll in human suffering every time we mistreat Nature."

John hit the podium with his fist and the sound reverberated in the room. Stunned faces turned to him. *Was he reaching anyone?*

He said quietly, "It's a paradigm shift in thought to have Nature as a political force, and not merely an object to be enjoyed on vacation or exploited for profit. The Earth can no longer be a piggy bank to raid. People say what we have done on Antarctica is radical—I say sensible! The only fundamental change to our approach is to include Mother Nature as a constituent in our government. And that is the revolution in thinking.

"We won over many opponents with the revenues generated by tourism to visit our vast wilderness. After the Melt, the population of the Earth squeezed the natural world into domesticated novelties. The frenzy to feed and house billions has devastated most of the once-untouched areas of the world. If we do *not* have a paradigm shift in the way we see ourselves as a part of the kingdom of Earth, I foresee the day when the wilderness is gone. And when that occurs, our demise will follow."

He pounded the podium again. "The problem with our world, my friends, is not just preserving the Earth's wild areas. We must create a sustainable way of living and control our population growth."

Like rotten cabbages, looks of disgust and anger came his way. Clusters of people rose and left the conference room. Population control and women's reproductive rights were not universally lauded. He ignored the retreating groups and only blinked as the door slammed after the dissenters exited.

In a see-saw motion, John gestured with his hands. "In simplistic terms, money equals food and comfort. We must understand how we fit into the entire spectrum of the world, not just our tiny microcosm of steel and concrete. And even there, Mother Nature hides beneath the veils of Civilization."

His eyes scanned the crowd. "Many cannot see the benefit in Mother Nature as a player on the political scene. 'Humans should come first! Growth is good!' they cry. But it is greed talking. We *are* doing what is best for the people. Balance, my friends, is the key to survival."

Frowns shot at him from a covey of lobbyists near the side door, and they too, left the room.

"War ravages many of the poorer countries and tyrants arise with the poverty and the hopelessness. In these countries, what is needed most from the world is a preemptive strike of economists. We need political and economic stability in our communities, so the fear, and sometimes the reality, of hunger and displacement no longer drive us to short-term solutions."

A few souls had moved closer to the front, taking seats abandoned by those angry individuals who had left. A group of students had entered the conference room and stood quietly in the side aisle. They gazed at him, innocent of the machinations of the world.

In a soft voice, John raised his hand upward. "Why are we running so? Did anyone tell you why?" He swept his arm in front of him. "Like a plague of locusts, the human race will annihilate everything in its path and ultimately destroy us all."

He looked at the lingering crowd, their faces riveted to his words. Or was it merely the entertainment value of his passion?

"The key to our survival is equilibrium between two opposing forces." He held up one hand. "The growth of the human family versus—" He held up his other hand. "—the existence of the natural world. That is the cornerstone of our philosophy—to balance human needs with those of nature."

A woman with an African headscarf around her hair smiled at him from the corner of the room. John gripped the podium, his throat closing with emotion. With her bright eyes and a beatific smile, she was a breath of fresh air in the room— she reminded him of Noelle. And she had heard his words.

He licked his dry lips and swallowed the spittle in his mouth. He whispered his final words, "Let's walk, my friends. Let's walk."

The room was eerily quiet as he left the podium. There was nothing more he could do, he had spoken from the heart—and for Noelle's memory. The blood pounded in his head as he reached the aisle. A few people shook his hand, and he nodded at their grinning faces.

But could his words penetrate the hidden agendas of the politicians and their puppet masters?

The audience regained their wits. Sporadic claps and calls of "Bravo" gained momentum as he neared the exit. With a wave, he slipped from the room. He knew their resolve to change was reflected by the hollow echo of their applause.

CHAPTER 34

The robocar stopped under the porte-cochere of the presidential residence.

John exhaled. *Home at last.*

The lights brightened along the entryway and the car door slid open. He stumbled out and stood for a moment, swaying with exhaustion. He gazed at the orange wisps of clouds on the horizon, then closed his eyes, inhaling the honey scent of the flowering Mata Negra hedges along the drive.

When John opened his eyes, the colors of the sunset had faded. In the deepening twilight, another wave of fatigue hit him. He glanced toward the rear of the car and muttered, "Come on, bag." His suitcase descended from the open trunk and hovered to his side. As the robocar left, he walked through the doors, shadowed by his bag and the Drots.

In a daze, he ambled toward the apartment, the muted floor lights preceding him, hypnotically drawing him along the corridor.

P whispered, "John, you passed the door to your apartment."

With a grimace, he stopped and shook his head. After the UN conference and his long flight from the States, he needed silence and solitude to reorganize his scattered thoughts onto the shelves of his mind.

"Thanks, P. My brain is fried."

"I know, John—you need rest. Welcome home!"

John retraced his steps to the front of his apartment and the Drots took their positions at the door. The security light scanned his face and the door opened with a whoosh. His bag trailing in his wake, he entered the foyer, now illuminated in soft lights. With a long sigh, he took off his coat and threw it on the hook beside the door. He said, "Bedroom" to the suitcase, and it drifted toward the back of the apartment. The foyer lights dimmed behind him as he walked into the living room.

John overheard Lowry saying, "Your dad is home."

He stepped into the room. Henry-dog and Leo sat on either side of Lowry, their eyes shining in excitement. They leapt off the couch and, tails wagging, bounded toward him. In the scramble, Leo knocked the suitcase onto its side.

Lowry rose from the couch. "Crazy dogs, be careful!"

The suitcase righted itself and continued resolutely to the bedroom.

John knelt to greet the dogs as they raced to him. They jostled each other to be the first to lick his face and bowled him over, flat on his back. Chuckling, he stroked the dogs. "Okay, guys, I missed you too."

Lowry walked over, and grinning, pushed them off of John. "Let him breathe." She reached her hand to him.

John clasped her outstretched hand, and with a grunt, rose to his feet. "Thanks for the rescue." With a tired smile, he drew her close and kissed her cheek.

"Anytime." She studied his face, then smoothed his hair back. "You look exhausted."

He gestured with his finger and thumb. "A wee bit."

She slid her arm through his, guided him to the couch, and gently pushed him onto the cushions. She grabbed a throw pillow and placed it behind his head. "Relax and I'll get you a beer."

He blinked in surprise. "No house service?"

She shrugged. "I turned it off for the night."

With a nod, John said, "Perfect." He set his phone on the side table. "P, good night."

"Good night, John, and sleep tight."

Lowry went into the kitchen. The dogs glanced at him, then padded after her.

John raised a brow. *I guess greeting time is over.* He propped his feet onto the coffee table and stretched his arms behind him, cradling his head. His eyes fluttered until he heard the *clip, clip* sound of the dogs' paws on the plank floor.

A twinkle in her eye, Lowry stood in front of him, holding out a frosted mug of beer. "Don't go to sleep yet—we have to get your hours switched back to Antarctic time."

A quick grin flashed on his face. He leaned forward and took the cold mug and raised it in a toast to her.

Lowry sat beside him and grabbed her glass of water from the end table. She clinked his mug. "Cheers and welcome home."

"Cheers." John gulped a mouthful of beer and sank back into the cushions. "I'm definitely glad to be home."

Leo jumped onto the couch next to Lowry. Henry leapt beside John, bumping his arm and spilling his beer.

He jerked the beer mug away from the dog. "Damn, Henry!"

Chagrined, Henry curled up beside him and laid his head on John's leg.

John sighed. "It's okay, buddy," he said, patting Henry's head. "At least I didn't lose the whole glass."

"Gotta love 'em." Lowry drew a tissue from the nearby carton and dabbed beer from John's sleeve. "Tell me about your trip. I assume Ginnie's back at school?"

With a warped smile, he replied, "The trip? Well, no matter how you slice a trip from the bottom of the world to the Northern Hemisphere, it's brutal." His smile faded as a knot formed in his brow. He looked at her. "Ginnie is okay, but it will take time for her to recover from everything that occurred—especially Noelle's death."

Nodding, Lowry whispered, "The last months have been rough on everyone." She touched his arm. "But she'll survive. Ginnie's a tough cookie."

"That she is." John took a long swig of beer. His shoulders relaxed as the alcohol took effect.

She turned to him with a smile. "On a positive note, I want to congratulate you on that amazing speech. Kisho and I found the feed from the UN conference. You knocked 'em dead, Mr. President."

"All three people who stayed to the end clapped." John pursed his lips. "But thanks. I wasn't sure anyone else was listening."

"Noelle would have been proud."

He chewed his lip, swirling the remains of beer in the mug. When the liquid stopped spinning, he glanced at Lowry. "I gave that speech in her honor."

Tears welled in Lowry's eyes. "Noelle was an amazing person. It was a beautiful tribute to her."

John stroked Henry's fur as he swallowed back his emotion. He drew in a deep breath, steadying himself.

In a quiet voice, Lowry said, "You must realize, that despite being the reluctant president, you've accomplished a lot on Antarctica. With us as an example, maybe other countries will consider similar laws."

He shrugged. "Hope springs eternal."

"As hope always does." She patted his leg. "As I watched you speaking, the thought crossed my mind that this might be your true mission in life."

"What do you mean?"

"Destinies dribble out and carry you in currents you aren't expecting. But if you stay true to yourself, you stay the course. You wanted to be a farmer. Perhaps your farm was too small. Perhaps Antarctica was the true garden for you to tend."

"Noelle said something similar." John grimaced. "My life has gone in a different direction than I expected. Ego makes fools of us all." He tapped his finger on his chin. "I remember an old saying:

We thrash our way through the wilderness, clinging to the vision of a shining city on the hill. And no matter how many times our wishes are entangled by weeds, we stagger on. We ascend the mountain, only to find that our precious desires have vanished in the wind, and now shimmer on the next ridge.'"

She hummed. "Sounds rather depressing."

John finished his beer and set the mug on the coffee table. "On our trek, I asked Noelle about the meaning of life. She said, 'Life is just being.'" He scratched his head. "Why is 'being' so hard?" A spasm swept across his forehead. "Why can't we, like a bee, simply drink the nectar from a flower, and then, dressed in pollen, drift away to the next open blossom?"

"You and I are both driven people." She shook her head. "But there's no doubt that the constant stroke of the metronome can wear on you."

Lowry shifted closer. She cleared her throat and glanced at him. "John, this may not be the best time, but I have something to tell you."

John's brow furrowed at her serious tone. His throat tightened as he faced her, studying her eyes as they searched his.

Her throat bobbed as she swallowed hard. A hesitant smile grazed her face, and then she blurted out, "I'm pregnant."

John felt his mouth open and close, but no words came out.

His mind adrift, he leaned his head onto the cushion, staring blankly ahead. The brass mantel clock sat facing him, its resolute pendulum swinging back and forth, mincing into his consciousness.

Lowry laid her head on his shoulder. He slipped his arm under hers and clasped her hand, her skin warm against his. Her breath touched his cheek.

John felt the rhythm of her pulse and the adamant ticking of the clock faded away. In the stillness of the room, he blinked against the tempest in his mind.

Control is an illusion constructed by our feeble brains, for the currents of our existence spring from the blood of our past. As organic as the ocean, the vagaries of life are like waves racing up a beach. Each wave gathers momentum in the depths and arches up to kiss the shore, then with a sigh, returns to build again.

With a smile, John closed his eyes. The only truth in life is that each day is utterly unique.

The End

ACKNOWLEDGEMENTS

My deepest appreciation goes to my friends, family, and supporters, especially my author friends: Lisa Tracy and Cristina Pinto-Bailey, early readers who believed in me and bestowed great feedback, and author Sonja Yoerg, for her prodigious support. Special thanks to my wonderful editors for this novel: Heather Webb and Jim Thomsen. Thanks to Kit Foster for creating the fantastic cover and Walter B. Myers for the flooded Earth imagery. Much gratitude to my family, for supporting me during the long process of crafting these stories. Thanks to my friend and 'cheerleader' Stevie Bond for reading and supporting my writings. And a special thanks to all my reviewers and readers.

ABOUT THE AUTHOR

K.E. Lanning is a writer and scientist. Born in Texas in 1957, she grew up near Houston in the small town of Friendswood, laced with white oyster shell roads and open fields dotted with huge live oaks, riding horses rather than bikes. But nearby, NASA's space program shepherded thoughts of astrophysics into her head.

Lanning received a bachelor's degree in Physics in 1979 from Stephen F. Austin St. University in Nacogdoches, TX and a MBA in 1986 from the University of Houston.

Lanning has long been a fan of science fiction, intrigued by the multi-dimensions of the genre, allowing the author to explore society, humanity, and our future, and bringing the reader along for the ride.

She now resides in the Shenandoah Valley of Virginia with her family.

Listen to the Birds is her third novel, and the last book in **THE MELT TRILOGY**, following *A Spider Sat Beside Her* and *The Sting of the Bee*, the first and second stories of the trilogy.

www.kelanning.com

CPSIA information can be obtained
at www.ICGtesting.com
Printed in the USA
LVHW041032070419
613259LV00001B/156